Praise for *Su*

"This is the most glorious mic
Literature. *Sugarbread* is such a te
the many celebrated voices in Singapore that represent minority
experiences through tokenism or ignore them altogether. Balli
Kaur Jaswal has made me feel like my ten-year-old self could be
someone's protagonist, like my skin belongs in the pages of books
in my country. She's turned the mirrors on Singapore and our
conversations about identity in a spectacular fashion. Her prose is
delicate, precise and aching. Her storytelling lingers with you for
days. This novel is triumphant and absolutely essential reading for
anyone who cares about living in this city."
—Pooja Nansi, author of *Love Is an Empty Barstool*

"*Sugarbread* is a warm and wry portrait of childhood, in all its
intensity and its confusions, and a deeply satisfying exploration of
prejudice, conscience, loyalty and reconciliation."
—Jolene Tan, author of *A Certain Exposure*

"A beautifully written companion piece to *Inheritance*. Balli Kaur
Jaswal uses the eyes of a young girl from Singapore's Sikh community
to revision life in the city-state, and explore overlapping conflicts
centred on ethnicity, nationalism, religion, social inequality, and
gender. As the story progresses, these tensions are elaborated in the
life stories of Pin and of her mother, embodied in the everyday rituals
of cooking and eating, and only resolved through an accounting
with a hidden past of exclusion and abuse."
—Philip Holden, Professor of English, National University of Singapore

"Pin is an earnest and enchanting child, through whose curious and clear-sighted eyes we see family life and complications and childhood cliques and racism. But this entertaining book also has touching insights into love, hope and wisdom and characters that will stay with you long after you finish it."
—Ovidia Yu, author of *Aunty Lee's Chilled Revenge*

"Balli Kaur Jaswal has written a profoundly moving story that is both a sensitive family portrait and a wild page-turner. With arrestingly vivid prose and carefully wrought characters, she draws readers into the world of ten-year-old Pin as she negotiates her Sikh faith and grapples with startling secrets. This is wonderfully crafted novel about food, faith and family."
—Pooja Makhijani, author of *Mama's Saris* and editor of *Under Her Skin: How Girls Experience Race in America*

"Movingly told, the narrative grips as it reveals the trials, tribulations and anxieties experienced by the growing protagonist as she learns secrets of her family in a multi-ethnic Singapore. Here is a powerful new literary voice in Singaporean fiction—and a voice that must be heard."
—Kirpal Singh, poet and creativity guru

"An elegant, evocative work that brings the seemingly-mundane world of everyday Singapore to magical life, drawing you in with its details and delights, inviting you to see things with the protagonist's eyes…and then insisting that you feel things with her heart though it may break your own to do so. A touching, poignant tale."
—Krishna Udayasankar, author of *The Aryavarta Chronicles*

SUGARBREAD

SUGARBREAD
BALLI KAUR JASWAL

A NOVEL

EPIGRAM BOOKS
SINGAPORE · LONDON

Epigram Books UK
First published in 2016 by Epigram Books Singapore
This edition published in Great Britain in September 2017 by Epigram Books UK

A CIP catalogue record for this book is available from the British Library.

ISBN
978-1-91-209866-8

Printed and bound in
Great Britain by Clays Ltd, St Ives plc

Epigram Books UK
55 Baker Street
London, W1U 7EU

10 9 8 7 6 5 4 3 2 1

www.epigrambooks.uk

For my mum, aunties and grandmothers

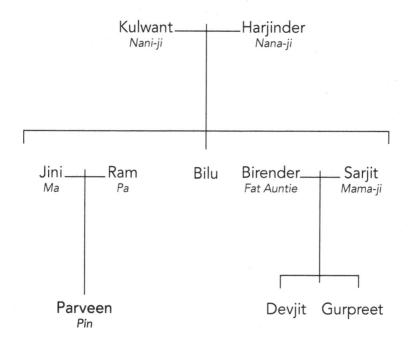

PART I

1

1990

IT WAS SINGAPORE and it was July. The early morning sun glowed orange and rose between the high buildings; streams of light poured through the still branches of trees and heat rose from the pavement. Ma and I walked in the shade under rows of canvas awnings. All around us, tin grilles were released and unfolded. They rattled loudly, like trains running right over my ears. Shopkeepers grimaced as they dragged out shelves and crates filled with Gardenia bread, jars of coconut kaya, sweet pandan bread, sticky pink cupcakes called huat kueh, packets of prawn crackers, buns plump with red bean filling, and Twisties snacks. These few things could endure the sun.

The shops were shadowy and cool caves inside. There were refrigerators for milk packets, and freezers for popsicles and Paddle Pop ice cream. The first few customers shifted sideways like crabs through the narrow aisles. Tall sacks of rice lay slouched in the back as if taking a break from the morning heat. Above them, red altars on the walls glowed with offerings of oranges and burning joss sticks. Some display cases were still chained and padlocked because it was early. The shopkeepers sighed as they squatted to fit their keys into the locks. They were always sighing; they were always tired.

Ma walked in brisk, long steps and I struggled to keep up.

I had short legs. I was the smallest girl in my class. I thought she should understand this but whenever I reminded her, she became impatient and said, "You'll grow, Pin." She had always been long-legged and elegant, so she could not sympathise. But being a little slower had its benefits. I noticed things while Ma just hurried along, and this was why she took me with her to the market. There were less crowded routes through the void decks of housing blocks but Ma preferred passing the shops because I could spot discounts. I had good eyes, and I added and subtracted quickly. Daddy called this "having good senses", and I liked to think that God gave me good senses deliberately to make up for what I lacked in height.

I looked out for deals from the shops, hoping that Ma would remember that she needed something and we could delay our trip to the wet market, even if it was only for a few minutes. "They are selling clothespins," I called out. Ma slowed down. I pointed to a basket sitting outside one odds and ends shop. This one was not as organised as the others. The old couple that owned it always looked puzzled when customers asked them for a set of anything. They sold every item individually—hangers, nails, pencil lead, paper towels, Tiger Balm. Ma called it the One-By-One shop, although its actual name, as printed on the sign above the stall, was Lee's Goods. I pointed at a tray sitting outside, filled to the brim with wooden and plastic clothespins. CLOTH PEG ONE FOR FIVE CENT.

"We don't need any," Ma said after reading the sign. Then she picked up her pace, leaving me to skip again to catch up with her.

"I like Twisties," I said, eyeing the bags on display outside another shop.

"Twisties are rubbish," Ma replied and I knew then that there was no more delaying. We were going to the wet market and we were going now.

On Sunday mornings, Ang Mo Kio smelled faintly like smoke and something sweet. On the short walk to the market, it was always these two smells—something burning and something tempting. The heavy smell of burning came from the smoke that rose from woks in nearby 24-hour coffee shops where red plastic chairs lay strewn around lopsided white tables. The smoke carried the aroma of onions and garlic sizzling in oil, rice noodles being fried in oyster sauce, softening vegetables stewing with chopped garlic, eggs and butter and dough, watery coconut gravy and fish curry. The sweet smell did not necessarily come from food, although it was overwhelming when we passed the Happy Garden Bakery with its gleaming display cases filled with chocolate mousse cakes and multi-layered kueh lapis. There was another kind of sweetness in the Sunday air. It came from the potted bougainvillea lined neatly along the paths, body lotion and deodorant mingling with sweat, morning greetings from one woman to another, the money being counted at the 4D lottery shop, the new rubber and leather at the bicycle shop. There was nothing else in the world like our neighbourhood on a Sunday morning. I had lived there my whole life. I was ten years old.

As we approached the wet market, both scents gave way to something else, a bitter taste that started in my throat. It was like this every time. Fear tightened my insides and turned my limbs into lead. I couldn't move or call out to Ma as she continued walking. Eventually, she looked over her shoulder and backtracked, her features crumpled with irritation.

"Come now. You're not going to get lost," Ma said.

I always clutched Ma's hand whenever we entered a crowded

place—the shopping malls in the city, the rows of hawker centres in Ang Mo Kio Central, the bus interchange—but sometimes, without realising it, she lost me. She never admitted it. A year ago, we went to the pasar malam down the street. Lanterns filled the ink-black sky like small moons and Chinese music crackled from loudspeakers. Shopkeepers shouted out prices for dresses, toys and cotton candy everywhere we went. I remembered feeling Ma's hand slip from mine as she drifted towards a good bargain. People filled the small space between us the way floodwater rushes into a gutter. She found me within a few minutes but in my mind, it had been hours, a lifetime. When I told her that she had let go first, she grew cross and asked, "Why would I do a thing like that?"

I could already feel the heat on my back now, sweat gluing my thin T-shirt to my skin. Around us, customers moved in different ways. Some sped past us in clapping sandals, others roamed heavily. There were straight backs, stooped backs, loose blouses and clinging T-shirts. I saw every shade of skin colour and the fine green veins that decorated the backs of knees. I saw jutting anklebones and flimsy rubber slippers. "Aiyah!" a man cried as his slipper came loose and skidded across the wet floor to land in a shallow corner gutter. I caught a glimpse of his eyes as they searched wildly for the person who had tripped him. I hid behind Ma in case he thought it was me but the fury only lasted a few seconds; he seemed to realise that if he did not keep moving, he would not get anything done. He ran to the gutter, pushed his foot back into the slipper and hurried along as if nothing had happened.

"Hold my hand," Ma said. I did as she told. "Now, what do you do?"

"Keep holding your hand."

"And what should you not do?"

"Panic."

"Or?"

"Cry," I said, a little bit softer because I was embarrassed.

"Ready?' she asked

I nodded and she brought me in. As the market rushed towards us, my first instinct was to twist away from Ma's grip and run away. Ma knew this—her grip tightened. There was no escape. The world became a stirring sea of people, voices and colours. It took time for my eyes to adjust to the dim lighting and for my nose to adapt to the dampness and the smell of blood mixed with flowers mixed with incense mixed with ripe fruit. We had entered through a narrow lane between a makeshift orchid shop and a poultry stall where skinned chickens hung by their beaks on C-shaped hooks. The greyish-pink shade of their pimply skin was sickening so I rested my gaze on another stall selling incense and paper money for burning and offering to ancestors. Further down, an elderly woman stood on a short stool and pointed at a tank crowded with grey crabs, their claws tightly bound with pink raffia string. They flipped and tumbled over each other, tapping steady threats against the glass. Their eyes were black beads.

There was no order here. All of Singapore was tidy and clean but the market was another world. I preferred the neat aisles and air-conditioning of the NTUC supermarket in Ang Mo Kio Central but Ma insisted that nothing was good unless it was fresh from the wet market. She glided through the lanes with ease, negotiating each stall with the swing of her hips. I could deal with the chaos of the market if I just followed her movements but I had to be careful not to let her see. Ma worried most when I walked like her.

That morning, Ma had woken me up by opening the door of my room and calling my name. "Pin," she said softly. I was already awake. Sunlight entered the room through the slats of my blinds. She closed the door and I listened to her feet moving quickly through the flat. My bedroom faced the main corridor of our building and on weekend mornings, I liked to watch the shadows of passers-by and match them to the neighbours. There was the young Malay woman who lived with her elderly parents. She was tall and bony, with short spiky hair. A family of four lived all the way at the end of the hallway. The mother always carried the baby, who added a lump to her silhouette. The toddler was too short to reach my window but I recognised the father's slouched figure as he guided him along.

"Pin." Ma opened the door again and was at the foot of my bed. "Wake up. Shower. Get dressed. I'm buying a lot of things today. I need you to help me carry bags from the market." I peeked at her through the thin sheets. Slender waist, hips jutting like narrow shelves—the shape of Ma.

"Five minutes," I mumbled.

Another shadow passed the window very slowly. I had to sit up to determine who it was. A sudden breeze pushed the blinds and distorted the outline. Ma came bursting into the room again even though it had not yet been five minutes. "Pin!" she exclaimed as though she had just caught me stealing. The shadow paused, startled by Ma's voice, then continued on its way. I pushed myself out of bed and got into the shower before I began to grumble so the water would muffle my words.

As I sat in her room and watched her powder her face and smooth out a small crinkle in her blouse, my irritation faded. Ma was too glamorous for the market. She insisted on wearing proper clothes; nothing fancy, but nothing she would only wear at home either. Most of the housewives who went to the market wore rubber sandals and baggy batik shorts with T-shirts. They did not comb their hair. Ma flipped her hair over and brushed it until it rested about her face like a dark cloud. When she disappeared into the bathroom, I tried to do the same but the brush got stuck in my curls. Another attempt didn't work—I had Daddy's hair and none of Ma's grace.

Now Ma's grip shifted away from my hand. I tugged her skirt to remind her. She nodded as if to say that she hadn't forgotten me, she was just looking in her purse for something.

"Fish stall first. Get it over with," Ma said. I let out a soft groan, then tried to hold my breath, but it was pointless. The fishmonger fanned his face with his hands as he called out prices. Fish with open mouths and glassy eyes lay in rows on trays filled with ice. Their fins fanned out like the ends of brooms. There were larger fish, whiter fish, fish with what looked like sharp long beaks. The sharp metal smell of blood was everywhere.

When the fishmonger saw Ma, he grinned and asked her in Malay, "Hello, would you like some fish?"

"Yes. Two first then tell me the price."

The man weighed two limp pieces of fish. "Eight dollars."

Ma squinted at the man to see if he was being truthful. After a moment, she said "Okay, then one more."

I made a face. I hated fish and this meant Ma would be frying some for dinner soon. The man caught my expression and laughed. "Your daughter," he said, more as a statement than a question. I smiled at him. I liked it when people recognised I was Ma's daughter.

"Yes," Ma said. "Thank you." She took the plastic bag from him and handed it to me. I slipped my wrist through the handles and let the bag sag from the weight, not caring if it broke. Ma trusted me with meat and vegetables; she carried eggs and heavy fruits on her own.

All four major languages were spoken at the market. The air was filled with Chinese syllables, swift as brushstrokes. Some of the older stallholders could speak in Malay. The dark-skinned man who sold chopped mutton negotiated in rapid Tamil. Some stallholders spoke uncertainly in broken English while others were forceful in their bad grammar. My family spoke Punjabi—a language that most people in Singapore didn't even know existed—and we used this to our advantage. At the fruit stall, Ma instructed me in Punjabi to inspect the redness of the apples while she tested the oranges for firmness. I was short enough to reach for them without having to bend towards the basket. Ma didn't like to show too much interest; to lean was to show need, and we didn't need to pay more than necessary for good fruit.

"They are ripe," I confirmed softly, even though I was speaking in Punjabi and the fruit seller wouldn't understand. We encountered very few Punjabi people unless we were at temple; if we saw them anywhere, we pretended not to because Ma didn't like to stop and chat. She said that most Punjabis were always looking for some gossip to bring home and even the most harmless bit of information could become national news in their hands.

"Sure? Look carefully." Ma replied. She eyed the stallholder.

"I'm sure," I said. The apple in my hand was round and ripe. I pressed my thumb into the skin and made a small dent.

Ma nodded and bought a few. The fruit seller was a delicate woman with a mess of short curly snow-white hair. As she handed the change to Ma, I could see her knuckles poking out of her pale skin.

"I'm tired," I announced to Ma as we moved to the next stall. The end of the market was still far away. There were leafy vegetables to be inspected, beans to be handpicked and chicken thighs to be weighed and packed. "I'm very tired," I said.

If Ma heard me, she pretended not to. I watched her bargaining like a Singaporean. "Give me same price but bigger one lah," she told the man who carefully cut slim slices of tofu from a larger slab. Ma was like my teachers at school—she didn't approve of Singlish though she couldn't help but use it sometimes. Usually when she spoke to strangers, she was crisp like a Channel Five newscaster. But proper English impressed nobody at the market—it made the prices go up. I had pointed out to Ma once that her nice clothes probably made the stallholders think we were wealthy, but looking tidy was something on which she would not compromise.

The handles of the bags dug into my wrists. The voices of stallholders and customers all melded together to become one loud buzz. I told Ma once again that I was tired. "And thirsty," I added. We were close to a set of stairs that led to a hawker centre upstairs. The first stall at the top of the steps sold ice-cold sugarcane juice. I was about to suggest a break but I knew the danger of this. It was not good to annoy Ma while she was buying groceries. It clouded her mind and made her forget important items.

After the tofu was the baby spinach. After that, tomatoes and carrots. I helped Ma to pick each item. "Don't rush," she warned me. "Choose carefully." But the air around me was becoming heavier, making it harder to breathe.

The night before, I hadn't slept much. My mind was full of numbers. "Four digits," Daddy had said, sitting on the edge of my bed. "Think carefully." Coming up with numbers sounded easy but they had to be lucky or he'd lose the 4D lottery. "Use your good senses, Pin," Daddy always said, his eyes locked into mine.

Every Sunday morning, he stood in the queue at the 4D shop fidgeting and hoping somebody hadn't already taken his combination. He had never won before but always came close. On my first day at school, I had given him my classroom number, which actually only contained three digits. I had added a random number at the end, making it 1123 because I thought it sounded likely. The winning number that week was close—1121. Every time Daddy scanned the newspaper to find out that he almost won, he clenched his fists, gritted his teeth and said, "So close!" When none of his chosen numbers appeared, he kept quiet and worked longer shifts at the hotel. Ma didn't believe in the lottery and called it a huge waste of money. Although she knew that Daddy queued up for tickets every week, she hardly mentioned it so the lottery was our secret, something only we could understand. Daddy truly believed that he would win one day. But Ma liked to say that gambling was as useless as praying when you were in trouble.

There were four more stalls to go but my legs felt rubbery. Ma did not tolerate such excuses. "Buck up, Pin," she'd tell me in English when the market overwhelmed me. We were at the durian stall when I knew I needed a different excuse, something more severe. A stallholder squatted on the wet floor in front of a wooden block and chopped through a durian's tough shell with a large knife. The two halves fell away, exposing the cream-coloured fruit, round and fleshy like a heart. For a moment before the pungent durian odour rose into the air, I was mesmerised by the stallholder's handling of the large, spiky husk. Most of them wore gloves but this man didn't bother. He grabbed each durian out of a straw basket as tall as I was and, after making a short slit with his knife, he pried both sides of the shell apart with his bare hands. I searched for calluses on his palms—surely they had to be rough from pressing against those sharp spikes. This was when I had my idea.

I started by fidgeting first, just a bit, then I stopped. Ma continued to look at the durians, deciding if she would buy them. These fruits were her specialty. I did not know how to check their barbed skin for ripeness. When Ma turned towards me, I squirmed again.

"Stop it," Ma said. She thought I was just being impatient, but I was working up to something larger. I stopped for a moment and then, when she moved on to the next stall, I continued. This time I raised my leg and scratched it until there was a long red mark. Ma still did not notice. Our next stop was the chicken stall. The stallholder there was a young woman with a son who clung to the hem of her shorts and stared at us. She shook the boy off her leg, gave Ma the prices and pulled a lumpy purple mess out of a skinned chicken all at the same time. I squatted on the floor and buried my fingernails into my flesh and dragged them across until I could hear the scratching noises.

Ma, in the middle of her negotiation, looked down at me. "Pin, what are you doing? What's wrong?" I made a face to show I was in pain and continued to scratch. Normally, when Ma tended to her own scarred skin, the noises were as sickening as the market smells. But now she was paying attention.

"Itchy," I said, shifting uncomfortably. I was starting to convince myself.

Ma squatted on the floor in front of me. She dropped all of her plastic bags. Water seeped through the hem of her ankle-length skirt, darkening the edges. She didn't care. She examined my leg, where I had built up an alarming rash. "We'll go home after this one," she told me as she rose to pay the stallholder, who quietly pocketed the change.

Ma ushered me out of the lanes, out of the drowning sounds, the yellowish lighting, the raw smell of blood. Outside, the dampness of market air was replaced by the familiar pressing heat. People rushed around in the bright morning and melted into the white air. We stepped out onto an even pavement and flowery bushes and rumbling buses slowing down to make stops. I let out a long sigh of relief. This was Singapore again—or at least, Singapore as I knew it.

•   •   •

A secret: I let Ma believe that I didn't like accompanying her to the market because I was scared of getting lost, but the truth was this was not my biggest fear. The market wasn't my favourite place in the world but I could pretend I was underwater or that I was a tourist interested in buying exotic fruit or I was a Martian coldly observing life on another planet. Eventually, I could even block out the smell of blood and the shouts from stallholders and I could walk carefully so I didn't slip on the wet floor. What I dreaded about our trips to the market was what Ma always said to me afterwards on the walk home.

"Promise that you will not become like me."

The first time Ma had said it, I waited for an explanation but there was none. I asked her why and she said, "There are many reasons, Pin. You're too young now to understand it all but you can avoid making my mistakes. I just want you to keep it in mind.

I was a little bit older than you when everything went wrong."

The second time she warned me, I reminded her that she had told me the previous week. She gave me a sharp look. "And I'm going to keep saying it until you learn, Pin," she snapped. "Do not become like me." I felt embarrassed. Ma would not have had to remind me if she hadn't seen me imitating her walk or trying to style my hair like hers. I thought that maybe this was just how it was—daughters and mothers were not supposed to be alike. It did not make sense to me, but Ma was adamant, and she repeated this only on Sundays, so it became our weekly after-market ritual.

I didn't like it because it sounded like I was in danger, and I wanted to know more, but Ma did not like questions. She rarely gave answers, and only when she wanted to. I was only certain about a few things with Ma. I knew that she had a beautiful face but scarred, wrecked skin on her arms and legs. I knew that she liked watching Hindi movies and she sometimes cooed to the potted plants outside our flat. If I wanted to know anything else, I had to look for clues in her cooking.

We walked towards our flat and Ma slowed down so I could keep up. She looked worried. "Let me take that," she said, pulling the bag of tofu from me. Going back to our block, we always took the route that led us away from the strings of people shuffling on their way to the market. "Good thing we went early. Look at all of these people going now. It'll be madness in there," she said.

Our block was Number 549. Daddy had bought a ticket with those digits before, combined with one new number each week. Directly opposite our block, the void deck of 547 was crowded with rattan birdcages. A few men helped to hang the cages from hooks in the ceilings, then they placed numbers above them. Inside the cages, brown songbirds chirped shrilly, as if trying to overpower each other. There was a sign in Chinese characters with the English translation scrawled underneath. It was for another community songbird contest. There was one under a different block every week. Old pot-bellied uncles, wearing white singlets and black shorts, sat underneath the cages with their heads cocked, listening for the sweetest song.

"They all sound the bloody same to me," Ma muttered as we walked out of the lift and down the corridor to our flat. We could hear the birds from our floor—the shrill whistling would filter in through our kitchen windows all day until a winner was announced.

Ma went into her bedroom and emerged with a bottle of ointment. She rubbed it on the rash I had clawed onto my leg. "Okay?" she asked, but before I could answer, she said, "Yes, you'll be okay."

I felt so guilty about pretending to have a rash that I lined all of the plastic bags neatly against the kitchen walls. Ma paced the length of the counter a few times, an army general. I opened the door of the fridge and moved a carton of milk to make space. There was an order to how the food was arranged in the fridge, and it all depended on the week's menu. I watched as Ma stacked spinach and bean sprouts in the vegetable drawer, put the chicken thighs and steely fish in the freezer, and the slab of tofu in a bowl of water. I tried to guess the food combinations for the week the way I searched my mind for Daddy's winning numbers, but nothing came up. Nothing made sense. Only Ma knew the plan. By the time she had finished, the fridge was crammed and blurred with colour, and it was almost noon.

I went back into my room, turned on the fan and stretched out across the cool tiled floor. Fierce sunlight softened as it entered in shreds through the slats of my blinds. In our small living room,

Ma arranged the furniture as an excuse to watch television, and eventually she slouched onto the rattan sofa. The blurry shadows of neighbours continued to pass and I guessed the owner of each one, knowing I was correct. I could guess at the events of the rest of the day as well. Daddy would come home soon from his night shift at the hotel and poke his head into my room to tell me about his lottery numbers. Ma would cook a simple lunch, nothing too filling, because it was Sunday and she liked to cook big meals for our Sunday dinner. I would eat, help to clear the dishes, then go into my room while Ma and Daddy sat on the couch together and watched television. I would drift in and out of sleep, songs from the afternoon Hindi movies trailing into my room as the sun set and light escaped our home.

· · ·

In our house, food was not just prepared and eaten to satisfy our appetites. Ma created meals based on her mood, the weather or unusual events. I always chewed my meals carefully, tasting for clues. Cabbage leaves soaked in sweet coconut gravy told me that Ma was feeling mellow. Perhaps it had rained that afternoon and I hadn't noticed it from the classroom window at school. Bay leaves and sour sauces were signs of sophistication—Ma was inspiring me to leave the narrow hallways of this block of flats where neighbours eavesdropped and tripped over each other's shoes. Cinnamon sticks were Ma's way of comforting me when she noticed a flaw in the way the world worked and she was softening the blow. The sharp tang of cumin added to any dish meant that Ma was bothered about something. There were many cumin dishes.

Daddy was the one who taught me how to find the hidden meanings in Ma's food. He said that it was a useful skill, especially when she was upset. The first time he told me about it, I was excited. I thought I would finally be able to figure Ma out. But all I discovered were her emotions. I could taste anger in the amount of red chilli powder and mustard seeds she sprinkled in a curry and I could tell that she was happy when she roasted chicken with light soy sauce and anise seeds, and served it over white rice. But I ached to find out more about Ma. She was full of secrets. I had known that from the very first time I saw her standing at the window, gazing intently at the buildings in the distance and the sky beyond that. She did this often, becoming oblivious to everything but the wide sky ahead of her. I was never sure if she was looking *at* something or looking *for* something. "Your Ma does not always say what she's thinking or feeling," Daddy said. "But when she cooks, she puts her whole mind and heart into the food and you're bound to learn something about her." So I searched for Ma in her spices and sauces, her mixed vegetables and her sweet desserts.

Ma had only started making the market a part of our regular Sunday routine when we stopped going to the Sikh temple. I couldn't decide which one I disliked more. I didn't mind wearing a salwaar-kameez or keeping my head covered and my feet bare. I liked the quiet peace of the prayer hall with its separate sections for men and women. I pretended I was a celebrity when I walked down the strip of dull red carpet and bowed low in front of the large Holy Book and the bearded priest who loudly read the script and never looked up. I could bear with the service—sitting cross-legged under fans that chopped the air, listening to the creaky accordions leading the hymns. But I dreaded eating at the temple, and for this I was sure that God would punish me.

Temple food was charred roti—wheat flour and water rolled into a soft dough, flattened and cooked on a flat iron stove. Cauliflower and potatoes mixed with spices and lumpy dhal were stirred in massive pots and pans over huge blue flames that flared like upside-down skirts. Thin, runny yoghurt contained strips of carrot and cucumber. They hadn't been cooked by Ma. The women in the back kitchen lived on gossip, trading stories about their friends' children and marriages. I always heard them talking when I walked in to put my plate in the sink. Once, one of them had caught my eye as I passed her and nudged her friend. "Isn't that…?" she asked. Her voice wasn't low enough. On the way home, I recalled the taste of their food in my mouth, dry and sour like their hushed gossip, and I told Ma I could no longer eat at the temple.

"It's God's food," Ma always said firmly, like that was an explanation for anything. I was to be thankful for being Sikh, she reminded me, because in our religion, everybody was treated equally when it came to eating. "Old and young, poor and rich—as long as you believe in Him, you are welcome to dine at the temple." I had to admit that it was quite generous of God to feed everyone. But I still wished He would make His food a bit more appealing. Whining around Ma was not a good idea; she didn't tolerate it. I never attempted the scratching trick at the temple because it was too risky with so many people watching. They weren't supposed to know about Ma's skin trouble. It was something the three of us kept to ourselves. She had a condition that made her skin itch and become frighteningly red. She went to a doctor who gave her a special ointment and advised her not to scratch, but she said it was unbearable sometimes. If she was upset, her skin got even worse. The rashes grew and spread, and took over her skin completely. Ma wore long sleeves to the temple, even on the hottest days, and pulled them over her hands if anybody stared. People were always staring—needle-nosed ladies with their large eyes and greying hair, younger women whose glances darted away only to look back again. The men held their looks longer. I had asked Ma once why they always looked at us. She shrugged and said, "When all of my skin trouble started, they all had their own ideas about it. A stupid superstitious lot they are."

To get me to eat at the temple, Ma had coaxed. She had pleaded. She had threatened. She had even allowed her voice to rise to a near-shout once, but so many people had looked up that she had to lower it, defeated. Finally, when I was about six years old, she came up with an idea. In her handbag, with napkins and a purse heavy with coins, she carried a small jar of sugar. Glancing around first to see that nobody was looking, she allowed me to sprinkle the sugar onto the hot roti. I always watched and waited until it melted into the dough before I tore off a bite to test. Every time Ma let me eat this sugar bread, she shook her head and muttered, "This is the last time." But she brought that jar with her every Sunday, to every temple programme. She told me once that roti was the only thing her own mother cooked when they were growing up. This was no surprise to me because my Nani-ji still ate roti for every meal.

"Sometimes we had to modify it too. Just for a change," she had said, a smile playing on her lips. It was the kind of smile she wore when she was remembering something that made her happy. It wasn't a look I noticed because often, the past brought shadows to Ma's face.

Nani-ji was at the temple every Sunday, sitting in the ladies' section, wearing her widow's white. Her hair was so thin that small pink strips of her scalp showed through the gauzy material of her scarf. Every time I walked in and noticed her, I quickly reached up to make sure that my scarf was covering my head, concealing my short ponytail. From the corner of my eye, I noticed Ma doing the same thing. Nani-ji knew that we cut our hair and she didn't like it, so we tried our best to hide the sin so she wouldn't notice and comment. Sikhs are not supposed to cut their hair or shave; the girls and women have plaits that hang down their backs like ropes, and the men wear turbans and thick beards that swallow their faces. Ma and I were modern with our short hair and Daddy too, with those faint dots of stubble on his cheeks. He managed to escape the temple most of the time because he took Sunday shifts at the hotel. He wasn't very religious, he admitted to me. He said that he had nothing against God, but he didn't think it was necessary to sit and drink tea in His home every week either.

Nani-ji was too old and slow on her feet to go to the temple on her own. Ma's brother, Mama-ji Sarjit, drove her early in the mornings. She always sat up front with his wife, my Fat Auntie, which was why we sat in the back. Ma and her brother only spoke few words to each other, and to Fat Auntie, even fewer. There had been an argument a few years earlier during which Fat Auntie had called Ma a disgrace for not attending her housewarming prayers. I knew this because Ma had said some unpleasant words about Fat Auntie's figure, specifically about her bum. After that, we avoided the temple for a few weeks, then Nani-ji got sick and had to go to the hospital, so they were forced to speak again. They politely said hello and gave awkward side hugs as we queued up for food. The tension between them lingered in the air and settled in the milky tea I was forced to sip to push the hard bread down my throat.

"I don't like it," I told Ma, shaking the cup at her. The black dots of tea leaves rose to the surface. "It's...unfriendly."

"Bitter," Ma corrected me but she had failed the test. I wanted to see if she, too, could taste emotions. "There's no such thing as an *unfriendly* taste. It's the cardamom that kicks you a bit, takes away the sweetness." So she was not aware of the clues she gave away every day.

Beneath his thick beard, my Mama-ji's mouth was set in a permanent frown. He greeted by nodding. He allowed Fat Auntie to talk as much as she wanted. At the temple, she was always the loudest. From across the women's section, I could hear her shrill voice bouncing between the steel plates and the pale yellow walls. She got along well with the temple ladies. I wasn't sure if my grandmother liked her because Nani-ji didn't like anybody, but Fat Auntie was always on her side. Every time Nani-ji stood up, Fat Auntie rushed to help her. Every time Nani-ji coughed, Fat Auntie patted her back with a look on her face that seemed more like concentration than concern. These gestures made Ma's lips become thin as if she had to swallow them to refrain from saying something nasty. Because she felt this way, I did too. I spent my lunches at the temple focusing on hating Fat Auntie, and couldn't eat the sweet rice pudding and greasy golden rings of jalebi because of the anger that coated my taste buds, stinging my mouth with bitterness.

We stopped going to the temple because Ma had had an argument with Fat Auntie. I did not know exactly what they had disagreed about because there was nothing they didn't disagree about. It happened about a year ago in the dining hall after a long service.

I had just finished eating my lunch and was staring at the portraits on the wall. There were five portraits of the Gurus and I tried to figure out the stories they told. One portrait showed Guru Nanak atop a horse, a gentle halo illuminating his long robes. Another showed three men charging towards an army with spears. In another portrait, all nine Gurus sat cross-legged in a line, a temple towering behind them. I let my legs swing under the table. Nani-ji and Fat Auntie sat opposite us. Fat Auntie's niece was there—a girl named Harpreet with long hair and a pointy chin. "We are cousins," she told me matter-of-factly. "My Auntie is your Auntie." I worked it out in my mind and we were not really related. Fat Auntie's sister was Harpreet's mother. But Harpreet was friendly enough and when I accidentally kicked her under the table, she cheerily said, "Never mind!" before I could even apologise.

Ma and Fat Auntie were speaking in English and Nani-ji was slowly eating her food, mashing the roti up with her fingers and shovelling it into her mouth. She frowned as they spoke because she did not understand what they were saying. The conversation was about her. "She's too old to be staying on her own," Fat Auntie insisted. "She can't live in my house. I've got my two boys to look after." She gestured to her two sons, my cousins Devjit and Gurpreet. They were teenagers and didn't look like they needed to be looked after at all. I only realised I was staring when Devjit scowled at me, so I turned my attention to Ma.

"We have no room in my flat," Ma said. "It's too small. At least there's a spare bedroom in your home. You know I want to take care of my mother in her old age. But it's just not practical."

"Do you want to take care of her?" Fat Auntie countered. "Or are you just making excuses?"

Ma stared at her and I could feel her boiling rage. "What is that supposed to mean?" she asked quietly.

"Nothing. It's just very typical of you. You don't like to take on family responsibilities. And it's hard to know when you're telling the truth." She looked pointedly at Ma's wrists, which poked out of her long sleeves. The sun had been strong that morning on our path from the block to the bus stop and Ma's skin was scarlet.

"Want to go outside and play?" Harpreet asked me. I wanted to say no but Ma turned to me and said, "Pin, go with your new friend." She gave Harpreet a warm smile.

"Your mother is very pretty," Harpreet said as we searched the racks outside for our shoes. I had placed mine on top of Ma's but then more people had arrived and kicked their shoes off and the floor was a mess of black leather shoes, sneakers, high-heeled sequined sandals and flat slippers. I finally found my shoes but Harpreet said, "Don't put them on. We're going to play a running game." We left the temple building and descended the stairs that led to a courtyard where I met the other children. Ma and I had never stayed at the temple for very long before, so I didn't know the other kids. "This is my cousin Parveen!" Harpreet said, clasping my hand. "I'm Pin," I corrected her. Nobody called me by my full name. Daddy liked to joke that it was too long for me.

The courtyard was a wide open space with high grey walls covered in moss and creeping vines. The ground below my feet was rough and uneven but Harpreet assured me I'd get used to it once I started running. She was in charge of choosing the game because she was the oldest. "Can we play catching?" a boy asked.

"Later," Harpreet replied, then I saw her turn her head to the side. "Choos," she said under her breath. She saw me looking and she looked around before she quietly explained it. "I learnt it from my friend at school. If you say something but it's not true, you have to say 'choos' afterwards. Otherwise God will punish you for lying." I kept this in mind.

We played "What's the time, Mr Wolf?" One person was named Mr Wolf and they had to stand against the wall with their back facing the rest of us. "What's the time, Mr Wolf?" we cried out, and Mr Wolf would call out a time. We crept closer to Mr Wolf according to the number of hours he called out. If he said it was three o'clock, then we took three steps. The moment anybody got close enough to Mr Wolf, they had to try to touch the wall and run before he tagged them back. The person who got tagged became the next Mr Wolf.

We played rounds of the game until a cluster of clouds briefly blocked the sun and cast shadows on the courtyard. "Rain!" Harpreet called out, dancing around as though it was already pouring. In the distance, we heard rolling thunder. A strong gust of wind carried the smell of damp earth from some other part of the island where it was already raining. I expected Ma to come out of the temple already but there were no signs of her.

"Let's play some more. I want to be Mr Wolf," one boy named Jaswinder said. It was not actually his turn to be Mr Wolf but everybody was tired and we were only half-heartedly playing anyway. He ran to the front wall. "Ready?" He called out. "Okay, ask me."

The adults began to trickle outside, looking up at the tin-coloured sky. "What's the time, Mr Wolf?" we asked. He did not answer.

"Oi! What's the time, Mr Wolf?"

Still nothing.

"WHAT'S THE TIME, MR WOLF???" we all screamed in unison.

Jaswinder turned around slowly and gave us a grin. And then he said, "Fuck". A hush fell over the group. Some boys began to giggle. The girls were appalled. "I'm telling your mother," Harpreet scolded him. She looked at me and shook her head. "I know his mother," she said to me. He did not seem to care. He announced the word again between giggles. The other boys shrieked with laughter but nobody dared to repeat what he had said. The girls huddled together.

Harpreet didn't have to tell his mother. She was one of the parents who had come outside when the sky began to darken. She rushed towards our group like a lightning bolt. "Say that again?" she challenged before slapping him hard across the face twice. I winced. Harpreet put her hands on her hips and looked satisfied. Jaswinder howled and whimpered as his mother dragged him off by the ear. "Saying vulgar words in the temple in front of everybody. Just you wait till I tell your father about this. He'll give you a bloody thrashing at home. Just *wait*."

We stood there in silence for a moment, as if mourning the loss of a soldier. "Maybe we should play catching or hide-and-seek," suggested a bony girl named Neelu. Harpreet agreed and asked me if I wanted to play too. I was about to say yes when I spotted Ma coming out of the temple entrance with my shoes in her hands. She was walking quickly and something was wrong. I could tell because of the way she looked at me, almost as if she was looking right past me because her mind was full of other thoughts.

"We're going now, Pin," she said sharply.

"We're playing hide-and-seek," I told Ma.

"No. Get your shoes. We're going now."

I turned to Harpreet. "Okay, next week," I said apologetically. I liked the temple more now that I knew the other kids. Running around and playing made me forget God's bad food.

"No. We're not coming back next week. We're not coming back here any more," Ma said. Harpreet's eyes widened.

After I put my shoes back on, Ma took my hand and led me out of the courtyard. The group of adults stepped aside quietly to let us pass. The children looked confused. Harpreet waved but Ma was pulling me along so hard, I did not have a chance to wave back.

At the bus stop, I noticed that the backs of Ma's hands were raw with scabs. She wrung her hands and bit her lower lip and tried to blink back tears that poured down her cheeks anyway. I put my head against her shoulder and my hand in hers but she shrugged me away. "God sees everything, Pin," she said finally as our bus approached. "You just remember that." I immediately felt a wave of guilt for playing "What's the time, Mr Wolf?" with that foul-mouthed boy Jaswinder now. God had seen the whole thing.

The following Sunday, we started going to the market and Ma made a religion out of buying food and transforming it into delicious dishes with her recipes. I knew that Fat Auntie must have said something terrible to make her so angry but I did not dare to ask her what it was. I just accompanied her to the market and when she first told me that I should never become like her, I said, "Okay." Then I turned to the side and said, "Choos, choos, choos." Thrice, because it was likely to be stronger that way.

•   •   •

I woke from my nap to the sound of the front gate yawning as it opened, the padlock snapping open. "Hi Daddy," I murmured as he stepped into my room.

"Hi Pinny," he said, a grin in his voice. "Not playing football today?"

"I don't play on Sundays," I told him. The boys in the neighbourhood sometimes let me join them in playing catching and football. I had a powerful kick and I was little enough to fit into the spaces in shallow drains where the balls sometimes ended up. I was also a girl, which made the neighbourhood people complain less if we accidentally hit them, because I was good at looking sad and sorry when I was scolded.

"I saw the boys downstairs," Daddy said. He folded his legs into a pretzel and sat on the floor, then he looked around as if to check for spies. He lowered his voice. "Promise you won't tell anyone?" I nodded. "Promise? Promise, *promise*?" He took out a stack of tickets from his pocket, folded like dollar bills. My eyes widened. There must have been over 20 lottery tickets.

"So many?" I asked, grabbing for the tickets. I spread them out on the floor and surveyed the numbers. Four of them were digits I had given him and the rest were unknown to me. I pointed to random tickets and asked about them. "Where is this one from? Why did you pick this one?" Daddy's explanations were varied. His numbers were like Ma's dishes—full of stories and combinations. 4402 was the license plate number of a wealthy hotel guest. 2421 was the cost of his new shoes, $24.21. 6748 had just occurred to him during a late shift and he took this as a sign that he needed to use it.

"There were so many important numbers this week, Pin," he said. "I couldn't just buy one or two." He didn't need to explain to me. If Ma found out, she'd be furious. She thought the lottery was a waste of money that we didn't have. "Why don't you get a better job instead of putting all of your wages in stupid 4D tickets?" she always asked in a tone that meant it wasn't a question.

"I won't tell," I told Daddy as he counted and stuffed the tickets back into his pockets.

"Thanks, Pinny," he said. He smoothed down the messy curls in my hair, but they sprang up again.

"I need to go for a haircut," I told him. The humid weather made stray curls rise from my head, giving me a monstrous halo. At school, I always kept my hair back in a tight ponytail because we weren't allowed to keep it loose. When Ma felt generous, she let me use a bit of her hairspray to keep down the curls, which she then pinned back with her black rhinestone clip so that my hair glittered.

"Why didn't you ask Ma to take you to the hairdresser today?" he asked. "After the market?"

I looked at the spot on my leg. The rash I had created had vanished. Daddy's eyes did not follow mine. He had a habit of asking questions and not really listening to the answers. I rolled over onto my back and watched my stomach rise and fall with steady breathing. The room was sinking into dusk. The faint chirps of the last remaining songbirds in the contest under the other block drifted into our flat in small waves.

"We had a lot of things to carry," I finally said.

"I noticed. Your Ma filled the fridge like it's the end of the world," he said.

"Maybe she has new ideas."

"Maybe," Daddy said, unconvinced. Faint worry lines appeared on his high forehead. The last time Ma bought this much food out of inspiration, she had gotten excited, then flustered. She rubbed cinnamon sticks on chicken thighs. Leafy vegetables were paired with snapped long beans—she usually insisted on decorating her dishes like colourful bouquets. That was the first week after the argument at the temple. Nani-ji had called our house a few times to speak to Ma, but Ma did not want to speak to anybody. "If you still think I'm a liar, then leave me alone!" she shouted into the receiver one day without even greeting the person on the other end. Gradually, the calls stopped and Ma began to create more peaceful dishes—velvety smooth fish curries, roasted and glazed pork slices, soft noodles mixed with finely shredded vegetables.

When it came to food, Ma always said that money did not matter. She bargained at the market but if forced to pay full price for everything, she would. It was afterwards, when we were at home, that she picked through her purse and laid out the notes and change on the table, sighing and clicking her tongue against her teeth. Daddy tried to make up for the lack of money by making it look like we had more. He liked to remind me that it was only a matter of time before he won big in the 4D draw, then all of this fussing and worrying would seem silly. I listened to him because Ma refused to and I tried to let him convince me, but it was difficult because he never even won a consolation prize. Daddy didn't just buy 4D tickets. He entered every contest and every lucky draw that was advertised. When the radio deejays announced that the first ten callers would win a Walkman or tickets to a movie, he leapt for the telephone and punched in the numbers. Sometimes I wished that he believed in God a little bit more because He would guide him to choose the right numbers for once, or call the radio station at the right time. There was something in Daddy's eagerness that made my heart ache. He needed to win something.

. . .

There were two phones in our flat. One phone sat outside in the living room—it was black and slick with extra buttons for functions we didn't need to use, like conference calling and speakerphone. Daddy had won it at his office lucky draw on Chinese New Year, the only lucky draw during which he had ever won a prize. We chucked the old phone—a basic cream-coloured phone—into the storeroom until I discovered an outlet under my desk one day. Daddy hooked the old phone to it but Ma insisted that he remove it because I was too young to have my own phone, even if it was on a shared line. "Pin doesn't need to talk to anyone in her room. There are no secrets in this house," Ma told him loudly. Daddy didn't want to remove it. He told Ma, "Wait till somebody calls and listen. You'll see why it's nice to have two phones." He was right. It sounded grand when calls came in, with two separate tones ringing through the air. It made the neighbours peek into our flat, impressed.

Daddy made me promise not to listen in on conversations from my extension. I tried to reason with Ma. "But if there are no secrets in this house, why can't I use it to listen?"

"Don't be cheeky, Pin," she said simply and it was the only answer she would offer.

When the phones rang that Sunday evening in July, both Ma and Daddy were in the kitchen, chatting in low voices. I was still too lazy to get up off the floor but then I remembered I still had chores to do before school the next morning. The prefects at school inspected our shoes every Monday and I had already gotten booked once for not washing and polishing them beforehand. The phones kept ringing—Ma's voice got louder and for a moment, my heart stopped. Had she found out about the lottery tickets? But then I heard the tone of Daddy's voice and he was not trying to defend himself. "If that's what you want, then go ahead and buy it. I'm not stopping you," he said.

"You're not stopping me but our bank account certainly is," Ma retorted. It was just a regular money argument, the kind that began and erupted in our flat and lingered in the air until it was picked up again. The phones rang one more time.

I must have picked up the receiver at the same time as Ma because usually, if I picked it up while she was already having a conversation, she heard the clicking sound and called, "Pin! I have it. Put down the phone." It was Fat Auntie on the line. I hadn't heard her voice since that day at the temple. I hadn't missed it much.

"Mother had to be taken to the hospital again today. I just thought you should know," Fat Auntie said curtly.

"What happened?" Ma asked.

"It's her lungs again. She's been having a very bad cough for a few days now. We had to convince her to go—you know how she is. The doctors say she's stable now and they want to keep her around to observe her for one or two days, but she insists on leaving the hospital tomorrow."

"Well, if she's feeling well enough—" Ma said.

"The thing is, she's really less capable now. It's like she's weaker every day."

"I know. We've talked about this."

"She's been talking about you a lot lately."

Over the phone, Ma's sigh was like a roar. "I can't change what she thinks. I can't change what anybody thinks any more. You can tell her that."

"You can tell her yourself. She told me to call and ask if she can stay with you."

"What?" Ma asked. I nearly dropped the receiver. Nani-ji *wanted* to come stay with us? It didn't sound right.

Fat Auntie sighed. "I don't know why but that's what she's been saying. She's been talking a lot lately about getting old and moving on from the past, things like that. She says that she wants to forget about what happened. It was so long ago. She wants to spend time with you and Pin."

"I need to think about it," Ma said. "We really don't have much space." Something brimmed in her voice. It was excitement. Ma was happy; I could hear laughter in her voice. I gently put down the phone and went to the living room to look at her, and I was right. She was sitting on the edge of the rattan couch, her knee jiggling nervously. A smile played on her lips like she was about to unleash a surprise.

She and Fat Auntie continued to talk to each other for a few more minutes before Ma told her she had not cooked dinner yet. She said goodbye and rushed into the kitchen, where Daddy sat with his newspaper strewn across the table. "I knew it," she said gleefully. "I woke up this morning, and I just knew it. I just had this feeling that my mother would call soon and ask to come stay with us. I didn't want to say anything, but I just knew it. She wants to forget about everything." The fridge door made a kissing sound as Ma pried it open and began unloading the shelves. "I bought so much food today and I kept asking myself what the occasion was, and now I know. I could feel it. She wants to forget. I knew it." Ma kept repeating this until it became clear that she wasn't really talking to Daddy, she was talking to herself. Soon the counter top was filled with gourds and leaves, powders and frozen meat. Ma laughed to herself. "What am I doing? She doesn't eat any of this… but she did say she wanted to move on from the past. Will she even try new food now?" Daddy just stared at her wordlessly.

"What's going on?" I asked innocently as I walked into the kitchen. Daddy opened his mouth as if to say something to Ma but she just came right out and said, "Your Nani-ji is coming to stay with us."

"For how long?" I asked.

"Pin," Ma said, annoyed. "That's rude."

"Where will she sleep?" I continued, glancing around the flat. I couldn't think of any place to put Nani-ji besides the storeroom.

"Nothing's been decided yet," Daddy finally spoke up. "We don't even know if she's really coming to stay with us." The deep lines on his forehead appeared again. He scratched his head.

"If I say she can stay with us, then yes, she's coming," Ma said.

"I don't want her to come here!" I blurted out. Daddy began to gather the pages of his newspaper and arrange them neatly. I did not understand how he could be so calm. Nani-ji liked him the least.

Daddy and Ma exchanged glances. Ma looked angry but the vibrant layout of her groceries distracted her. She turned her back to me and started arranging the vegetables and meat into neat piles. "I'll take you out to eat, Pin," Daddy offered. "Just for tonight," he told Ma. She shook her head and muttered something about how her mother would have whacked her for being so spoiled but she was in such high spirits, she just left it at that.

"Come on, Pin. Stop being silly. Let's go downstairs. We'll have a bite to eat, then come up and eat whatever your Ma has made." Daddy gave me a kind smile. He was always doing this, making sure both Ma and I were happy.

"Okay," I said and went into my room to change into the long denim shorts I had worn to the market that morning; the red T-shirt was balled up in the corner. The sour fish odour from the market still clung to the fabric.

A cool evening breeze swept through the air as we stepped out of our block. I took Daddy's hand, lacing my fingers in his. Sunday evenings meant empty streets and less noise. We walked down the street as if it belonged to us. The hawker centre glowed under fluorescent lights and signs. I chose Hokkien noodles with bean sprouts and chopped chillies. Daddy had Point-Point rice. We called it that because the dishes were laid out in small platters behind a glass case and customers had to ask for a bowl of rice, then point to what they wanted—tofu; fish cake; fried long beans; spinach; steamed chicken. The sign above the stall said Very Tasty Economy Rice because the food was cheap—three dollars bought Daddy a plate piled so high that I couldn't see the rice. We did not speak as we ate.

My noodles were flat and slippery, difficult to keep on the chopsticks. The chillies stung my lips. It was spicier than I had remembered. I studied the hawker's expressions behind the smoke that rose from his hissing wok. Framed by the steel counters and glass casing of his tiny stall, he looked overgrown and uncomfortable.

Daddy finished his food before I did and let out a contented sigh. I thought of Nani-ji as I ate and tried again to feel some guilt or even a bit of sadness. Something like it rose in my stomach but after considering, I decided it was just the food.

"What are you thinking?" Daddy asked. "Are you ready for school tomorrow?"

I made a face. Daddy laughed, shook his head. "You have a

long way to go, Pin," he reminded me. I made another face.

"Why does Nani-ji have to stay with us?" I asked.

"She doesn't have to. But your Ma wants her to."

"Why?" I pressed.

Daddy paused. He looked like he was selecting the words he would use, Point-Point style. "For one thing, she's ill. And she and your Ma have a lot of things to resolve… It's very complicated, Pin. It's really not for me to explain to you." He looked down and fumbled with his hands.

This was why I had never asked Daddy to explain why Ma didn't want me to become like her. She was just as big a puzzle to him as she was to everyone else. Sometimes when she spoke, a look crossed his face as if he had just met her. Around Ma, we were both awed and slightly confused.

"She doesn't like you," I reminded Daddy.

"Nani-ji doesn't like many things. She's had a tough life."

"Where will she sleep? And for how long?"

"Listen, Pin," Daddy said. "I don't want you dwelling on this any more. Whether you like it or not, your grandmother is coming to stay with us. She's your mother's mother. She's family, and sometimes, we make sacrifices for family, okay? If I wanted my father and mother to come and stay with us, your Ma probably wouldn't be too thrilled, but she would accept it, wouldn't she?" I wasn't sure if she would. Daddy's parents had both died by the time he married Ma anyway.

"Push it out of your mind. It will take some time—maybe a week or two—before Nani-ji moves in anyway. It's not like she's on her way right now. Don't think about it."

A spotted stray cat wove between my ankles and went for Daddy's next. I reached down to pet it. If Ma had been there, she would have pulled my hand back and exclaimed, "Dirty!" But Daddy let me stroke her long grey fur. I scratched the nook behind her neck until she dipped down and stretched out on the floor, her claws spread and extended. Daddy looked under the table and coaxed her to his side with small piece of fish cake. As she crouched towards his hand, sniffing it, he reached into his pocket and took out an old receipt.

"Got a pencil?" he asked.

"No," I said.

He pulled out the pen he always carried with him in his shirt pocket. "You start," he told me, nodding towards the cat. I shook my head and pushed the paper back to him. "You first," I said. Daddy took the pen and started a rough outline of the cat. Slowly, she began to take shape on the paper.

At school, I didn't take art class very seriously. The assignments were boring: draw a bowl of fruits, make a Chinese New Year card, pick a leaf from outside and trace the veins. But sitting with Daddy and drawing was not like assignments. We spent many evenings after he came home from work sitting in our flat and sketching the buildings across from ours. When we were out and there was nothing to say, he always dug out a piece of paper and found something for both of us to draw.

The cat changed positions. This time, flat on her belly, she looked regal. She narrowed her eyes at me as if I had just insulted her. Daddy laughed, adding some roundness to the slender figure he had drawn.

"She's fat."

"Well-fed," Daddy replied. In the distance, there were more cats rubbing against the legs of customers and weaving their way between the tables. They all had the same low bellies that swung like pendulums as they walked. Pieces of noodle, fish, potato and clumps of rice littered the floor.

Daddy fished in his pockets for another piece of paper. "Your turn to draw," he said, pointing the pen towards me. I saw his own drawing on the receipt and knew I couldn't do anything better than that. Daddy told me that he had taken up drawing during his long shifts guarding the hotel downtown when there was nothing else to do. Mostly, he drew what he saw on the security screens since he wasn't supposed to take his eyes off them. Doors, hallways, sometimes the streets outside from a narrow angle. Ma complained that his pockets were full of useless drawings of black and grey squares, but I didn't let her throw them away. I kept them clipped together in my desk drawer and carried them to school with me, sometimes flipping through them during Silent Reading.

I took the paper from Daddy reluctantly. "Want something to drink?" he asked. I shook my head but he got up anyway, and came back with iced chrysanthemum tea in a tall glass. He pushed the glass towards me.

"No," I said. The cat's head rested on a crook between her paws. The folds of her skin stuck out in rings. I couldn't get the shapes of her ears correct—they were sharp, precise cones without softness in my drawing. The more I drew over them, the rounder they became, but then they were wrong again, lumpy this time.

"You should have some of this, Pin. It's sweet," Daddy insisted. Impatience rushed through me—Daddy was not good with his own combinations. Chrysanthemum tea didn't go with noodles or his mixed rice.

"I don't want," I said. I pressed the pen into the paper and pushed the glass back towards him. It tipped and spilt onto my paper. I didn't mean to ruin my drawing but as the ink spread and blurred, it looked as though the cat was in motion. Daddy moved out of the way and switched seats so he wasn't opposite me. He looked down at the drawing.

"It looks like her," he said encouragingly. We both looked over at the cat but she had walked to another table. "The ears were good."

I turned over the paper to see if the ink had spread through to the table. There was writing on the other side—a row of numbers.

"Hey! You have to keep this!" I told Daddy, giving him back the lottery ticket. It stuck limply to my fingers.

Daddy peeled it off carefully. He spent a minute looking at the numbers, rereading them and mumbling them out loud. Then he balled up the ticket and tossed it into my bowl of unfinished noodles.

We got up without saying anything and walked home. I filled the night silence with stories about school—things my teachers had told us, and games my friends had invented during recess. I talked and talked so Daddy wouldn't have space to say anything. I didn't ask him why he threw away the ticket because I already knew why. We weren't going to win. Nani-ji was moving in with us. Our luck that week was not very good.

•   •   •

That night, I fell asleep thinking about the last time Ma, Nani-ji and Fat Auntie had been at the temple. I tried to figure out what Fat Auntie had said that made Ma so furious, but when I thought of her anger, the redness of her scabs flashed into my mind and I recalled the people at the temple with their accusing looks. I woke up in the middle of the night because I thought I heard Daddy telling me to wake up, but he was speaking to Ma. His voice sounded more urgent than I had ever heard it and it scared me. I thought that she had found out about his lottery tickets and he was trying to defend himself, but as his voice rose, I could make out the words.

"I'm telling you frankly, Jini," he said. "She's not coming here to fix the past. There's more on her mind. She never took your side and she never will. You have to think carefully about your mother moving here." I was surprised. I had never heard Daddy sound so forceful before.

Ma responded, but her voice was too low for me to hear what she was saying. I crept closer to the door but they both became quieter, as if suddenly aware that I was just down the hall. I fought to stay awake after that in case anything else was said, but eventually I sank back into a blank, dreamless sleep.

2

OUTSIDE THE GATES of First Christian Girls' School, I felt like the smallest Primary Four girl on the island. Stark white buildings propped up by long columns, steeples with stained-glass windows and an enormous bell tower loomed over the pavements and glared against the blue sky. The cluster of white buildings sat at the top of a steep hill so the school looked like a majestic ancient castle in Europe.

At the main gate, I could imagine I was walking into a storybook kingdom but it was difficult to pretend for very long. Every morning, the humid air pressed against my skin and branches holding waxy tropical leaves swept the air and carried a bitter earthy smell that seeped into my nostrils. The man who sold cakes of ice cream sandwiched between coloured bread stood at his pavement cart and yelled, "Lai, lai, seventy cent, seventy cent!" A dense tangle of tree branches blocked some sunlight and in the distance behind them, the pale outlines of office buildings peered between clouds. Everything looked like Singapore. I could not have mistaken it for any other place.

There were girls at First Christian whose mothers and grandmothers had been students there too, and they carried stories of ghosts settling in the hallways after the war. French missionaries and settlers had built the school during World War

Two and those stark white buildings had been hiding places for anybody escaping the Japanese. Pastors in long black cloaks secretly sneaked in strangers to stay in the classrooms while bombs and gunfire rained all over the island. The girls told these stories like they had been there themselves; the rest of us only half-listened because the war was a lifetime ago and we had heard all these stories already. Those were girls whose mothers wore fancy jackets and silk blouses everywhere even if they were housewives like Ma. Their jewellery matched their shoes and they spoke in crisp British English with glistening cherry-red mouths.

The others were like me—Bursary Girls. Our parents could not afford the school fees so at the end of every month, we queued up in a corner of the school canteen and collected a donation from the school and a bill that showed what we owed. The other girls did not tease us because the principal, Mrs D'Cruz, always reminded them that it was not the Christian way to look down on those who had less. She gently told them to introduce us to the Lord instead, for He brought good things to those who believed in Him and feared Him. Most of the Bursary Girls were apparently not very familiar with the Lord.

You weren't supposed to be able to tell the Bursary Girls from the others because we all wore the same uniforms—dark blue pleated pinafores over white blouses, white Bata canvas shoes and white ankle socks. We all wore the same silver badges with a small cross covered in vines. But some girls' pinafores were a lighter shade of blue or too short because they were second-hand. The elastic on their socks had snapped at the beginning of the year so their socks dropped at their ankles like excess skin. Those girls looked like Bursary Girls. Ma made it a point to buy me a new uniform every year because she didn't want me looking poor at school. "And we're not poor," she often reminded me. "We're not as well-off as other people but look—we have a roof, we have a television, a phone line, electricity and you have good food to eat every day."

Ma was always curious about what I was taught at school. I figured it was because she and Daddy paid more to send me to First Christian than they would have if they had sent me to a neighbourhood school, and she wanted to make sure they were getting what they paid for. She wanted to know everything I learnt, and sometimes I felt like a teacher. I recited my times tables, told her how the reservoirs collected rain and summarised stories we had read for English before she was satisfied. She nodded quickly with each new fact. I started to wonder if she already knew everything, or if she was also learning as I was. One of the few things I knew about Ma was that she'd had to leave school after her O-Levels so she could work to support her family after her father had left.

I decided to trick her one day. I gave her all of the wrong information, starting with a maths problem sum with a wrong answer. Then I moved on to science. I told her that plants could survive without water. She just nodded, listening, but not really letting the false facts sink in. I could tell because her eyes were glassy. Then I spelled a few English words incorrectly. She did not protest. I racked my brain to think of what else we had covered in school that day. Social studies: we had learnt about Singapore's early settlers. I told her that Singapura was named after Sang Nila Utama saw a tiger, not a lion. I told her that Singapore was never a part of Malaysia, that it had always been a city-state of its own and they hadn't chucked us out and told us to go fend for ourselves. I also told her that the Japanese had never attacked

Singapore during the war; they had helped us.

Ma's eyes widened. "How can you lie?" she cried. "Stupid girl." She pulled my plate of steaming baby corn and carrots and honey-glazed chicken away from me. I was surprised at her outburst. I sat there with my fork and spoon suspended in mid-air.

"I was just joking," I told her. "What's wrong?"

"There is no joking about the past."

"But history is boring," I said. It was. My social studies reader was the neatest book I had because I tried not to touch it. When I opened it, the pages drowned me with facts and figures and sepia-printed pictures of rickshaws and dirt roads and crooked signs hanging from dingy shophouse balconies. They were not places I recognised as home.

Ma was clearly upset. She leant towards me as if she were about to tell me a secret, but looked concerned as she searched for something in my face. "The past may be distant," she said. "And we might not care about it as much as we do the present. But it is wrong to change the facts."

I knew she would only give my food back once I gave her a sign that I understood, even though I didn't see what the big deal was.

"Okay," I said.

She raised an eyebrow doubtfully.

"O-*kay*," I emphasised. I was tired of her rules. She pushed the plate back across the table and shook her head. "Pin, Pin, Pin," she simply said, shaking her head as I stuffed the vegetables and meat into my mouth. I did not speak for the rest of the meal— my big mouth had already almost cost me lunch that afternoon. Sometimes with Ma it was best to say less.

• • •

The day after Ma had announced that Nani-ji would move into our flat, I struggled not to think about her. Daddy's advice had been to push it out of my mind, so I shrank the image of Nani-ji until she was a tiny white ball of fluff. I lugged my school bag on my shoulders and took long steps up the hill into the field where morning assembly was held.

Assembly at school was the same every morning: we stood in straight rows and sang "Majulah Singapura" as two prefects raised the red and white flag on its rope. Like our voices, it bounced and jerked unevenly. After the National Anthem, we made fists with our right hands, put them over our hearts and recited the Singapore pledge about building a democratic society. Then Mrs D'Cruz took over and gave the daily devotion. Those of us who weren't Christian were told to bow our heads in respect. "Pray to your own god," the teachers had urged us on the first day back in Primary One, "or listen."

I knew it was useless praying to my own God because He would not be at the First Christian Girls' School. He would not even listen to me unless I had my head covered and I was sitting on the carpeted floor of the temple listening to the drone of Punjabi prayers. He did not understand English, which was the only language we were allowed to speak at school. It was the language of my thoughts once I left our flat every morning and stepped onto the school bus.

Mrs D'Cruz wore thick woolly skirts with matching jackets and had stiff, short hair that framed her head like a helmet. When she smiled, it was an effort and her whole body showed the strain. Spider's web wrinkles cracked the corners of her eyes, her shoulders rose slightly and even her pink ears seemed to perk. She only smiled during devotions.

"Your parents and some of you older girls might have bank accounts," she began. We shifted and nodded. "To have a bank account, one must first earn money. To access this bank account, one uses an ATM card."

"Or a chequebook," said the girl behind me, in the same pitch that Mrs D'Cruz had used. Her comment sent a ripple of giggles through the class and caused a teacher to come marching towards us. I wiped the smile off my face, feeling her glowering behind us. Mrs D'Cruz was too far away to notice. She continued.

"God has plans for you. He wants you to prosper. Throughout our lives, when we do good deeds, God deposits money in our bank accounts. Our *spiritual* bank accounts." She enunciated each syllable and dragged out the R. "When we sin, what do you think God does? He withdraws this money. At the end of our lives, God will check your account in Heaven. Will you be wealthy or will you be bankrupt?" Mrs D'Cruz looked up with triumph. "Let us pray," she said and we all bowed our heads. Daily devotions often had something to do with money and Mrs D'Cruz explained once that this was the only language Singaporeans understood. "I say money only and wah…the whole sea of heads before me looks up."

There were a few things I did not understand about God, like why He was invisible. It seemed like somebody who had done so many good things for the world would want everyone to see who He was. I also didn't understand why He created animals that suffered unnecessarily, like the stray dog with the lame leg I often saw roaming outside my block in the mornings. The most confusing thing to me was this: the God at school was surely not the same God that I knew at home. The God Mrs D'Cruz spoke about had a son named Jesus. My God had a few sons but none of them were Jesus. His name was Guru Nanak. He had eight other gods helping him win wars against the Muslims and the Hindus so He could turn people into Sikhs. Mrs D'Cruz liked to remind us that God did not have a face, and that He dwelled in everybody's hearts but this could not be right. I knew exactly what God looked like. He had watery deep-set eyes, a white beard and wore a turban.

Ma had bought a portrait of God from the temple a few years ago after Nani-ji had pressured her. With some stern words, Nani-ji also urged her to buy a calendar with God on it, a prayer booklet with the same picture, and a postcard. God only had one pose in all of these items. His robes were bronze, matching the soft, blurry light around His head. His turban was white. He looked sad and stern.

Ma had stood dangerously on a rickety chair and knocked three nails into the wall to make sure that God would remain on our wall. She placed the other items in different parts of the house. "Just as they say," she told me brightly, "God is everywhere." He stared from the back of her bedroom door and from the top of my dresser. Ma seemed to think that this God's presence in our flat would do us some good. That was the year when Daddy was being given fewer shifts at the hotel and he spent a lot of time searching through the classified ads in the newspaper for a different job.

But it was only a matter of weeks before God started to bother Ma. The first thing she put away was the calendar. "Why do I need God to remind me which day of the week it is?" she asked me. The prayer book went next, when Ma decided that books were meant for telling stories, not religious chants. God's image on the cover was distracting. She wrapped the books in a nice cotton scarf and placed them in her dresser drawer. God in the postcard suffered the worst fate—He was damaged one day when strong gusts of wind blew rain into our flat. I found it odd that Ma had left the window open that afternoon because she scolded Daddy all the time for being careless. But as she peeled a soggy God off her dresser, she shook her head and loudly expressed her remorse. "Oh dear," she sighed. "What a pity. I paid a dollar fifty for this." A week later, I came home from school to see Ma struggling to pluck God off the wall. She didn't give a reason for His removal, so I came up with one on my own: God didn't match our furniture.

"He's still everywhere," Ma had warned. "But you don't see Him. You don't have to see Him." I did though. After a month of seeing God all over our house, I saw Him hanging from the trees like a heavy leaf. I saw Him floating in the muddy water that surged through the canals when I played football with the neighbourhood boys. I mistook turbaned and bearded old men for God all the time at the temple—skinny Gods, Gods in collared shirts, Gods who made jokes, Gods who slipped into taxis alone after the service, Gods who drove cars with their families. The only place where I couldn't see God was school. He hovered outside the school gates and didn't dare enter, choosing instead to sit quietly on the kerb while I had my lessons.

It was Monday, which meant that there would be Chapel after assembly. We shuffled out of the courtyard in single file. I hung back as the rest of the class disappeared up the stairs to the chapel. The Muslim girls stayed back as well, and we waited for the Malay teacher to tell us which classroom we'd be going to while the rest of the school sang hymns and listened to Pastor William delivering his weekly sermon. Nobody was supposed to skip Chapel—the Hindu and the Buddhist girls went and stared blankly at the hymn lyrics. The Muslims were the only girls who were excused because their religion was strict and their God did not allow them to be in the presence of other Gods even if they shut their eyes tightly and pretended not to listen.

I used to go for weekly Chapel when I was in Primary One. Ma and Daddy told me to quietly sit and be respectful. At the end of every Chapel session, Pastor William and Mrs D'Cruz would hand out pieces of paper with instructions to circle one option: *I want to take this precious chance to know the Lord* or *I am happy with my religion.* I always circled the second one and returned it to the prefects. Nobody bothered me about it. The choir usually led the school in peaceful songs about saviours, redemption and deer lapping at gentle waters. I kept my lips pressed tightly together but the tunes remained in my mind. At home, I sang them quietly.

Then Ma heard me singing "Amazing Grace" one day. "Pin, we're sending you to that school because they have high standards and you're a smart girl. It's not a neighbourhood school—we want you to speak good English and have better opportunities. We're not sending you there to become a Christian."

I tried to explain to Ma that the songs were harmless. I did not believe in them. I liked the tunes and they played over and over in my mind even if I tried to think of something else. I made a mental note that day to ask my God to introduce better music in our temple programmes instead of the usual mumbling drone the priests delivered every week.

Ma was not convinced. The next day, she wrote a note to give to my form teacher, Miss Yoon. *Please excuse my daughter from all chapell services from now on.* I used correction fluid to ink out the second "l" before I gave it to Miss Yoon. Since then, before

Chapel, I would quietly exit the assembly hall with the Muslim girls and two strict Hindu girls whose mothers had also written notes. There was also a Punjabi-Sikh girl, but she was in Primary Two, and if I spoke to her, the other girls would tease me for being friends with a baby. Among the Muslim girls was Farizah, who was my best friend. She pulled her socks all the way up her legs and her pinafore was extra long so it hung loosely around her waist like a sack.

The Malay teacher, stout in a baju kurung that covered her arms and legs and hair in shiny floral-print fabric, led us to a classroom that smelled like her: sweet rose perfume and talcum powder. She unlocked the cupboard doors and pulled out board games from the shelves. A few girls rushed for the Monopoly and others took Snakes and Ladders. Farizah and I sat in a corner of our own. She came to school prepared every Monday with stacks of cards.

"Old Maid or Donkey?" she asked, pushing the two stacks of cards towards me.

"Old Maid," I said and we set up to play. Another group of girls formed a team to play Five Stones but when one of the bean pouches broke, they came to watch us.

"Hey Pin. Is that girl your sister?" Siti asked. She pointed at another Punjabi girl. Her face was buried in a book.

"No," I said.

"She looks like you."

She didn't look anything like me but most people thought Punjabis looked alike. "She's not my sister," I said.

"Her last name is Kaur," Siti said suspiciously. She looked back and forth between me and the girl. "Don't they look alike?" she asked another girl in Malay.

I exchanged a look with Farizah, who endured questions all the time. We had that in common. Girls were always asking her why she wore her socks so high and why she was so religious. "Other Muslims don't wear high socks," they said, pointing to the other Malay girls as proof. They asked me questions as well. "You say you're Indian but why do you have fair skin? Why don't you take Tamil as your Mother Tongue language like the other Indian girls?" I had heard these questions a dozen times. The questions about my last name were not new either.

It was Kaur because all Sikh girls and women kept Kaur as their last name. All males were Singh. Daddy said that it made us all part of one united family, but when I explained it that way to the other girls, they thought I was related to every Kaur or Singh they knew. Last year, we had a relief teacher named Miss Kaur and some girls spread a rumour that I was her daughter or her sister. It bothered me so much that I came home and told Ma about it.

"What's her first name?" Ma asked.

"Satwinder," I said.

Ma thought for a while. "We don't know her," she finally said with relief. It always concerned her when Daddy and I discovered other Punjabis anywhere.

Siti kept insisting that I was the girl's sister. "I'm not," I told her.

"But you're both Kaurs," Siti said.

Then Farizah spoke up in rapid Malay. "Okay, yeah, Siti. She's her sister. Everybody who has the same last name is related in this school." Everybody started laughing and making jokes, pairing all of the people whom we knew with the same common last names. Melissa Tay and Tay Wan Hua were twins then! Mrs Lee the science teacher and Miss Lee who taught art could be mother and daughter! Old Mrs Chia who taught home economics to the older girls was married to Mr Chia, the man who worked at the drinks stall! This last pairing brought on shrieks of laughter. The Malay teacher looked up and told us all to settle down. Siti scowled and walked away.

Farizah sat with her legs tucked behind her. The long skirt flowed around her like a blanket. "Old Maid!" she declared, turning over my cards to expose an image of a skinny gap-toothed woman with straw-like hair. "You're not paying attention."

I wasn't. I was looking at the Punjabi girl who was reading her book intently. She had short hair, tied back in a high ponytail like mine. I wondered why she was also in the group who didn't go for Chapel. There were a few other Punjabi girls at our school with long hair. They went to the auditorium for Chapel and they listened. I wondered about their mothers and what they were like. Why weren't they afraid of their daughters coming home singing Christian songs?

• • •

The school bus on the way home was always stuffy no matter how many windows we opened. I was always one of the first to get on the bus because I didn't stay back to buy snacks from the tuck shop. My stomach rumbled, waiting for Ma's food. I tossed my bag on the seat I wanted, furthest from the old bus attendant, whom we called Bus Uncle. The other girls began to trail in, clutching packets of shredded cuttlefish and French fries soaked in chilli sauce. The driver climbed in through his entrance, followed by Bus Uncle.

Bus Uncle was an old Chinese man who sat in the very front

seat. He was there to make sure we didn't misbehave and to collect the bus fees in a small envelope from our mothers every month. In a loud, screeching voice, he talked to the bus driver in Chinese, sometimes glancing at us. "What is he saying?" we always pestered the Chinese girls, but they shrugged and said that he was talking rubbish. He said that we were too noisy even when we were perfectly still. He told us to shut the windows because it would rain soon, even when the sun was shining brightly and the sky was an intense blue. Sometimes, when we talked back, he pulled a thin rotan from under his seat and threatened to cane us.

"Sit down," he screeched but it always came out as "shit dow". We changed it to "shit now" and chanted it back to him. "Shit now! Shit now! Shit now!" Puzzled and angry, he would get up and slowly come at us, the movements of the bus making his body tip and wobble like he was on a boat in turbulent water. His white knuckles shone like pearls as we squealed and told each other to shut up.

Today started out quiet. Farizah had lent me her Donkey cards to take home and I was spreading them out on the floor in the back of the bus, while the other girls crowded around and asked if they could play. Siti, too proud, sat on her own and waited until I called out to her.

"Oi, you playing or not?" I asked her after I gave out cards to everyone. She shrugged and took the last few from me. The bus shivered as it started, then it slowly rolled past the narrow school gates. As it picked up speed, wind rushed in through the open windows, making my hair fly into my mouth. We wove through the neighbourhoods of Toa Payoh and Bishan, brick-and-concrete numbered blocks of flats above shops, squares of basketball courts, overhead bridges lined with creeping vines and bright pink bougainvillea. Shiny palm leaves burst from the tops of some trees, while others had thin branches that stretched across the sky like spiders. Daddy always told me to pay attention to the trees when I drew our neighbourhood with him because I often forgot about them. They were so neatly lined along the paths that I confused them with the buildings, the roads, the shops and everything else in Singapore.

The wind had started out as a whistle, but became a roar as the bus continued. My voice rose to be heard over it and the other girls did the same. Soon we were shouting just for the sake for being loud and Bus Uncle was twisting in his seat. The bus jerked forward to stop for Susheela Surangam, who watched us from the front with envy. She was the last one to get on the bus every morning, so she had to sit in the most undesirable seat, right next to Bus Uncle. On the way home, she was the first to get off, which meant that she couldn't join our games for very long, so she just didn't, choosing to sit in the front seat again instead. Bus Uncle gave us a warning to be quiet and to return to our seats. We ignored him and continued to shout until Bus Uncle slowly advanced on us. Squealing and pushing, we scrambled to our seats. "Shh…shut up!" we hissed at each other between giggles. "He's coming, shhh!" Close up, Bus Uncle's face was a series of folds and flaps, one layer of skin covering the other. His wrinkles were so deep that they had shadows. He wore glasses with large frames that covered part of his face.

"Shit dow," he croaked, aiming his glares at the girls directly in front of him. From my angle, I noticed that his ears were lined with dark hairs. I nudged the girl next to me, Shu Ping, whose face was already red and bloated from keeping down her laughter. "Eee, look at his ears. Like a monkey," I whispered.

Shu Ping exploded, laughter pouring out of her like confetti. "Shut up," I said but I was laughing too. Bus Uncle turned slowly to face us. He asked Shu Ping something in Chinese and she didn't respond. He looked at me then he asked again. She shook her head and made herself look serious, gulping down her giggles until they were completely gone. Then he shifted his gaze to me.

"You. What you say? You so funny? What you say?" he asked in broken English. He asked me the same thing in Malay. I hoped that one of the girls behind us would imitate his voice to distract him but the bus became strangely silent. He stood there for two more stops, asking me over and over again what I had said. I just shook my head and replied, "Tidak, tidak." *Nothing, nothing.* The girls being dropped off filed past Bus Uncle, leaving me trapped under his stare. His eyes were like marbles behind those large frames. I shrugged at him and looked out the window. Eventually, he moved away and went back to the front. Giggles rose again but they were nervous and unfamiliar. One girl asked me what I had said.

"Nothing," I told her, annoyed that nobody had tried to help. I collected my cards and put them back in my bag. For the rest of the journey home, I stared out of the window and watched the way the sunlight bathed the bricks and concrete golden-brown. The spaces between the painted lines on the road below disappeared, then appeared again once the bus slowed down. My neighbourhood was one of the last on the bus route. There were four girls after me who all lived around my block. When Irene Seet got off the bus, I got my things ready—bag, folder and water bottle—and carefully made my way to the front seat. Bus Uncle turned to stare at me again. This time, I looked back at him for a long time. I saw Ma doing that once at the market. The vegetable stallholder had pulled his hand back quickly after handing Ma her change, having caught a glimpse of her scarred wrist under her sleeves. Ma had stared at him until he pretended to be distracted by a noise and turned away.

"Apa?" I asked Bus Uncle boldly. He didn't respond and it seemed like he didn't hear what I had asked. I was a bit relieved. I could get into trouble at school for being rude to Bus Uncle. Mrs D'Cruz might make me stand up in front of everyone at Assembly and apologise for my behaviour. She might make all the students and teachers pray for me and Ma would hate that, probably pull me out of the school altogether.

Then a look of recognition came over Bus Uncle's face. His eyes lit up and a smile lifted the corners of his narrow lips. It was not a friendly or forgiving smile. There was something mean in his eyes. The bus jerked to a stop and the door creaked as it opened. As I stood up, Bus Uncle softly said a word I thought I knew but I was so eager to get off the bus, I dismissed it and ran towards my block, the windows glinting like eyes in the afternoon sun.

•　•　•

The corridor leading up to our flat was made narrower by potted plants, doormats, shoe racks and parked bicycles. All of the flats in our building were identical, but you wouldn't have guessed it from what was outside. Everybody seemed to try hard to make their homes look unique—strange grille patterns and bright curtains were popular. Sometimes I walked past the other flats slowly on purpose, because some families liked to keep their doors open if they were at home. Through the bars of their front gates, I peeked into their flats: rattan furniture and television consoles, wooden dining tables, cushions covered in faded printed sheets, beaded curtains that rattled as the residents stepped in and out of the kitchen. One time, a neighbour had caught me looking, and waved her hands and stomped in my direction as though shooing away a bird.

The door to our flat was open but I had to ring the bell so Ma could come out and unlock the gate. "Coming!" she called, but before I heard her voice, I smelt the food. Noodles stir-fried in oyster sauce with prawns and bean sprouts. Red chillies cut and soaked in soy sauce. Honeydew cut in cubes and piled on a side plate to soothe my mouth if I got stung by a hot seed. I could barely wait for Ma to open the door because I hadn't eaten anything all day. During recess, Farizah and I had continued our mini-championship of Old Maid in the courtyard. She didn't eat because she was practising ignoring her appetite. She didn't have to start fasting until the weeks before Hari Raya Puasa in November but she wanted to do better. Last year, she had to fast for nearly a month. She had fainted during two separate assemblies and had to be sent home.

Ma opened the gate and gave me a kiss on the cheek. "How was school?"

"Okay."

"What did you do?"

"Nothing." I went into my room and shrugged my bag off my shoulders before coming out into the kitchen again, where Ma was sitting.

Ma rolled her eyes. "I'm glad I sent you to a good school to do nothing and come home," she said sarcastically. I giggled. Normally, I wouldn't know if Ma was making a joke or not but the food and the kiss indicated a good mood. It meant that she was not angry about what I had said about Nani-ji the day before. I hoped that she would forget about Nani-ji altogether.

"Your hair's a mess, Pin," Ma said. She ran a wet hand over my curls, flattening them only for a few seconds.

"I need a haircut."

"I'm sure we can find a way to pull it back so you don't have to go and get it cut all the time."

"Why?"

Ma shrugged. "It doesn't matter. I'll bring you for a haircut next weekend if you want. I just thought you might want to try something different for a change."

"No," I said.

I took a plate from the shelf and scooped the noodles onto it. Ma had already put the soy sauce with chopped red chillies in a small bowl. "Remember to eat your fruit," she told me, pushing the cubed honeydew towards me. She watched me eat for a while.

"Tasty?"

"Mmm," I said. The noodles were sticky and she had sprinkled crispy fried shallots on the top. There was a hint of garlic, but not too strong, which meant that Ma was alert. She asked me the regular questions about school—what did you do in maths? Science? English?

"What did *you* do today?" I asked. I had to be careful about asking questions like this. On a few occasions, she took it as an insult when I asked her what she had done. "What haven't I done?" she would snap, gesturing to the bowls and plates of food and the sparkling clean stove. But I was better now at detecting her moods in her meals. She was never upset when she made Chinese dishes because they were too light. White rice and pale yellow noodles were often used as quiet peace offerings. Malay dishes were warm, suitable for early dinners. The Indian dishes, with their fiery reds and their stabbing spices were the ones that warned me. They caused me to suck in my breath and think hard before I said anything.

"I cleaned up the flat, I washed the clothes and I visited Nani-ji," she said.

"How is she?" I asked, because I knew it was polite.

"She's...she's okay," Ma said. She looked down at her hands and began to clear the plates.

As I turned to follow her into the kitchen, something in the living room caught my eye. I turned around and saw a portrait on the living room wall. God's portrait. He looked the same—old with sad eyes and a long, snowy beard that hung from His chin like drapes. He was holding up one hand, the lines on His palm covered by a single string of beads. His eyes followed me as I walked towards Him. I quickly jumped away and His eyes were still fixed on me. We started a quiet staring contest.

"Ma..." I called out.

Ma came out of the kitchen. "I found that in the storeroom this afternoon while I was cleaning up. There's so much junk in the storeroom, Pin. We can throw out your old bicycle, can't we? And I tell you, the stacks of newspapers and phone books in there. You need to remind me the next time you hear the karang guni man coming. We can clear out all of our old things and get some money out of it."

"Why did you put it up?" I asked her, my eyes still locked with God's.

She drew her stomach in a bit and placed one hand on her hip. "Why not?" she challenged.

"Nothing," I mumbled, pushing past her into the kitchen. I

scraped the few remaining bits of bean sprouts and shallots into the garbage chute and washed my plate. Ma seemed to have forgotten that she had banished God to the storeroom for a reason.

Somebody rapped on our door loudly, then shook the gates so they rattled. I rushed to the door to find my friend Roadside standing in the corridor with a football tucked under his arm.

"Hi, Pin. Can you come out and play?" he asked.

"Hold on," I said and called out to Ma to ask her permission.

"Wash up first," Ma said.

I groaned. Roadside grinned. "Okay, see you downstairs." He disappeared before Ma could come to the gate to say hello to him.

"Why do I have to wash up when I'm going to get dirty again?" I asked Ma.

"Because it's my rule," she replied.

"But I'm going to play football!"

"Pin, don't argue," Ma said. "You know what my mother used to say when I wanted to race down the street with boys? Cheap, she called me. Cheap and dirty."

I had always known that it was a privilege to be allowed to play with Roadside. A year ago, he and I had started our own detective club. We were very busy; there were many mysteries to solve in our block of flats. There was the Lift Button Pusher Mystery that Roadside and I tried to solve by staking out different floors of the building and making notes on who entered the lift at which times so we could figure out who was pressing all of the lift buttons at once and causing the lift to stop at every floor. Then there were several shoe thefts that we took upon ourselves to solve, but the town council put up posters reminding residents to keep their shoes inside and the thefts stopped on their own. Our last case was a vandalism mystery: we set out to discover who had spray-painted "OP" in red on the gates of an elderly man's flat on the third floor. We stopped working on that case after Roadside's father explained to us that the man owed money to loan sharks, and that we were better off playing outside than letting our imaginations run wild in the hallways of our block. Now Roadside joined the boys in football and I tagged along. Sometimes Ma still mentioned that she was very liberal to let me play with boys outside where everyone could see.

My towel was clipped to the bamboo pole outside. I had to lean out of the open kitchen window to pull it off. It was warm to the touch because it had been a hot day. There was a light afternoon wind, enough so the clothes on all of the bamboo poles on our block swayed as if to music. The jagged rhythm made them look lifelike. I thought about God breathing onto our block and I glanced back at Him again on the wall. He sat still in the frame, His eyes surveying the flat.

The boys had already started by the time I got there, so I sat on the grass edging the basketball court and watched them. Their T-shirts were thrown together in a pile, a slight odour of sweat drifting from them. There were a few boys whose names I didn't know because they only joined us occasionally, but the regulars were Roadside, Malik, Samuel, Deven, Wei Hao and Kaypoh. They trusted me with the scoring but I daydreamed when the games were slow. I was also in charge of timing. I checked one of the watches on the ground. We had 20 minutes before the older boys came to the court and claimed it.

There used to be more space in Singapore, my parents often told me. People didn't have to live piled on top of each other, lined up in hallways. There were dense forests and wide roads. Daddy missed those days but Ma did not. "That was such a long time ago," she argued. "Why does it matter? Look at what we have now." She gestured around her so we knew she meant the safe, well-lit streets, the sturdy concrete buildings and the trees sheltering the pavement like roofs.

The boys were red-faced and sweating, their ribs showing through tan skin, light skin, skin the colour of tar. They ran and laughed and stumbled and pushed. As I watched, I envied their swift angling. Sometimes Malik's sister would come, and she'd sit on the grass with me. She was more insistent about playing, and she threw tantrums, but Malik wouldn't let her join in. "You and Girl just sit on the grass and take care of our things," he instructed her. All of the boys except Roadside referred to me as "Girl." I didn't like it and Roadside knew this, but he had never corrected his friends.

Then the older boys showed up with their familiar sour smell of cigarettes. "Okay, get out," one of them said jokingly, snapping his fingers. Roadside tucked the football under his arm and directed us towards the blocks. "Girl, any games under your block?" Malik asked.

"I don't think so," I replied.

"We go her block lah," Malik said to the others.

The boys set up the game in the void deck after checking to see if anybody else was playing there. Every void deck in the neighbourhood was the same: there were concrete mahjong tables and small shops on each end, and in the middle there was enough space to play football, even though a few pillars that held up the building sometimes got in the way. On the walls facing us were signs that said "No Soccer" but the walls were dotted with dusty circles from where footballs had impacted.

After a short argument over the scores, the boys picked up

the game where they'd left off. They darted through the maze of walls and their yells echoed through the space. I got bored waiting for somebody to get injured or tired so I could take his place. I went over to one of the mahjong tables and sat down on its cool cement top. The mahjong squares were painted on and the old Chinese ladies from the block only had to bring their tiles. I had seen them before in their silvery pyjamas, with their teased white hair and jade earrings that stretched their lobes like dough. They played swiftly, swapping tiles and chatting loudly. One of them always smoked cigarettes and she liked to croon at me in Malay when I walked by. *Cantik!* she would call out. It always made me smile and look down at my feet, then she'd laugh and say, "Don't so shy lah, pretty girl!"

The ball hit the wall with a loud smack. "Bloody hell!" one of the boys shouted. The rest of them broke into laughter. I traced the tabletop with my finger. It was rough and stained with cigarette burns. The older boys who lived downstairs from me smoked, then tried to mask their breath with mints before they got home to their mothers. One time, Deven's mother spotted him holding cigarettes for one of the boys while he showed him how to do a banana kick, and he wasn't allowed to come down to play with us for a whole month.

The boys shoved and tripped over each other's ankles, and swore loudly in every language. They called each other names, then laughed and lightly shoulder-punched each other. Malik teased a Chinese boy about being so pale that he couldn't see him against the white walls. The boy retorted that the walls under my block were all so dirty that they matched his dark skin better. There was a quick pause, a tension in the air, before Malik burst out laughing and cuffed the Chinese boy on the cheek. They continued playing.

Their exchange reminded me of the twist of Bus Uncle's lips as he said that word. Mungalee. It was a mean and ugly word for Indians and I only knew it because Daddy told me once that people used to call him that when he was a young boy because of his dark skin. They mistook him for a South Indian because he was friends with lots of them and when they walked down the street together, their classmates shouted, "Mungalee lai liao! Mungalee lai liao!" *The Indians are coming! The Indians are coming!*

I asked Daddy what he did when people said those mean things, and he said there wasn't really anything he could do. He said it was always better to let ignorant people make fools of themselves. But hearing about it made me angry, and I wanted to go back into Daddy's childhood and shout ugly names right back at those people.

"You're lucky, Pin," Daddy said. "People in this country have learnt to tolerate each other. Even our own teachers used to call us Blackie and Darkie and all kinds of names. They wouldn't be able to get away with it now." Bus Uncle was old, so maybe he did not know that Singapore had changed. It still bothered me, though, and it made me think of something else that had happened the previous year on the school bus.

Before somebody had the idea to bring cards, pick-up sticks and sticky balloons onto the bus, we occupied ourselves on the journeys home playing the Question Game. It was pretty simple. We split up according to race, then asked each other questions in our own language. The person answering would have to reply either "yes" or "no", without understanding what the question had really meant. Sometimes, a person would say yes to questions like, "Are you the smartest girl in the school?" or "Will you have a rich husband?" That person got points. Sometimes a girl answered no to a good question and she got no points. Or sometimes without realising it, a girl might have admitted to having ten ugly boyfriends or a crush on Bus Uncle. The Chinese girls asked the Malay girls, the Malay girls (whom I usually joined) asked the Chinese girls, and the Tamil girls asked all of us. Their language was the most fascinating—fast and rough like pebbles rolling around in a tin can.

Margaret Lee, whom everyone called Maggie Mee like the noodles, asked questions in French because she had attended a bilingual school in Canada when she was very little. I liked Maggie Mee; she knew what a Punjabi was and asked me once if she could come to my house one day to eat real Punjabi food. Her best friend in Toronto was Punjabi. She told the other girls they were stupid and narrow-minded when they asked me why I didn't understand Tamil. "You think all Indians are the same?" she asked them, shaking her head. Like Farizah, I could always count on her to speak up for me, although sometimes I wished I could do more speaking up for myself.

There was a girl on the bus named Gayathiri Vengadasalam and nobody really liked her very much. She was loud, she pinched people when she wanted their attention and she didn't speak proper English. She was a Bursary Girl who looked and talked like a Bursary Girl, who shamed the rest of us who couldn't afford to go to First Christian without our monthly allowance from the school. Her old pinafore was faded and spotted like denim, her blouse had a yellow tinge, and she wore her school badge too high so it glistened from her shoulder instead of above her heart where the crest was supposed to sit. She also had very dark skin.

It was Abigail Goh who invited her to play. "Want to join the question game?" she asked brightly. Gayathiri nodded. Abigail ducked into her seat with her friends and they began to whisper and giggle.

"Okay. We're ready. Are you ready, Ga-ya-thi-ri?" Abigail asked. She stretched out the syllables unsurely like it was the title of a newly discovered species.

"Yeah, ready," Gayathiri said.

Abigail asked the question. Nobody laughed but everybody seemed to be holding their breaths. I only knew one word in the question because in kindergarten I had to learn all of the nursery rhymes in English and Chinese. I had heard this word before in "Baa Baa Black Sheep". At first, I thought they might be asking her if she was a sheep because of her curly hair. But then Abigail said it again. "Are you black?" she was asking.

Maggie rushed at Abigail and stuck her chin really close to hers. "My mother says people like you are a disgrace," she reprimanded.

Abigail did not budge. She gave Maggie a steely stare and said, "Go back to Canada then, Maggie Mee." Some girls began to giggle while exchanging uncertain glances.

Gayathiri did not understand. I wanted to warn her, but I was frozen with shame. If I said something, would the other girls call me black too? She watched the two girls stare each other down, then she said, "I choose Yes! No…no…yes! Okay, yes." My heart sank. Some girls looked down into their laps while others separated themselves from Maggie and Abigail, starting their own quiet hand-slap games. The Malay and Tamil girls looked confused; they asked their Chinese friends what Abigail had asked, but nobody would say it because Gayathiri was still giving her answer. "Yes! Yes!" she said excitedly.

I hated her then. I wanted to push her back into her seat and tell her to shut her mouth; she was only making things worse. But she just kept repeating her dumb answer, grinning like she had won a prize.

A loud cry interrupted my memories. Two of the boys I didn't know lay crumpled on the void deck concrete, their ankles knotted together like pretzels. The rest of the boys ran over to them, laughing at first, but their expressions quickly changed when they noticed that one of them could not get up.

"Oh shit," said Roadside, bending to help his friend. I walked over to them and watched from a distance. I didn't want anybody to be hurt but if he was out, I'd be allowed to play football.

The boy winced. He tried to get up, then collapsed again. Tears glistened in his eyes, but he looked away when he noticed me. "Look at what?" he muttered, and I quickly turned away. The boys were reluctant to bring him back to his block, knowing that whoever brought him home would be given a scolding by his mother. They pushed the task to each other for a while and finally decided to settle the matter over three rounds of scissors-paper-stone. Malik lost and grudgingly told the boy to put his arm around his shoulder as he dragged him off. I stayed around while they decided what to do without the boy. Finally, Roadside turned to me. "You be the goalie, Pin. You can catch, right?"

"Yeah," I said, trying to sound casual, but I was really excited.

"Okay. Wei Hao, you take over Azmi's place."

Wei Hao pointed me towards one of the goal posts. I ran over, forgetting to maintain my poise. I wanted Daddy to come back from his shift right now and see me at the void deck, saving the day.

"Oi, goalie! You ready?" Wei Hao called.

"Yeah!" I called, waving my arms. Wei Hao's face changed and he turned to Roadside to point something out. Then Kaypoh said something, and they all turned to look at me.

"What?" I asked.

"You'll have to take off your bangle," Roadside said.

I touched the kara on my wrist. Most of the time I forgot it was there because I had worn it since I was a baby. "I can't take it off," I called back.

"Why not?"

"It's too small," I said. "And it's for religion." This was something I had had to explain to the prefects at school who always booked me and tried to give me demerit points for wearing jewellery.

"What religion?" Kaypoh shot back, but I ignored him.

"If you wear that, you'll injure somebody," said Roadside. "We all take off our watches and put down our keys. Take off the bangle or you can't play."

"But I *can't*," I insisted and demonstrated my point by trying to pull off the bangle. It couldn't slide past the bone where my wrist widened into my hand.

"Try soap," one of the boys suggested. There were faded grass stains on his white shorts and tracks of dirt on his legs.

"*You* should try soap," I muttered.

"Sorry, Pin," Roadside whispered as I walked past him on the way back to the mahjong table. I tried to push the bangle off my wrist again. I got it a bit further along this time but it left long red marks that Ma would surely notice. Maybe I could convince her to buy me a new kara at the temple, something I could easily slip off when she wasn't looking. She insisted I wear the kara all the time. "It's bad enough that you're singing Christian songs," she frowned. "And it's not like we go to the temple or keep our hair long or eat Punjabi food all the time. It's the least you can do to show some respect to God."

Strokes of orange and red painted the sky as the late afternoon sun sank through the trees. The boys played for the final goal, their shouts becoming louder as the sky slowly darkened. I was so focused on their game that I didn't notice the two women passing through the void deck until Roadside hollered, "Stop! Two aunties passing!" The ball escaped them and rolled into a nearby drain.

I recognised the first woman by her size. It was Fat Auntie. She was huffing and puffing from carrying a duffel bag that added to her own weight. Her salwaar-kameez was pale blue, making her thick stomach and her trunk thighs look even wider. As she struggled along, one of the boys turned around and nodded in her direction. *Do you know her?* he seemed to be asking. I gave him a stern look—eyebrows raised, eyes narrowed—that said, *No!*

The woman behind her was shrouded in white. At first I thought I recognised her because of her outfit, but she was skinner than my grandmother and slower in her movements. She looked at the ground as she walked, as if she dreaded each step. Her shoes made a scraping sound as they dragged against the concrete. The boys backed against the wall and their gazes shifted from Fat Auntie to the old woman. Fat Auntie disappeared into the lift lobby. The woman opened her mouth to tell her to wait and it was the scratchy voice that I recognised. It *was* Nani-ji. I had never seen her move so slowly. In fact, when she walked, she usually had the appearance of somebody escaping—eyes darting around to survey the area, legs moving faster than the hips. I got off the table and ran up the stairs to beat them to our flat.

"Ma! Nani-ji is coming!" I called through the gate between gasps. Then I stopped. Something was different in our flat, and it wasn't just God staring from the wall. The smell of smoke and charred dough drifted out the door. Panicking, I rattled the padlock, thinking that there had been a fire in our flat. But Ma was very calm. She seemed to float towards the gate.

"I know, Pin," she said. "She's here already?"

"No, I saw her downstairs with Fat Auntie. Why is Fat Auntie here?"

"She had to help Nani-ji carry her things."

Her things. The duffel bag and the two large shopping bags Nani-ji had hanging from her limp arms. She was moving in with us now and she was going to stay for a while. Nani-ji living with us meant that two kinds of food had to be cooked. The smoky smell came from the roti. I peeked into the kitchen to see that the deep woks and frying pans had been replaced with a single iron plate for heating the flat dough.

"How long will she be here?" I demanded to know as I stepped into the house.

"Pin, you're sweaty. Go take a shower," Ma replied. I repeated my question but walked into my room as I did it so Ma would think that I was obeying her. As I walked towards the closet to take out a fresh pair of shorts and a T-shirt, I noticed that my room was different from before I had left to go downstairs. New sheets covered my bed and a thin mattress lay on the floor next to it. My school bag, which I usually tossed on the bed when I got home, was neatly propped in the corner. The scattered school books and folders on my desk had been organised in a neat stack. Ma walked in after me. "Well, where else is your grandmother supposed to sleep?" she asked, as though we were already arguing. I could think of plenty of places other than my room—the living room, the toilet floor, the corridor outside.

"How long will she be here?" I asked. Ma ignored me. I opened my mouth to ask again, louder this time, but somebody was rattling the padlock again. "Coming," Ma called, then she turned to me.

"Pin, your grandmother is very ill. She needs somebody to take care of her. This is what we do for people we love. If I don't have Nani-ji here, what kind of daughter would I be? I certainly expect that when I grow old, you'll open your doors to me as well."

"Why can't she stay with Fat Auntie?"

"You know your Auntie works and she's got two boys. And I *want* Nani-ji to stay with us." I remembered the conversation from the previous night, how Ma and Daddy had argued about Nani-ji's reasons for moving in.

Ma left the room, and went to greet Nani-ji and Fat Auntie. I stayed in my room and sat on the edge of my bed because it didn't seem to belong to me any more. I knew I'd have to sleep on the floor because Nani-ji had a bad back. I was furious with Ma for agreeing to have Nani-ji move in so early. I thought I had at least a week. In that time, I could have tried to get on God's good side. I could have done a few good deeds, like extra floor-sweeping duty after school and not making fun of Bus Uncle. Surely God would have seen my efforts and granted Nani-ji better health so she wouldn't have to live with us.

I wondered if Daddy had known that Nani-ji was coming over so soon. He probably hadn't; he would have told me. Then again, I knew that he kept some things to himself. He said I was too young to know about them or that they were Ma's stories to tell when she was ready. Daddy spoke about his childhood freely, like it was just yesterday that he was climbing fences and sneaking off to the rivers on the edge of the island with his buddies. But Ma's stories were closely guarded.

The smell of smoke, musky and dull, wafted through the flat. It swallowed the light, tangy scent of sesame oil that usually remained after Ma made Chinese food or the slightly sour smell that followed a spicy Malay dish. I shut the door to my room but I could not block out the smoke smell. I heard the doorbell ringing twice and saw the shadow of Ma's feet flitting by under the door. Our flat was about to become crowded. Nani-ji would take up too much space with her raspy voice, and her mothball-scented clothes and her grumbling about everything. In a moment, I would have to face Nani-ji and I pleaded with God to stretch this moment for as long as possible. It was the first true prayer I had ever uttered.

3

THE FLAG FLUTTERED and waved across the television screen above a background of tall buildings that lined the glittering Singapore River. A familiar tune began faintly in the background. I was on the living room floor doing my maths homework. I timed myself on each one—whichever answer I worked out in under 30 seconds, I wrote out on a separate piece of paper. I considered these numbers lucky because I was terrible at problem sums. These would be my lottery number suggestions for the week.

The flag waved again and the buildings faded into old shophouses, tinged brown on the edges like toast. The Singapore River was suddenly filled with debris. A shrill violin note began the slow song, "We Are One". I had to learn it in school for the National Day celebrations, and could sing it without having to read the lyrics that marched across the screen. The shophouses faded from the screen, which was then filled with still photos from the war. Japanese soldiers, their teeth bared as they pointed their bayonets at a group of huddled women. Hungry children who held out their cupped palms for rationed food. Rickshaws caught in mid-stumble past a mess of shops and houses with dented tin roofs.

God observed from the wall. I hid the paper from His view

because I didn't want Him to know that I was helping Daddy to gamble. I didn't even know there was anything wrong with it until Nani-ji pointed it out last week. "Gambling is sinful," she'd told Daddy.

"It's just a hobby," Ma had said. She gave Daddy a hard look.

"When I win, I'll buy you a gold jewellery set and we'll see if you complain then," Daddy joked with Nani-ji, who did not look amused.

The violin music swelled and was accompanied by a harmonious chorus. *We are one island, we are one nation, we are one people!* The photographs of different sections of old Singapore faded into modern video clips. Serangoon Road, once an unpaved and chaotic market, suddenly transformed into Little India with bright garland and sari shops. Chinatown, red and fantastic with sequined dragons and paper lanterns and frail samsui women in their red headgear, became tidier. The dragons came out only for festivals and the samsui women were no more. Housing estates lengthened, filling a vast sky with concrete and glass. I thought I caught a glimpse of our neighbourhood, but it could have been any housing estate in Hougang or Jurong or anywhere else in Singapore.

Most National Day song lyrics were about change—"A fishing village, a bustling city. A home of beginnings, a home of progress. An uncharted island, a bustling seaport. O Singapore, together as one nation. O Singapore, together as one island! O Singapore, together as one people!"

I did not see what was so great about change. It only seemed to bring more trouble. Everything in our flat had changed since Nani-ji had moved in and it had only been a few weeks. She had a lot of rules, and within those rules, there were more rules. I wanted to ask her whose house she thought she was in, but if I ever talked back to my grandmother, Ma would kill me. She had already threatened to rub chilli on my lips because I had called Nani-ji for dinner one day by shouting, "Oi, Nani-ji! Come and eat!" Ma was furious. "You don't 'oi' your grandmother, you idiot!" she scolded.

One rule was that we had to pray before dinnertime. The prayers were long, not like the quick blinking grace the Christian girls said before eating their meals at recess. These prayers lasted 30 minutes, which was a lifetime when I was already starving. And I was always hungry nowadays because Ma cooked less for lunch. She did not have much energy. She cared less about which spices went together and how the onions should simmer before sauces turned bitter and how ginger could sting if she was not careful. This was also Nani-ji's fault. She made Ma uncomfortable, and said things that made Ma grow quiet.

Nani-ji thought Singaporean food was vulgar and disgusting. She told Ma to stop showing off when she cooked. "You grew up eating simple Punjabi food. You can't afford to spend so much money on groceries. Why do you bother?" she asked one day. Ma kept quiet. Nani-ji continued. "It's a waste of money. And you're not even working. You chose this life. Accept it and stop trying to be a fancy chef over here." I readied myself for an argument. Ma was aware of what we could and could not afford. She didn't need anybody telling her. But Ma did not come up with any clever retorts. To my surprise, she mumbled something into her food that sounded like an apology.

One day, before Daddy left the flat to go for his night shift, I tiptoed out of my room and asked him why Nani-ji was so mean. I could only see his shadow and a small strip of light from outside on one side of his face but I could tell that he was thinking very hard about how to answer. "Your grandmother grew up one way. She expected life to remain that way. But so much changed when she came over from India. Some people like things to be different after some time, but Nani-ji is not one of those people. Too much happened too quickly. Your Nana-ji left, your uncle had to get married, her…" This was where he abruptly stopped talking and muttered an excuse about running late. He would not tell me anything else. He became curt when I pestered him. "I've said it before, Pin. Your Ma's stories are not for me to tell."

The song faded along with the images. National Day was on Tuesday. Some of our neighbours had hung flags from their windows, but we did not do that. Ma said it was not necessary to show how much you loved something just by displaying its picture. She had said this loudly yesterday in the living room, in front of God and Nani-ji.

Nani-ji shuffled out of my room. I heard the door opening first so I turned up the volume on the television. Then I heard her feet brushing against the floor. She walked over to the television and shut it off.

"It's too loud and you're sitting too close. You'll go deaf and blind," she said.

"I wasn't watching," I told her.

"Then why did you have it on?" she asked.

I made a face. Nani-ji's back had turned by then but God could still see me from the wall. He was keeping a very close eye on me nowadays and He showed his disapproval often. Daddy didn't believe me when I told him that God moved in the frame, but I had witnessed it a few times. "That's just a painting of God, Pin," Daddy said. "Use your good sense before you let your imagination take over like that." This was what Daddy said sometimes before we started drawing as well because I liked to add details that weren't in the pictures. He said it was important to be precise.

But I knew better. God was living in our flat; He had moved in along with Nani-ji. His expressions changed with His moods. The corners of His mouth curled slightly when He was amused or pleased. His eyes narrowed when He knew I was lying. I was most aware of His open palm. When I left the flat in the mornings for school, He seemed to be waving or telling me to be careful. But if I disrespected Ma or Nani-ji, His palm was steadily raised as if to slap me. Daddy said I had a strange imagination. He wasn't afraid of God. He said that he worked hard and did good things so what did he have to worry about? Ma was anxious around God. She pulled her sleeves over her hands when she passed Him in the hallway.

This was another one of Nani-ji's rules—Ma and I were not allowed to wear shorts at home. "Shorts are not decent," Nani-ji said, giving my bare skin such a hard look that I instantly felt ashamed. Ma's skin had gotten worse since Nani-ji moved in. I inspected my own arms and legs to make sure I was still okay and so far I was, but Ma's skin had started to erupt when she was a bit older than I was. I searched my skin every day. The smallest scrape or cut made me nervous and I only calmed down when I remembered how it got there—a nail sticking out from a desk had grazed my leg or a piece of paper had put a thin slice into my hand while I was helping Miss Yoon distribute worksheets.

I spent most of my afternoons in the living room these days, trying very hard to ignore God as He watched me. He just stared and stared and didn't care that it was rude. I wanted to get away from Him but I was not allowed in my room while Nani-ji napped because I made too much noise shifting about and arranging my pencils to do my homework.

Nani-ji stretched and I heard the soft cracking of joints. "I'm going to make some tea," she announced before shuffling into the kitchen. "Ask your mother if she would like some."

Ma was resting and I didn't want to bother her. She took long naps in the afternoons nowadays. She told me it was because she was tired from cooking two separate meals each for breakfast, lunch and dinner. "You're all a lot of trouble," she said. But sometimes she didn't sleep. I peeked into her room one day when she left the door slightly open to let the breeze in. She lay on her bed and stared at the ceiling, her mouth set in a grim line.

I got to my feet and followed Nani-ji. The kitchen looked different now. The iron plate was permanently fixed onto the stove and there were other objects I'd only ever seen at the temple before Nani-ji had moved in. There was a rolling pin and a heavy marble slab to flatten the dough on. There was also a strange and heavy bowl that appeared to have been made out of cement and a small club that went with it. Ma used it to grind the spices and powders for the gravy that went with Nani-ji's roti. The kitchen countertop was dusty with wheat flour.

Nani-ji guarded the pot closely as if my presence would ruin the flavour. The can of condensed milk, jar of tea leaves, some fennel and a cardamom pod lay on the counter.

"Ma puts these in curry," I informed Nani-ji, picking up the greenish pod. It had a small slit in the middle as though it had been cracked. When I pried apart the soft pod, three black seeds spilt out. Nani-ji turned and made a clicking noise with her tongue. "Don't touch those," she ordered, pushing me away. But she didn't tell me to leave, so I stayed and peered into the pot.

Tiny bubbles began to speckle the water. Nani-ji tossed in the black tea leaves with her hands and stirred until the water seemed to rust. Steam curled from the pot, carrying the aroma of tea into my nostrils. I decided that if sunlight had a taste, it would be that of black tea leaves. Nani-ji continued to stir, then she added the fennel and cardamom seeds. After that came the condensed milk, which thickened the tea and gave it a creamy colour. The water nearly came to a boil; it rose and bloated in the pot, making the dark leaves spin to the top. Nani-ji hastily pulled the pot off the stove before it had the chance to overflow. The blue ruffle of flame remained until I reminded her to turn it off. "I know," she said crossly.

Next, Nani-ji took a strainer out of the drawer and with her unsteady hand, she carried the pot over to the sink and drained the tea into a cup. The leaves fell in clumps into the strainer. The cup was filled to the brim when I realised she had made too much. Knowing that Nani-ji hated to waste, I took another teacup off the shelf and asked if I could have the rest.

"Just a bit," Nani-ji said but the excess filled over half the cup. She sat down at the dining room table with a great sigh that filled the room like smoke. I was about to take a sip when Nani-ji pulled my cup away and poured my tea into hers.

"Hey! You said I could have some!" I protested. Nani-ji made that clicking sound again, which instantly quieted me. She poured the tea back into my cup, then back into hers again. Steam billowed from the thick column of tea as she poured back and forth. I recognised this cooling method from the temple, where the women always left a great distance between both cups as they poured so that the heat could escape. Sometimes they even poured the tea into deep plates, letting the stirring fans above them cool the large surface.

Nani-ji slid my cup back. The top was frothy from all of the pouring. I took a sip. It was warm and spicy, different from the regular Lipton tea bags that Ma dipped into hot water and mixed with milk and sugar in the mornings.

"This isn't like Ma's tea," I said. I wasn't certain if it was a compliment. It tasted a bit like the temple tea, but not as bitter. It was sweet and filling.

"Your Ma doesn't make this kind of tea," Nani-ji said. "Your Ma doesn't make anything the way I do." I took another sip to see if I could taste the sadness that lined her words.

"I like Ma's food," I proudly informed Nani-ji. "She cooks well. I don't even eat in school because I prefer Ma's cooking. And when I go to the hawker centre with Daddy, I don't eat anything that Ma can cook because I know she can make it better."

Nani-ji took a slow sip from her tea. When she moved the cup from her lips, I noticed that they were shiny and I realised that she had once been young. Her eyes, which seemed like heavy window shades, had been a source of light many years ago. Those creases in her face used to only appear when she laughed.

"You want to be like your Ma?" Nani-ji asked me.

I nodded.

"You know why your Ma cooks like that?"

"Why?"

"Because she always wanted to do things differently. It got her into more trouble than you'll ever know."

I took another sip. A pointy fennel seed had somehow escaped through the strainer and bobbed to the surface of the tea. I pressed it between my lips. The flavour seeped into my mouth and I knew it was no mistake that it had entered my tea. It tasted like something old but still alive.

A memory.

"Why?" I pressed.

Nani-ji shook her head. "Don't become like your Ma," she told me. She rose from the table and washed out her cup in the sink. I sat and tried to drink the rest of my tea but suddenly, there was no more room left in my stomach. I glanced at God. From that angle in the kitchen, His features were crooked. I wasn't certain, but He looked to be in agreement with Nani-ji.

•   •   •

They fought a few days later.

I was back from school earlier than usual that afternoon because early rains were bringing on the flu and some students had not come to school. There were fewer girls for the school bus to drop off, so the bus driver took a different route, skipping Bishan altogether. During assembly, we were asked to bow our heads in prayer for our ill friends. Some girls envied those who could stay at home, but I did not. I prayed to my own God and asked that He not make me sick as well, because I could not imagine spending an entire day in the flat with Nani-ji.

I got off the school bus and saw Roadside on the other side of the street. I envied him for being old enough to take the MRT home from school. We waved at each other. "You coming down to play today?" he called. Traffic roared between us on the busy main road.

"Don't know. I'll see," I said. Nani-ji did not know that I played with the neighbourhood boys downstairs—when I left the flat, I told her it was to run an errand for Daddy, like going to the hardware shop or buying him a can of Coca-Cola. He went along with my lie every time but we kept this secret from Ma. I could only play with the boys if Ma was locked away in her room and Daddy was at home. I also had to be sure Nani-ji would be busy with her evening prayers by the time I got home so she wouldn't notice how long I'd been gone and that I always came back empty-handed. I had to avoid God's intense gaze as well. But I also got tired of going through all of that trouble just to sit on the sidelines and watch the boys play; I still couldn't take off my kara and they still wouldn't let me join their games unless I found a way to remove it.

I heard voices rising as I walked down the corridor, but this was normal. Passing any window on our floor, I heard conversations in languages I suddenly wished I understood. It was only when I got closer to our flat that I realised the voices were Ma and Nani-ji's. The shards of their words pierced the dense air.

"When you stop shouting, I'll listen to you," Nani-ji said steadily.

"I won't stop shouting because you won't listen to a damn thing I say," Ma replied.

"Jini, I came to live with you so we could talk about it and move on. God wants to forgive you," Nani-ji said.

"I thought you would finally listen to my side of things. You don't know what happened that day. All you want is to believe what you heard from Pra-ji and all of those gossiping neighbours."

"God wants to forgive you," Nani-ji repeated.

"But I didn't do anything wrong!" Ma cried. "Why don't you understand that? Why doesn't anybody believe me?"

"How is anybody expected to believe you when you called Pra-ji a liar? Pra-ji—a wise man, a religious man, a righteous man. And look at you. Look at your skin. When you were about to get married, he warned me that it would get worse if you kept on lying."

"Pra-ji is a liar and I'll swear to God on that fact. I won't ever change my mind about him and if you don't believe me, fine. But don't you try to tell Pin that her mother did something terrible when you don't know the facts," Ma declared. "That's why you wanted to spend time with my family, isn't it? To warn Pin about becoming like me. To watch her."

I sucked in my breath.

There was a long pause before Nani-ji said, "Fine. Suit yourself. God sees everything."

My heart pounded. Who was Pra-ji? Pra-ji meant older brother in Punjabi and the only older brother Ma had was Mama-ji, whom Ma called Sarjit if she ever spoke about him. Ma would not add "ji" to the end of any title for her brother, because you only called people Ji if you respected them. But it didn't sound like this Pra-ji was someone Ma looked up to either.

I heard another voice echoing down the corridor, then the rhythmic thump of metal against the concrete steps. "Karang guni! Karang guni!" The rag-and-bone man who recycled old newspapers and telephone books was making his way through the building with his large trolley and weighing scale. He didn't pay very much but there was nobody else to give our old things to. I strained to listen to what was going on in the flat, but Ma and Nani-ji had stopped speaking. They were probably in separate rooms now, brooding. I knocked loudly on the door.

Ma gave me a blank stare when she opened it. "I got a letter from your school today saying there's been a flu outbreak," she said. She pressed the back of her hand to my forehead. "I'll make you chicken soup."

"I'm not sick," I told Ma.

Ma retreated into the kitchen. I heard the clicking of the gas igniter before the hiss of stovetop flames. It sounded as if she were talking loudly to herself, but everything she said was meant to reach Nani-ji's ears. She did this sometimes when she was angry with Daddy or me. "Nobody believes me. All thought I was lying then, think I'm lying now. She'd rather believe a bloody sick old man than her own daughter. Righteous man, she calls him, after all these years."

Then she came out of the kitchen and leant against the doorframe, her head tilted towards the front door. At first I thought she was listening to something God was saying but then I realised that she was just listening for the karang guni man. He called out and honked a small horn like there was something to celebrate in taking our old things. The commotion of his clanging trolley, his horn and his loud calls made it sound like there were several people parading down our corridor, but the karang guni man was of small build and practically invisible. A sudden smile lit Ma's face.

"Pin, help me bring out all of the old newspapers," Ma called. "Open the door for the man and give him everything. We need to get rid of all these old things." Her voice bounced against the walls of my room, where Nani-ji could surely hear it. I went to the storeroom and began taking out stacks of yellowing newspapers. I was not afraid of the storeroom any more, now that God did not lurk in the dark corner behind my bicycle with training wheels and a box of shoes I had outgrown. I tripped over a pile of twisted wire hangers and a puff of dust entered my lungs, making me cough. If Nani-ji saw the state of our storeroom, she'd surely have more to say about dirt and Ma's skin. This was where Ma hid everything she did not want to deal with.

"Karang guni!" the man called out, passing our window. He peeked into the flat. Ma told me to deal with him, then she hurried into her bedroom. "Karang guni!" he shouted, tooting the horn.

"Here," I said, feeding him newspapers through the railings of the gate. In her rush, Ma had forgotten to unlock the gate. I gave the man two old telephone directories and a few furniture catalogues that had come free in the mail. The karang guni man looked as old as Bus Uncle but he did not have that mean look. He would not call me names. As he weighed, he asked me questions in broken English.

"You how old?"

"Ten," I said.

"Primary what?"

"Four."

"Wah. So big girl. Speak English also good. You go to which school hah?"

I waved in the direction of the school. Past our corridor, past the blocks of flats and the glossy leaves of trees were shapes of neighbourhood schools, short and boxy. I did not want to show off and tell him I went to a Christian school.

"Study hard, ah," he warned me. "Otherwise, become karang guni man also hard. Must go here go there, carry heavy thing, give money. Wah," he exclaimed, wiping sweat from his forehead. "Difficult."

Ma would have said that this was a tactic to get me to feel sorry for him so I accepted whatever price he offered for the things we no longer needed. But he really did look tired.

"Uncle, you want water?" I asked him.

"Huh? No, lah!" he chuckled, dismissing me as if I had been crazy to offer. "So nice ah you. Don't need lah. No trouble." He swiftly tied a few long pieces of pink raffia around the entire stack I gave him, then he hooked his scale to the fat knot in the middle. His slight frame trembled as he lifted, did a quick calculation, then dug into his pockets to search for change.

Then Ma came out of her room, the keys dangling from her fingers. "Take these also," she said after she unlocked the gates. She thrust a stack of loose cards at the karang guni man. "Make sure you recycle them properly," she said.

The karang guni man looked at the cards, then backed away. He told her he would not take them.

"Take. Just take," Ma said, pushing the cards to the man.

"No, no, no," the man said, frowning. "I don't take this."

I looked at what Ma was giving him. They were not cards. They were old black-and-white photographs of different shapes and sizes, with perforated edges. There were five of them altogether and they would weigh almost nothing. At first I wondered why Ma wanted to sell them if they would be worth nothing, then I realised it was just that. She wanted somebody to tell her they were worth nothing.

"Give them to me," I told Ma. The only old pictures I had ever seen were the ones of her wedding. Before that, there were no traces that Ma even existed. I wondered where she'd been keeping these photographs this whole time.

"Take," Ma said, violently thrusting the pictures at the man. His arms flew up to protect himself. I flinched as well, thinking that Ma had hit him. She certainly looked wild enough then. I turned around and looked at God. *Do something,* I urged Him. But He just watched like an amused passer-by.

The karang guni man's hands struck the photographs just as Ma loosened her hold on them. They shot out in every direction and littered the floor. The man handed me the money and hastily dragged his cart away. "Sorry," I called after him but he did not turn around.

Ma did not pick up the pictures. She stepped over them calmly, went into her room and shut the door. Then she cried loudly. Her sobbing made me feel like I was being split inside. One part of me wanted to cry along with her, but the other part wanted to shake her until the truth escaped her lips, until her foggiest memories cleared, so I would understand what she had done wrong.

I sat on the floor for a long time before I fanned out the pictures and studied them. There were Nani-ji and Nana-ji, too young then to be known by those titles, their faces like stone slabs, harsh angles in black and white. Shadows misted their eyes and there were no smiles, not even a hint of happiness. There was Ma, a toddler, looking past the camera with round eyes. There she was again, a teenager with slick plaits down her back and stiffness in her shoulders, like she was preparing to take over the world. There was Mama-ji Sarjit standing next to her, skinny and sharp-chinned, less stern in those days; he looked startled. They all did. And then there was another boy. He was a baby in one picture, sitting on Nani-ji's lap, and then he was taller, leaning against Ma in another shot. After that, there were no more pictures of him. He must have been a cousin or a neighbour's child. I noticed him because he was the only one who smiled, but in a slightly crooked way that made him look cheeky.

Ma did not come out again for dinner. The soup kept on boiling and I knew it was all she could cook for tonight. Nani-ji came out of her room, made me sit with her for prayers, then made roti for the evening. She gave me two pieces and wrapped four more for Ma and Daddy, which I thought was kind, considering the fight she'd just had with Ma and how much she despised Daddy. The surprise must have shown on my face. She caught me watching her.

"You think I'm cruel, don't you?" she asked softly.

Yes, I thought, although I knew I'd get the chilli for sure if I agreed with her. I hated trick questions and thought Nani-ji was quite sneaky for trying to get me into trouble.

"I'm not, Pin. I love your mother like your mother loves you. But your mother lies. Your mother did something terrible when she was a bit older than you. She kept secrets and she made up stories."

"She did not," I said.

"Somebody died because of your mother," Nani-ji said evenly.

I took in a sharp breath because the word "die" was so harsh in Punjabi. It pushed into my chest and settled there like a stone. And then it made me furious. How could Nani-ji say something like that about Ma?

I waited for her to leave the kitchen before I threw the roti down the garbage chute. Wasting food was a sin, but what good was it if I already knew what it would taste like? It would be sour like resentment, sour like lies and it would churn in my stomach, a heavy burden. I was loyal to Ma because of how she ducked at the market to check my skin, how she leant dangerously out of the window to hang my clothes. She stayed at home and waited for me. She let me play with the boys in the neighbourhood. A clear, weightless laugh from Ma was rare but it was unlike anything I had ever heard. She was more beautiful than other mothers—all of my classmates told me so when she came to school last year on Report Card Day. Later that evening, as I struggled to eat her tasteless soup, I thought about how happy she would be to see me forgive the lack of salt and sweet prunes. How proud she would be of my loyalty.

• • •

It was the first of September and the first of the month meant that the school bus fee had to be paid. Daddy placed two ten-dollar notes, two fives and three dollar coins all in the envelope. "Be careful not to let any of it spill, Pin," he whispered. Nani-ji opened her eyes and shot us a look. She required absolute silence from all of us while she did her early morning prayers.

"How did she hear you?" I asked Daddy. He smothered his laugh with his big shovel-like hands. "Go on," he said. "You'll be late."

"I haven't eaten breakfast yet," I told him. Ma was in the kitchen, sleepily boiling an egg. She used a spoon to scoop it out of the pot and peeled away the shell gingerly over the dustbin. Then she split the egg in the middle and poured a few drops of sweet soy sauce into the yolk. She came out into the hall to give it to me. Nani-ji's chants filled the flat, and she swayed slightly. God looked pleased.

"How come we've never done morning prayers?" I whispered to Ma.

"We're not old ladies," Daddy said. Now it was my turn to stifle laughter. Ma gave Daddy's shoulder a gentle shove. "Go to work. You, go to school," she ordered. Nani-ji looked up again. I finished my boiled egg, put the bowl in the kitchen sink and straightened my uniform. Nani-ji stood up to finish her prayers.

This time, the chanting became a tune, rising and falling. God's head bobbed, slightly enchanted by Nani-ji's praising music.

Outside, a strong breeze stripped the trees of their leaves and made them circle the ground. It looked like it might rain. Monsoon season had arrived earlier that year and dense clouds often made the sky seem lower. I waited for the school bus under the shade of a skinny tree. On the pavement ahead, a Chinese family huddled together over a patch of grass. It was the beginning of the Hungry Ghost Festival and they were offering meals to the spirits of their ancestors. The father laid out two oranges and a plate of rice. The mother added a plate of cookies. Together, they lit red joss sticks and clasped them in their hands. Smoke trailed from the glowing tips of the incense as they waved and muttered their offerings. Then they stood up and lit a fire in a large red oil barrel as tall as I was. The father struck a match and lit it from a hole in the bottom. I stepped back as the flames leaped and seemed to lick the sky. They threw sheets of paper money into the flames. The money quickly blackened. Pieces of ash drifted across the pavement, crumbling as the wind hit them. I started to cough, and was relieved when the bus arrived.

I handed the envelope to Bus Uncle, who counted the bills carefully. Then he spilt the coins into his palm and sorted through them. A grin spread across his face. He shoved the envelope back at me. "No enough," he said.

"There's enough!" I insisted, pushing the envelope back to him.

"This one only thirty-three dollar. School bus fees thirty-five," he said, emphasising his point by holding up three, then five fingers.

I looked at the girl sitting closest to the front. She said,

"Yeah, it was in the school newsletter." I vaguely recalled Daddy complaining about the bus fees becoming more expensive but he must have forgotten.

I reached into my pocket. I had enough in my coin purse to give Bus Uncle the rest of the fees but then I wouldn't have enough left to buy something from the canteen for lunch. I couldn't trust Ma's food any more. Yesterday, she had left the wrinkled shells of seeds inside her coconut gravy.

Bus Uncle laughed unkindly and a sneer formed on his wrinkled face. He leant so close to me, I could feel his hot breath on my face. "Mungalee," he said loudly so everyone could hear. I shrank away from him and went to the back of the bus. My face was still hot but this time, it was from embarrassment. "Shut up," I muttered under my breath.

Elizabeth Rodrigues asked me what the word meant. "I don't know," I told as her as truthfully as I could. "He's just talking nonsense." But the girl who sat across from us, Dinavati, knew exactly what the word meant. She glared at Bus Uncle. "If he calls me any names, I'm telling my father," she said.

The elastic on my hair band was stretched and worn. We had PE for first period and by recess, my hair had come loose from my ponytail. Farizah and I went to the toilets so she could help me tie it up. "It's almost long enough to plait," she remarked. She turned on the tap and wet her hands before running her fingers across my scalp. The water trickled down my neck and darkened the edges of my blouse collar. I squirmed a bit.

"Stay still," Farizah commanded.

"Yes, ma'am," I said and our giggles bounced off the walls. The second-floor toilets always smelled like urine and strong disinfectant. Both our noses were wrinkled in disgust. But my hair had to be fixed. Since Nani-ji forbade haircuts, Ma wouldn't take me to the hairdresser. She kept trying to convince me it would look better long anyway. "Maybe the weight of being long will straighten it out," Ma had said doubtfully.

Farizah was taller than I was but I had never noticed her height until she stood behind me. In the mirror, I could see her forehead clearly above mine. She seemed so much smaller because of her high socks and long pinafore. It billowed around her knees like a tent.

"Isn't it warm for you?" I asked her, pointing at her shins. School rules said we had to have white socks so most of us wore sports ankle socks. Farizah's socks were thick and they looked woolen. A tiny sliver of her leg skin showed as she shifted the weight from one foot to the other.

"I'm used to it," she said. This was her response to every question about her religion. "Aren't you hungry?" I had asked her pointedly at lunch the other day. She was really fasting now and wasn't allowed to even swallow her own spit. I was the only person she tolerated questions from, and she never asked any in return because she seemed to know everything already. She knew about how Sikh men braided their hair and tucked it into their turbans. She knew about my kara.

"There," she said. "Happy?" We both looked in the mirror. The ponytail was taut and my hair looked gelled back. I instantly looked neater than I had that morning, when Bus Uncle had called me that word. The only thing that worried me was the wetness of my hair. It looked like oil and Bus Uncle would double his insults if he suspected I had smoothed my hair with oil. The girls who made fun of Gayathiri said that she smelled like coconut oil.

"It will dry," Farizah said. "Do you like it?"

I nodded. Outside, the bell clanged, signalling the end of recess. Farizah looked relieved because it meant she didn't have to stay in the bathroom any more. She had a hard time being in the canteen during her fasting period because there was food everywhere.

"Let's go," she said.

"Hold on," I said. I took the bar of soap from the sink, ran it under water and scrubbed it on my left wrist. When there were enough suds, I tried to slip the kara off. It moved a bit further than it had without the soap, but it still couldn't get past my wrist. I tried a few more times before washing the suds off my hands and walking out with Farizah, defeated.

"I think you need a saw or something," she told me, inspecting my wrist. "Is it real silver?"

"I don't think so."

Farizah shrugged and looked at her own wrists. They were slightly paler than mine, with dark hairs in rows following one direction. We queued up with our class and bowed our heads while the girls around us said an after-meal prayer. Most of them fidgeted but Farizah stood still. The only time I saw her move was after the prayer was finished. She reached down to adjust her socks. She pulled them so high her knees disappeared, turning her into a pillar.

• • •

The full-length mirror was built into my closet door, which was wide open. Nani-ji stood in front of it and twisted her thin white hair into a bun. Patches of her scalp showed at the top of her head, and she ran her small comb over the exposed parts of it.

Long bands of cool light entered my room through the blinds. Our neighbours shuffled past in shadows and outlines. I wanted to watch them and play my guessing game, but Nani-ji insisted on going to the temple early.

"What's the point of going there after the service is over? A free meal?" she had asked, pointedly staring at Daddy. He had held up his arms like criminals in movies when they surrendered. She had been making comments about his not going to the temple lately. Ma explained that he often worked Sunday night shifts and had to sleep in the day, but Nani-ji clearly thought of this as an excuse. "What's so difficult about his job that he has to sleep so much?" Nani-ji had retorted.

Daddy was the only person in our flat who always looked God squarely in the eye. It was as though God was some stranger passing him on the street, powerless and equal. Nani-ji always looked at God's feet when she prayed. Ma tried to avoid His gaze. I looked at Him in the eye sometimes but it was only because I saw Him moving so much and I wanted to see if there was anything else He wanted me to know. But Daddy was confident around God. He didn't seem to think he had anything to be afraid of.

I went to take a shower and when I got out, Nani-ji was still standing in front of my mirror. This time, she was inspecting her own face very closely, tracing the deep lines that ran from the corners of her eyes. She was breathing heavily, something I had noticed lately. At night, she mumbled nonsense in her sleep. During the day, she took in the air with large gulps, her chest heaving from the effort.

"I have to change clothes," I told her. I was wrapped in my towel and the water dripping from my ears formed a small puddle near the door. Nani-ji looked up from her reflection.

"You shouldn't be walking around the house half-naked like that. It's indecent," she said. She wandered out of the room. The fight between her and Ma had caused a silence that I hoped would last for a long time because the flat had become peaceful, although in a strange and uncomfortable way. But within a few days, Nani-ji was breathing down Ma's neck again. Ma protected herself by coming out of her room, cooking quickly, then rushing back inside like a mouse hurrying back into its hole in the wall. She shut the door behind her so quickly that there was little time for Nani-ji to find something to say.

Ma usually laid out an outfit for me to wear to the temple but this morning, she looked tired. "They're all ironed—just pick what you feel like wearing." It was a luxury to be able to choose. I could pick what I wanted to wear when we went anywhere else, but the rules changed for the temple. People stared, judged and calculated in the temple. But that Sunday, Ma was too busy making herself look presentable. I chose a light yellow salwaar-kameez with a deep orange lining and small diamond-shaped buttons. It was one of the few salwaars I had with an elastic band and not a drawstring that I had to tie into a knot. I walked into Ma's room, hoping she wouldn't notice I had worn it two weeks before.

Daddy was snoring lightly, the sheets pulled up to his chin and his big toes poking out at the ends. Ma put her finger to her lips and said, "Shh," as I pushed the door closed behind me.

"He won't wake up," I told Ma. Years of working the night shift had made Daddy able to fall asleep at any time. His days and nights were reversed, as if he was living in another time zone.

Ma was wiping dots of talcum powder off her blouse. Her outfit was a deep green embroidered with pink flowers. She dabbed on a bit of blush and some brown lipstick. The make-up gave her a stern Sunday appearance. When going to the market, she wore the same shades because they were good for negotiating. She often said that praying was like bargaining with God and always coming up short. She told me this now, her voice lowered so Nani-ji wouldn't hear. Daddy stirred and Ma smiled.

"Look at him," she said tenderly. It made me smile. Ma and Daddy didn't talk to each other as often as they talked through me, but what they loved about each other was always made clear in these exchanges. I was also relieved; lately, with Nani-ji around, Ma had been looking at Daddy with doubt. But his eyes were closed now, the dark lids a deep shade of purple. He was still and free from worry; he looked younger than he was.

"I don't know how he manages to look so calm all the time," Ma said, reading my thoughts. "Your father is the happiest person I know. And all he wants is for everyone else to be happy." For a brief moment, her lips twisted in a small display of envy. "You know what I mean?"

I thought about Daddy's drawings and how he always made me draw the world as something bigger than it was. He drew in small squares and lines, but I was always instructed to fill the entire page, corner to corner, so nothing was wasted. "Yeah, I know," I said.

I pushed myself up onto the dresser and sat with my legs dangling down. I asked Ma if this was why she married him, because he wanted the world to be happy. It seemed like a good reason to marry someone.

"She married me because I looked like a movie star," Daddy said with a grin. Ma and I both gasped and began to laugh. She took a pillow and tossed it at his head. The pillow missed him but bumped their wedding photograph. It rocked on the wall like a pendulum.

"You were awake!" I exclaimed, jumping from the dresser to the bed. The mattress creaked and Daddy let out an exaggerated groan as I fell on him.

"How can I sleep when you ladies are trying to get ready with your hair spray and your make-up cases and your clips?" he grumbled and closed his eyes again. You ladies. I beamed, thinking of myself as somebody dignified and grown-up.

Ma turned around to inspect my outfit. "You look nice," she said.

She dabbed a bit more powder on a cluster of red scars on her throat. "You're not wearing any jewellery?" I asked. Her disguises for her scars usually consisted of long-sleeved blouses, close-toed shoes, long pants with stiff cuffs and a gold necklace that concealed the spots that appeared on her neck.

Ma shook her head. She had worn the necklace for her wedding. A pair of round matching gold earrings were also missing. "They're with your Nani," she said. "I let her keep my wedding jewellery when she moved in."

This didn't make sense to me. "But it's your jewellery," I said.

"They were given to me for my wedding. They were your grandmother's," Ma said. "She'll give it all back. It's the only valuable thing she ever really owned and she likes keeping it with her. Remember how you liked to carry that smelly pillowcase everywhere when you were a toddler? It's like that."

My mind went straight to my room. I tried to think of what I might have to hide in case Nani-ji decided to claim it as hers, but I didn't own anything of great value besides my sticker collection and the small stack of bus tickets I had been saving all year. I decided she could have the dirty pillowcase.

Ma shrugged in the mirror. Her eyes in the reflection met mine. "It's not important, Pin. Gold is gold. And those designs are outdated so I won't pass them on to you when you get married one day. I'd get it shaped into something more modern. People shouldn't hold on to things like necklaces and old clothes. It's unhealthy." She brushed on a bit more powder and hurried out of the room.

I poked Daddy's arm. "Want to come to the temple?" I asked.

"No," he said.

"Why not?"

"Sleeping."

"Liar."

Daddy reached for the drawer next to him. There was a glint in his eyes. "Give me some numbers."

"I didn't think of any," I lied. I had thought of plenty that week, but I was afraid of what God might think.

"Hurry," Ma said and she came back into the room. "Your grandmother is starting to grumble."

"Starting?" Daddy said. I laughed. Ma turned around and gave Daddy a look. He rolled onto his side and pretended to be asleep again. I passed Nani-ji in the hallway on the way back to my room. She was breathing very hard through her nose.

"Are you sick?" I asked with hope. I wanted to spend my Sunday watching the boys play football, queuing up with Daddy at the 4D shop, sitting in the kitchen while watching Ma.

Nani-ji shook her head. "Turn around," she said.

I did as she told and felt her bony fingers on my scalp. "Are you going to the temple like this?" she asked me. My ponytail hung loose and wisps of hair stuck to my neck.

"I'm going to comb it, then tie it tighter," I informed her. It was getting harder to get my ponytail to stay in its place. I had to use a bit of baby oil to weigh down the curls that stuck out of my head like scribbles.

Nani-ji shook her head again. She put both her hands on my shoulders and steered me towards my room. Her fingernails dug into my skin but when I tried to shrug her off, she clung on. As I closed my door behind me, I heard Nani-ji calling for Ma in her raspy voice. I got dressed with an uneasy feeling, straining to hear the conversation between the two of them after Ma came out into the hallway.

"Okay, fine!" I heard Ma say. I opened the door to see her standing in the hallway with her hands thrown up in the air, surrendering. Nani-ji gave a satisfied nod and said, "Be quick. I don't want to be late again."

"What's going on?" I followed Ma into her room. Wordlessly, she grabbed a brush, a fine comb, a bottle of baby oil, and a handful of clips and rubber bands. "Outside," she told me, pointing with her chin towards the living room. "Your grandmother says I have to plait your hair," she said.

"What? Why?" I asked. I gave God a glance. He looked quite pleased.

"Because it's not proper to go to the temple with your hair in a ponytail if you can tie it up neatly," Ma said. But I had seen girls there with long ponytails. I'd even seen short-haired girls with their hair untied. They got dirty looks from the women and the more daring boys gave low whistles as they passed but God didn't do anything. I protested to Ma and looked to God for support. His expression was blank again. Nothing.

"Sit down, Pin," Ma said. She sounded exasperated, as though she'd been asking me to sit down all day. She pulled the brush through my hair a few times first, making my hair a fluffy cloud. Then she opened the oil bottle and rubbed it in her hands. She ran her fingers through my hair, making it slick.

"Hold still," Ma said, and this meant that she was going to do something that would make me want to jump up and run away. I heard a small ripping noise before I felt the sharp pain on my scalp.

"Ow! Why are you pulling my hair out?" I squealed, trying to wiggle away from Ma. But she had my hair in her hands and the more I resisted, the more it hurt.

"I'm not," Ma said grimly. In her voice, a struggle was evident. She drove the comb through my hair again. When it got stuck on my tangles, she lifted the comb and used it to pick at the knots until they came loose. "Stop moving," she said in a raised voice.

"It *hurts*!" I replied, my voice almost as loud. Ma's hands dropped.

"You do not talk to me like that," she said in English. "Especially not in front of that person."

At first, I thought she was talking about God because she gave a quick nod in the direction of the wall. But then I noticed Nani-ji shuffling from the kitchen to the living room. It seemed that all she did was drift from one room to another to stir up trouble. And Ma had been in a good mood that morning as well. Usually, temple Sundays were the worst days. She was always anxious in the mornings, and she changed her outfit several times and snapped at me for not being ready on time even if she was the reason we were running late. On the bus, she always wrung her hands the same way she did that time I thought we were leaving the temple for good. Nani-ji lowered herself onto a chair that creaked under her weight. Ma separated my hair into three sections and began to plait tightly.

"You should do this every morning," Nani-ji said to Ma. "She shouldn't be leaving the house with her hair all over the place. A Sikh girl should look respectable."

I scowled. Ma did not say anything. She tied the end of the plait with a rubber band. I scrambled onto my feet and looked in the mirror. My head glistened and my ears stuck out too much. I looked funny and I told Ma so in English.

"Just be quiet," Ma said under her breath. She wrapped my shawl around my neck, picked up her keys and motioned for Nani-ji to step out the door with us. On the bus ride to the temple, she only spoke when the bus conductor asked her where she was going. The people on the bus gave us odd looks for our sequins, our bright patterns, the decorations hanging from Nani-ji's ears. I didn't say much either, but I leant close to watch Ma. I couldn't decide if what she said was meant for me, Nani-ji or God peering from the wall, his arms crossed over his chest as we left our home to go to his.

• • •

It was a long service. At the temple, God was not supposed to see our feet. Everybody sat cross-legged or with their feet tucked under their bottoms. The older ladies sat with their backs against the walls and pillars. I had to keep shifting. Every time I moved, Nani-ji looked up sharply from her prayer book. Ma also had a prayer book but she had trouble keeping up. She paid less attention to me and more to the barbed-wire letters, trying to read along with the mumbles of the rest of the crowd. I knew that she wasn't good at reading Punjabi, but in front of Nani-ji, she had to at least pretend.

"Ma," I whispered. "I have to go to the toilet."

Ma shook her head. "The programme will be over soon," she said. "Wait." Nani-ji looked up at us again.

I was bored. I thought about how I would draw the temple if I had a pencil and a piece of paper. Large ceiling fans stirring dust from the old carpets. High square windows with dark green shutters. A podium at the front, covered in gold sheets and sheltered by a white canopy. It was surrounded by flowers, coins and dollar notes strewn everywhere. The priest sat behind the podium and he waved something that looked like a wand over the large holy book. A bigger portrait of God, framed in heavy gold, sat on the wall. I had never paid much attention to it before, but now I focused on Him. Had He followed me from the flat, or was this just His picture? I searched His face for a long time until I remembered what I wanted to ask Ma. I tugged on her blouse.

"I need a new kara," I told her. I showed her my bangle. It did look small on my wrist now.

Ma shook her head. "That one is fine," she said. "You don't need a new one yet."

"It's too small!" I tried to twist it off my wrist to show her.

"It's supposed to be small so it doesn't slip off while you're at school," Ma whispered back.

Nani-ji leant over and told us to stop talking. "Have some respect," she hissed. Ma drew away from me and lowered her head into the book again. All around me, I could hear the soft buzz of chatter. The women, in their clusters, were sharing gossip. The teenagers had formed their own corner from which giggles rose then subsided quickly. The men on the other side of the room talked in serious tones; they were so unlike Daddy with his goofy grins. On the rare occasion that he came to the temple with us, he did not talk to the other men just as Ma did not talk to the women. He was polite but he sat in his own corner and looked straight ahead. On the way home, he'd mention details I never noticed, like how many times the priest cleared his throat or a black crow that had spent the entire time crouched on the window sill, ready to swoop into the room.

At the end of the service, we waited for the priests to come around to give us dheg—a soft sweet dough fried in butter and oil. To receive it the proper way, we had to hold out our palms and turn them into small bowls. Ma searched her purse for a piece of tissue to blot the oil off my fingers. I wiped my hands and followed her into the dining hall. Nani-ji lingered behind us but she stopped to talk to the other old ladies, other Nanis and Dadis. I wondered what my Dadi-ji, Daddy's mother, would have been like if she were alive. Would she be as grumpy? Would she warn me about Daddy the way Nani-ji had warned me about Ma? I grabbed Ma's hand and pulled, hoping to lose Nani-ji in the crowd. Ma winced and shrugged me away. Then she glanced in both directions as if we were crossing a street, and pulled her sleeve up a bit to reveal her skin. It was a deep, screaming red, like the inside of a mouth.

"Why is it so bad?" I asked.

Pulling her sleeve back down, Ma replied, "It's been like that since your Nani-ji moved in." It wasn't an explanation but it was all she said.

We shuffled into the dining hall with the crowd. My bare feet slid slightly on a puddle of water. "Careful," said a woman next to me. All around me, arms reached for steel plates and spoons and forks. People were talking excitedly, greeting their friends, pushing to get in the queue, rushing for open seats. Ma grimaced as the crowd jostled us along. When she grabbed my hand and pulled me towards her, I was grateful. At the front of the queue, I got the usual—one piece of roti and a scoop of yoghurt. I shook my head when the man serving dhal held out his ladle. "Are you sure?" he asked me, eyeing my colourless meal.

"Yes," I said and my scarf slipped off my head. I let it dangle on my shoulders until I reached an empty seat between Ma and Nani-ji. I quickly adjusted it before Nani-ji noticed. She always kept her scarf pinned to her hair, even if she was nowhere close to a temple.

Nani-ji chewed her food slowly. Ma ate in small, quick bites and she was halfway through her food when she realised that I was waiting for her.

"Oh," she said, remembering. She unzipped her purse and pulled out a small pepper shaker. Looking around her first, she sprinkled the sugar onto my plate. "You're getting too old for this, Pin," she whispered. I pretended I didn't hear her. I was sure I would never grow into liking temple food.

"What are you doing?" Nani-ji asked, leaning over. Ma quickly shoved the pepper shaker back into her purse.

"Nothing," I said.

"What was that?" Nani-ji demanded to know. *Why are you so nosy?* I would have asked her if I had dared to.

"Nothing," Ma insisted.

Nani-ji reached over and inspected my plate. The grains of sugar glittered. She looked back and forth between Ma and me. We both looked down at our plates.

"Learn how to eat God's food the way it is prepared for you," she said sternly. "You are too big to have your mother putting sugar on everything to make you eat it."

"She doesn't put sugar on *everything*," I protested.

Nani-ji looked at Ma. "You used to put sugar on everything," she said. Ma cleared her throat.

"I only put it on the food Pin doesn't like to eat," Ma said.

"I'm not talking about Pin," Nani-ji said. "I'm talking about Bilu. You put sugar in everything he ate."

Ma looked at Nani-ji in shock. I was surprised too—who was Bilu?

Then Nani-ji went back to eating, but Ma's hands were caught in mid-air. When Nani-ji was finished with her meal, she turned to Ma. "What? You think I didn't know you used to do that? No wonder he was always looking for you when you weren't there."

Ma didn't say a word. She adjusted her scarf again, this time so it fell over the side of her face, concealing it from view. She finished her meal quickly and I did the same, stuffing the sweetened roti into my mouth, scooping up the yoghurt until there was nothing left on the plate. It hardly tasted like anything. We didn't stay for tea. Ma pulled me out of the door with Nani-ji trailing behind. She seemed to want to get out of the temple as quickly as possible.

"What was Nani-ji talking about?" I asked Ma as we searched the piles of shoes outside for my sandals. I found them and squatted on the floor to pull on the straps. When I stood up, Ma had disappeared. I spotted her talking to a man sitting on a sheet near the entrance. He had a spread of karas—gold, silver, thick and thin. I recognised him as the man who had sold Ma all of the pictures of God for our flat. Ma handed him some money and came back to the shoe rack with a plastic bag.

"Here," she said cheerily. "This is for you." She handed me a thin but slightly bigger kara, one that I could easily slip on and off whenever I wanted to. "I'll ask your Daddy to saw off the other one when we get home, okay?" Her voice was strangely high-pitched and her smile looked like it was hurting her face.

"Thanks, Ma!" I said. It slipped over the other kara as I put it on.

Nani-ji trudged out from the dining hall and joined us to look for her shoes. Ma and I stepped back and watched her. Both of us could see her brown sandals but neither of us offered to help. We just watched.

•   •   •

At home, Ma entered her room and did not emerge until evening. I had planned on cornering her in the kitchen, but then she drifted from room to room like a ghost and it was hard to make eye contact with her, let alone have her listen to me. I wanted to ask her who Bilu was, why Nani-ji had said what she said, why she was suddenly so unhappy. The list of questions went on and on. I could not stop thinking about them; they floated into my mind like Daddy's lottery numbers on a rare day when I felt confident we would win.

We had left the kitchen windows open all afternoon. "Thank goodness it did not rain," I said, following Ma into the kitchen. "Or everything would be soaking wet. It started raining earlier this year." She cast me a sideways glance and began rummaging through the fridge. There was nothing in there that satisfied her. She threw the door shut and walked over to the window. The songs of the remaining songbirds from that week's contest trailed into our flat like a fine mist. "I think it sounds peaceful," I volunteered. My mouth was dry. Questions screamed inside my head but somehow, I could not force them out.

"Can you hear the individual birds?" Ma asked me. "Or is it just one loud noise to you?"

"I…I guess it's just one loud noise. But there are fewer now so I think it's easier to tell which song belongs to each bird," I said. She sounded so matter-of-fact, like this was what she had been contemplating all afternoon in her room.

"Listen carefully," Ma said. She leant closer out of the window. "Come here and listen."

I obeyed. Both of us strained to hear the calls of the birds in their wooden cages. Sometimes I thought I could follow the tune of just one bird but then another song intersected it and I wasn't sure which I was listening to.

"Everything overlaps in this city," Ma said. "Do you see that? Everything merges together." I did see it. Concrete pavements over grass, flats over hawker centres, Malay food over Indian food over Chinese food over McDonald's. Leaves pointing towards the sky in every possible shade of green—jade; emerald; a deep sea green; a sickly yellowish-green. Beneath them, spotted branches spread in crooked lines across the sky. Behind them, buildings. Underneath those, the MRT snaked across the city. A city; an island; a state; a country. Everything overlapping.

"The trick, Pin, is to be able to see everything on its own," Daddy had always said when I told him I was lousy at my drawing assignments in school. "Just think about what you're drawing one bit at a time and you'll get it." It sounded like Ma was trying to tell me the same thing but she was struggling to find the words.

"Who was Bilu?" I asked her.

Ma looked out of the window again. She asked me to listen to the birds again. I listened. I stared past Ma's shoulders at the trees, slowly dissolving into dusk. As the sun began to set, the buildings and the trees would become bare frames. I strained to listen to the birds until it seemed like there was only one. Then I heard scattered applause. The winning songbird had been chosen.

Ma left the window and pulled out a chair in the corner of the kitchen. She began to speak when I went to sit with her. "Bilu was my younger brother and I loved him more than anything in the world. He died when I was fifteen."

4

1967

FROM FAR AWAY, it resembles a house. It has a roof and a fence and gaping windows and a door that swings on its hinges at the slightest breeze. Up close, it is a series of angles and shadows, of uneven shades of white paint and a rusted tin roof that threatens to slide off. If you listen to it from any distance, you will hear three things: the deafening drumming of rain, the uncomfortable creak of floorboards, and voices from the neighbours that filter in through the rips in the mosquito nets of the windows.

This is where Jini lives. She is twelve years old.

It is a hot day. Beads of sweat roll down the back of her neck as she walks down the road. A man selling sweets and nuts in paper cups wobbles by on his bicycle, calling out his price. Two stray dogs with speckled fur and broad grins circle each other, their tails swaying. Her mother has given her a list of things to buy for dinner and has instructed Jini to bargain. "We cannot afford everything. If you can get Shop Uncle to give us half a dozen eggs for the price of three, do it. Tell him we'll pay him back. We're not going anywhere."

Jini finds haggling for eggs embarrassing. Every week, she stands among the housewives and argues with Shop Uncle. He speaks so rapidly that she doesn't know what she is agreeing to pay most of the time. He can be nice sometimes, when business is good and there are several wives in the shop at the same time, babies propped on their hips and toddlers winding around their ankles. If the shop is empty, she is less likely to get a bargain. Just last week, he chased her out for demanding too much. "You think this is a free shop?" he barked at her once. "Indians always like that. Want everything for free." She ran out of the shop without half of the groceries her mother had asked her to buy.

Jini has not been allowed to buy groceries for two weeks, but she begged to be let out of the house all week, to be able to do something, and this morning, her mother finally relented. School is closed for the holidays now and Jini is bored. Some of her girlfriends from school live in her neighbourhood but her mother has instructed her not to talk to too many Punjabis nowadays. She's afraid that Jini will accidentally reveal that her father has been gone for weeks. Jini doesn't have the heart to tell her mother that everyone already knows.

As she carefully crosses the road, Jini thinks she hears a familiar voice but it might just be her imagination. On this stretch of road, the sound of birds calling to each other and the screeching of tyres are like human voices. Then she hears it again.

"Big Sister!" She spins around. It is six-year-old Bilu, jumping and waving from the other side of the road.

"Stay right there!" she shouts, holding up her hands. "You move, I'll kill you." Her brother's eyes get big, then he suddenly sits down in the middle of the pavement, folding his legs neatly under his bottom. This makes Jini laugh as she dashes back across the road but she quickly grows cross again.

"Does Mother know you're out here?" she asks. He nods. She gives him a stern shake, a tug at his collar and he quickly changes his answer.

"No-no-no-no-no-no-no," he says. A man wearing a pair of paint-streaked shorts passes and gives Bilu a sideways glance.

"Okay, then go home."

"No."

"Yes. Bilu, go home." She points in the direction of their slanted house.

"No-no-no-no-no-no-no!" he shrieks. The man stops in his tracks and stares at Bilu, startled.

"Leave us alone," Jini says to the man. She is not usually this rude to her elders but this man is giving her a look she has seen before. With his eyes, he is asking her, what is wrong with your brother? If she knew, she would give an answer to each and every person who has given her that look. The best she can come up with is the reply her mother gives women at the temple: "He's not right." This gets them plenty of pity and clicks of the tongue. Nobody wants the burden of a child or a sibling who is not right. It is when they continue to ask questions that Jini grows impatient and wants to tell them all to mind their own business. Why do they care if he was fed properly as a baby or what will be done with him when he grows older and becomes more difficult to control? Her mother turns pale at such questions; Jini turns red.

Bilu writhes and screams. He rolls on the ground, getting sand and dirt in his hair and eyes. Tears stream down his cheeks. The man walks away but continues to keep his eyes fixed on them. "I said, leave us alone!" Jini yells. Momentarily, Bilu stops, bewildered. He looks at the man, who is now hurrying down the street. Even Jini is surprised by the sound of her own voice.

"Go out?" Bilu asks. Tears are dripping onto the collar of his T-shirt.

"No. *I'm* going out. *You* must stay in the house," Jini says almost pleadingly. Bilu dissolves into sobs again. He clenches his fists and rubs them into his eyes. Jini feels her heart breaking. Even when Bilu is trying to trick her into letting him do something he has been forbidden to do, she pities him. "It's not fair. He doesn't know any better," she tells herself. She has heard her mother use these excuses as well. Jini thinks of what her mother would do. She pulls Bilu to her chest and sings into his hair. Bilu's sobs fade and soon all she can hear is light sniffling.

"Okay? Now you go home. I'm just going to the shop," she tells him. He scrambles to his feet and charges back into the house as if nothing has happened.

Bilu cannot go to school, so every day for him is like the dull June holidays. School is too difficult for him. He cannot hold a pencil or write his own name, he cannot walk very fast and when he tries to run, he stumbles. He cannot be away for a whole day from those he is familiar with. Jini's father insisted on sending him to school but he screamed and clung to the legs of his desk, and scrambled into corners when his teachers tried to discipline him. In his second week, he went missing for hours and was found sleeping in a shallow drain, a puddle of dirty water soaking into his uniform. There is something wrong with him but there is no room to find out what, not with Jini's father disappearing every two weeks and leaving them with no money or food. Jini's mother prays constantly because it's the best they can do.

Shop Uncle is standing behind the counter, engrossed in a Chinese book. He is a middle-aged man with a few streaks of silvery hair and a tattoo of some Chinese characters on his arm. Today, he looks like he is in a good mood. He is scanning each character in his book with his finger. He chuckles at one part.

"Uncle," Jini says. "I want six eggs. I only got money for three.

Can I take now, pay later? Please?"

His smile disappears. "Indians always cheat! Always cheat me!" he shouts. She stands and waits with her hands behind her back, her head bowed. "You got money for three, you only buy three."

"Five. My father is coming back tomorrow, then I'll pay you. Okay?"

Shop Uncle shakes his head but he puts an extra egg in the bag. It's just as well that they have only four eggs—one for each member of the family, minus her father.

"Why you look so sad? I give you one for free already," the Shop Uncle says.

"Thank you, Uncle." Jini forces a smile.

"Girl, I tell you a secret. I always happy," he says. "Never sad. Sad no good. No use. Must always be happy. Understand?"

Jini nods. "Happy," she croaks. Shop Uncle grins.

"Happy! Must always be happy!" he says, sitting back in his chair. Sunlight streams into the shop windows, making the shelves gleam. Jini tries to keep the man's words in her mind on the short walk home but as she approaches her house, his voice fades, then dissolves into the stifling afternoon heat. She wants to take Shop Uncle's advice, but with her father leaving them with barely enough money, Bilu's problems and her mother crying herself to sleep every night, she doesn't know how to be happy any more.

• • •

On weekdays, the noise in the house comes from Jini singing songs at the top of her lungs, from her mother pounding spices in the kitchen, from Bilu expressing his changing moods—squeals and cries, shouts of glee and sorrowful sobs. The neighbours contribute without even knowing it. Jasbir Kaur next door calls her sister an ugly pimple-face. The Jeyanathans a few doors down play their Tamil songs loudly on the radio. The widow with four grown sons wails about how much she misses her dead husband. There are several Punjabi homes scattered around the neighbourhood, and the children sometimes get together and walk down the street in a pack, calling out to their buddies to play football.

Weekends are a bit different because they don't feel like school holidays. On Saturdays, Sarjit comes back from the army and Mother looks lighter, happier. He is 19 and doing his National Service. He stays in the barracks because he says it's a hassle to come home and go back every day. The army has given him a desk job because he is good with numbers. Mother calls him her soldier; her face always lights up right away when she hears the creak of the gate outside and the sound of his boots pounding against the soft grass.

"Son!" she cries, flinging her arms around his neck. Ever since their father left, she cries each time she sees Sarjit. "We've missed you," she coos, helping him pull the laces off his boots. "Jini, there is tea on the stove. Bring some for your brother," she says. Jini rushes into the kitchen to get the tea. She can hear muffled crying again from the living room. The rattan furniture squeaks and groans as Sarjit sits down wearily. Every week he says the same thing: "I'm tired."

"How's school?" he asks Jini as she serves him the tea.

"It's the school holidays, Dumbo," she says. He pulls one of her plaits and she twists away from him, laughing.

"You're the Dumbo. Where's Mr Bilu?"

"In the room somewhere," Jini says.

"He's not still following you all over the house?"

"No. But be careful. If he starts again, we'll never get him to stop," she says.

"Speak Punjabi," her mother instructs. She does not approve of English being spoken in the house. "How am I supposed to know what you're saying if you don't speak in a language I understand?"

Sarjit rubs his eyes with the back of his palm. "I'm going to find Bilu, then take a nap," he tells Mother.

"Okay, son," she says. "Jini, don't go anywhere. I need your help with dinner."

On Saturdays, Jini is allowed to help in the kitchen. Her mother often complains that girls usually start helping in the kitchen at a much younger age. "Look at Jasbir and her sister. They can make saag with their eyes closed and they're two years younger than you. Why is it so difficult for you?" she always says. "I was seven when I started cooking."

But Jini can't help it. When she tried helping in the kitchen before, she only seemed to slow things down or make a mess of the ingredients. She was clumsy and asked too many questions. "What is this? Which tree does this grow from? Is this spicy?" She grows listless when her mother starts ignoring her, and she thinks the food they eat at home is boring anyway. Dhal, roti, dhal, roti. Saag sometimes, if there is enough money for spinach. Chicken and potato curry on a rare occasion, if their father has sent home money. Jini would rather eat like other Singaporeans—nasi lemak like the Malays, kway teow like the Chinese, dosai like the South Indians. She has seen the British with their straight brown moustaches, their accents that sharpen the edges of words. She envies them most for their thick steaks and hearty potatoes.

I knew everything by the time I was your age, her mother always says. What more is there to know, Jini wonders, looking out of the window onto the stacks of tin roofs and yellowing grass. She knows her school work, she knows her friends and she knows which buses can take her all over the island, to streets of cramped shophouses with carved wooden shutters, to the heart of town where more shiny buildings are slowly sprouting like trees, to corners of the island where sand and silt spill into the sea so you feel like you're on the edge of the earth.

Her mother takes out a bag of flour from under the kitchen cabinet and pours the contents out into a steel bowl. "Check it for insects," she tells Jini. "Last week, I found a small spider sitting in the atta."

Jini washes her hands, dries them off, then begins to sift through the flour for anything suspicious. "Nothing," she says when she's finished. Her mother wordlessly hands her the bowl of green lentils. Jini sorts through the little beads looking for stones. Last week, Bilu got very upset when he bit down on a stone, which made him throw up his dinner. Her mother looked furious for a moment but then a look crossed her face, and it was one Jini could not forget. Her mother was momentarily stunned and frightened. She looked at Bilu like she wasn't sure how he got to this house, this dinner table.

Jini picks out two small stones and tosses them into the sink. "Finished," she says. On the stove, a pot of boiling water gurgles. Her mother empties the lentils into it and takes out a few jars of powder—some yellow, some brick red, some that look like fine sand.

"I have to teach you how to make roti," Jini's mother tells her. "Otherwise when you have a husband and children of your own, what will you cook for them?"

Chilli crab. Tofu with peanut sauce. Chinese vegetables with plump stalks and juicy leaves. Hainanese chicken rice with sweet soy sauce and ginger chilli. Noodles—both thick and thin—with fish cake and pork balls. Red-hot South Indian curries served with sticky bread and milk tea. Durians, longans, rambutans for dessert. Chendol. Ice kacang. Jini can think of a million things she'd cook if she had her own kitchen. She would work hard in school, she would have a good job and earn lots of money. She would never be short of ingredients.

As if reading Jini's mind, her mother says, "We can't even have a bit of chicken this week. I was going to make curry for your brother. Poor thing eats the same thing at the army every day. They just give them beans and bread, beans and bread every day. That's no meal. After a while it gets boring, doesn't it?" Jini knows better than to reply. Admitting that yes, it does get boring will only make her mother sadder when she realises that's what they eat every day. Beans and bread—just the Punjabi version.

"Okay, first we have to make the dough. Sprinkle some water on the flour. Go ahead, do it. Just a bit. Now gather the flour together and make it stick. See how it clumps? Now keep gathering and mixing like that. You're trying to make one big ball of dough out of all of this flour. Don't even waste a little bit." Her mother's way of instructing is softer when it comes to making roti. She coos to the flour because she believes it is important to show care when a person is cooking. "When you don't care, the person eating can tell. If you are angry or upset about something, your bitterness seeps into the food like a poison. It enters the mouth of the person eating, and then they become angry and upset."

Jini adds more water. Her mother cautions her not to make the dough too sticky or they'll have to absorb the water with more flour. "The first time I made this in India for your father, I was so nervous, I kept spilling too much water into the bowl. My hands were shaking. Then I added more flour to make it less sticky. Then I spilt more water, added more flour, spilt more water…the final ball of dough was huge! I wondered what your father would say. Luckily, he was pleased. He thought I'd made him a lot to eat on purpose." She laughs and it seems like the first time, the sound jingling like wedding bangles. Jini is not as amused. An image of her father, greedy and expectant, crosses her mind and brings with it a flash of anger so bright that it blinds her for a moment.

"Now you knead the dough. This is important. You have to make it soft." Jini's mother grinds her knuckles into the dough, which sinks. Then she uses the heel of her hand to flatten and roll it back up repeatedly. Jini notices how hard her mother's hands are and how young she really is. She thinks about the British again. She has seen wives on the army base near her school wearing cotton skirts and paper-thin blouses. They have smooth, pale skin and light eyes that glisten in the tropical sun like precious stones. When they walk, they appear to be dancing, and she can only imagine what they must be like when they cook. Always happy, using their fingers delicately, pampering their roughened skin with scented lotion afterwards.

Jini has noticed a small change in her own skin lately but she thinks it has something to do with the heat. On hot days, small rashes break out on her arms and legs and they disappear at night, when the air is cooler. Sarjit noticed a small rash on her elbow once and scrunched up his nose. "Eee. Dirty. Somebody didn't bathe today," he told her. "One of my army mates never bathes and his body has dark patches all over." She cringed and took more time in the shower that evening, until her mother banged on the door and told her to stop wasting water.

She and her mother take turns kneading the dough. They add a bit of ghee to it to make it softer so her knuckles can just slide across and bits of dough don't get stuck to her skin. Then they hear a scream. At first, it sounds like it's coming from the neighbour's house and they simply look up, then continue what they are doing. Her mother always says it's not nice to listen too carefully to what the neighbours are saying and doing because they will do the same thing back to you. Then they hear it again, a tortured noise, and Jini realises that it's coming from the living room, from Bilu.

She and her mother rush out to find him lying on the floor, writhing and twisting. His face looks pained and his mouth is open but he's not making any sound. But when her mother steps towards him, he lets out a shriek and scrambles to the wall. Her mother sits down on the floor.

"What is wrong now?" Sarjit is standing over Bilu, just staring at him. "What did you do?" she asks him angrily.

"Nothing!" he says. "I went to see him, I tried to hug him and he called me Papa. So I said, no, not Papa, this is your Pra-ji, your big brother. He kept insisting, Papa, Papa, so I just walked out. Then the next thing I knew, he was…like this."

"Idiot!" Mother cries. "Never tell him that Papa isn't around."

"I didn't! I just said that I'm not Papa."

"You must have said more than that," she says. She turns her attention to Bilu, who is crawling underneath the furniture and sucking his thumb. Jini feels sick inside watching the scene. Sarjit flings up his hands and walks out of the room. "I didn't say anything else," he mutters, exchanging a glance with Jini. They both know what their mother is like when it comes to protecting their little brother. He always comes first, because he needs more care than either of them. They will need to take care of him one day when she's old and gone, she often reminds them. If not his own family, then whose? This is why she pushes Jini to study hard, and she has been dropping hints to Sarjit about marriage. "After the army, when you're earning money, settle down with a nice girl, somebody who won't mind taking care of Bilu if something happens to me." She is very hopeful about this idea, even though people in the temple have told her to stop mentioning Bilu's condition and bringing him out of the house. "Which girl is going to be so understanding?" they ask gently.

Bilu's face is swollen—eyes, nose and lips all red and puffed so he looks like a cartoon of himself. His long hair has come undone from the bun on his head. Jini has often thought of suggesting to her mother to just cut it. People would probably talk, but once they realise how difficult it is to keep Bilu still and manage him, they'd sympathise. But she's afraid to bring it up to her mother, knowing that she'll suspect that Jini is trying to ask for permission to cut her own long plaits. Jini would never do such a thing to dishonour God. On occasion, the thought slips into her mind and she thinks about what she would look like with a short bob that curls under her ears. It frightens her. She would be a completely different person.

As she watches her mother coax Bilu to stand up and walk towards her, the pity she feels quickly turns to rage. If not for their missing father, Bilu wouldn't be like this. He wouldn't be screaming so loudly that there's a roaring in her ears even after he has stopped. Her mother wouldn't be sitting on the floor, struggling to keep the patience in her voice as she speaks to him. Jini is furious now, anger boiling in her chest and moving down to settle in her stomach. She remembers the first image that came to mind when Sarjit took her aside and quietly told her that their father was gone again. She was worried; she imagined him on a back road somewhere at night, having been robbed or run over by a car, confused about his surroundings. She even imagined him imprisoned by some mistake. Now all of those images flood to mind but instead of fearing for the worst, she relishes it. Nearly a month has passed now and all they know is that he has returned to India. He sends back money occasionally but it is never enough. She is certain that he will not be coming back. There is some comfort in thinking of him being injured. It numbs the pain she feels from hearing Bilu's inconsolable cries.

"The food!" her mother suddenly shouts, jerking her out of her thoughts. She rushes back into the kitchen and turns off the stove. The dhal must be burnt and stuck to the pot now—the fire has to be shut off at just the right boiling point or the lentils become soggy and tasteless. She can hear her mother cursing in the kitchen.

Bilu is still sobbing. Jini squats down on the floor and closes her eyes. Then she begins to sing to him the way she did yesterday afternoon when she caught him following her. She begins with a hum and notices his short, shaky breaths becoming longer. "You are my sunshine, my only sunshine…" she sings softly. The lyrics enchant Bilu. She is surprised when he points outside to the evening sun, descending behind rooftops and fences. "Sa-shine," he says. "Sa-shine." He crawls to Jini and she holds him until she hears her mother calling her to come into the kitchen and help her finish cooking dinner.

• • •

The first time their father left, it was only for a few hours, but it was enough to make Jini's mother panic. There was fear in her eyes as she paced the house and looked at the clock on the living room wall. Before storming out of the house, he had told her not to expect him for dinner. He said he was going out to find more work to support the family and when Mother questioned him, he became enraged. "And what if I go out for drinks after a long day's work? What is wrong with that?" "Everything is wrong!" her mother retorted. "Sikhs do not drink and smoke! It's disgraceful!" But he simply shook his head and left the house. Jini knew then that it was the beginning of a longer disappearance, because there was something final in the way he left that evening, the way he forced his eyes away from hers and Bilu's as he left.

Jini's father came home the next morning but he left again the following week and he was gone for three days. He returned with a present for Bilu, a wooden car. Jini didn't get anything. "You're too big for presents," her father reasoned. She was eleven, but suddenly she felt much older. She smelled something strong on his breath; Sarjit told her later it was whiskey. It made her feel sick and she had to force herself to eat later at dinner.

Jini's father left for good a few days after her birthday in May. He had been making extended trips to somewhere for a long time now—she did not know where—and her mother suspected he was on the run from loan sharks. "He must be gambling and borrowing to pay for drinks and opium," Jini overheard her telling Sarjit when he returned for the weekend. "He thinks he can just run away and nobody will find him."

She knew that her father had land in India, although she wasn't sure what that meant, but it sounded like a hopeful prospect. He could sell it and come back. She didn't miss him all that much because he rarely spoke to her anyway. They didn't have much in common. He used to talk to Sarjit about politics and government, about Singapore's landscape changing in the future. "More and more people are coming in. Soon this patch of land will be precious. They are planning on building high-rise flats everywhere. It's more efficient." He spoke of a new Singapore like it was some enchanted kingdom. Jini thought of the hotel and bank buildings sprouting up in town. On clear days, one could see the faint skeleton of a forming skyline. She might live in the sky one day.

Everybody in the neighbourhood knew about the opium dens because they had friends who had seen her father there. Jini could tell that they knew because they looked down uncomfortably whenever they saw the family at the temple without their father. They didn't ask where he was. Nobody wanted to say anything. The person who finally told them was Pra-ji.

Pra-ji is a wise man who converses with God then conveys His message to those who seek His help; he wears white from head to toe and has a long beard that is turning grey. His eyes are small but when he speaks, they well up with life. At the temple, he leads the singing with his deep voice, and the men and women follow along.

After the service, he talks to individual families in the courtyard. They flock to him with questions. My daughter is sick—will she get better? I have a pain in my back that won't go away—will you ask God why He is doing this to me? Will my mother be able to make it here from India? Who broke my shop windows? What should I do when my son talks back? He addresses all of these questions quietly, keeping his answers discreet. The crowd only diminishes when they begin to get hungry and somebody announces that langar is being served. Then their questions can wait.

Jini's mother has a question for Pra-ji and as people trickle back into the temple, she remains outside, but tells Sarjit to bring Jini and Bilu inside.

"She's going to ask him to find you a wife," Jini says as they queue to get their food. Mischief dances in her eyes. Sarjit reaches out to pinch her on the arm but she shrinks away and moves closer to Bilu, who is sucking on his thumb. She notices Sarjit blushing.

"I don't want a wife," he mutters. He told her one day that he wants to study physics at university, but the thought of finding money for the fees is laughable. He is making a good salary in his army job; if he leaves, what will the family do? Her mother would never forgive him.

They receive their food on steel plates, similar to the ones they have at home. The men and women serving are solemn, with their heads covered and their eyes cast downwards. Mother has told Jini before to remember how great God is when she receives her roti and dhal and yoghurt. "Ours is the only religion in which the poorest man will never starve," she always says proudly. "As long as you come to the temple and pray and believe in God, you receive langar in return." Behind the men and women, clouds of smoke billow from clay pots, and flames from large kerosene stoves lick hungrily at the air. Jini nods in appreciation and goes to sit down on the women's side of the hall. She saves a space on the floor for her mother, who doesn't show up. A sudden fear grips Jini. What would she do if her mother abandons her too?

She looks across the hall at Sarjit and Bilu. Sarjit is trying to get Bilu to stay still as he eats. He is careful about not pressuring

Bilu too much—anything can set him off and they don't want to deal with the embarrassment of having the entire Punjabi community witness Bilu at his worst. Bilu squirms and ends up spilling most of his food on the floor. Sarjit looks exasperated. He tries to make eye contact with Jini, and she shrugs back at him, secretly pleased that he is dealing with Bilu for a change. She envies him sometimes for being able to stay in the army barracks for the whole week, away from the family.

After they eat their lunch, they put their plates in the back kitchen and wash their hands. The floor in the kitchen is wet and greasy under Jini's feet. The sinks are overflowing with dirty dishes and grey suds. She scrubs her hands, remembering what her brother said about his army mate who never showers. On her thumb, there is another mysterious little mark, one that she's never seen before. When she scratches, it becomes irritated and red. She runs water over it until an old woman behind her tells her to hurry up. "Stop using up so much water," she grumbles at Jini, who quickly apologises and steps away.

Their mother is still in the courtyard talking to Pra-ji when Jini, Sarjit and Bilu come outside. Sarjit is trying to steady Bilu, who twists and whines and keeps his eyes fixed in a sideways glance at the sky.

"Sat sri akal, Pra-ji," Jini says. Pra-ji greets her back. "Growing big, dear," he says. She blushes. Everybody says she's growing bigger and she knows they mean that she's getting taller and looks more mature, but sometimes she can't help but wonder if they notice that her chest is beginning to swell. Some of her school friends have mentioned that she could pass for a secondary school girl with her body. She throws her scarf over her chest so Pra-ji can't see but his attention is now on Sarjit and Bilu.

"How's the army?" he asks Sarjit in English. Jini's mother quickly looks to her for a translation but Jini shakes her head to let her know it's nothing important.

"Good," Sarjit says. Next to Pra-ji's big frame, Jini's brother is a bag of bones. His knees and elbows jut out awkwardly and there is very little hair on his face.

"Very good. Your mother tells me you intend to get married soon," he says. Jini snorts. Her mother gives her a sharp look.

Sarjit shrugs and looks at the ground. His cheeks are turning red.

"I know a family in Ipoh who is interested in marrying off their daughter here. Good family. The father is a police officer," Pra-ji tells Mother. She nods vigorously, only giving Sarjit a quick glance. Bilu strays from Sarjit and begins to play with the mess of shoes people have left outside. After rubbing his hands over the soles, he puts his hands in his mouth.

"Don't do that!" Jini calls. She claps to get Bilu's attention. He stares at her, frozen for a moment, before he pushes his whole fist into his mouth. Jini opens her mouth to call out again but she stops when she realises that several people in the courtyard have turned to stare. They seem to think that from a distance, the family won't notice them gawking at Bilu as if he were some strange animal.

Pra-ji lowers his voice and tells Mother, "This girl will be quite accepting of…the family's problems. I can assure you of that."

"How do you know for sure?" Mother asks worriedly.

A smile spreads across Pra-ji's face. "She doesn't have many suitors. Sarjit will be her best option."

. . .

At home that evening, Jini's mother is crying. She cries every Sunday as Sarjit packs his bags to leave the next day. Jini is sitting in the room with him, watching him fold his clothes.

"Coming back next weekend? You can meet your new girlfriend," she teases. He swats her on the mouth and it stings so much, she begins to tear up.

"Stop it," he hisses. "It's not funny. Can't you hear Ma crying?"

"She's sad because you're leaving. She cries every week."

"It's not just that."

"Then what is it?"

"I think Pra-ji told her more things about Pa and what he's been doing. I think he's moved to India permanently."

"Permanently?"

"Yeah, that means he won't come back, you understand?"

"Cannot be."

"Can be. When you two were getting your shoes and helping Bilu, he pulled me aside and told me I might become the man of the house because Pa is not coming back," he says grimly.

"How does he know?"

Sarjit shrugs. "I don't know. He knows everything. He says he spoke to Guru-ji who told him to tell us not to hope for a return. I have to get married now, Jini. There's no way I can refuse to do so."

Jini feels the rage growing inside her again. It makes her heart pound inside her ears. She thinks of all the evil words she knows—four-letter words in English, Chinese swear words she has heard in school. She imagines herself throwing them at her father like daggers until he collapses.

"I'm going early in the morning tomorrow, probably before you wake up. Take care," he tells her, reaching out to tug one of her plaits. Then he stops. "Do something about your skin, will you? It's getting disgusting."

She looks down at her arms and sees three new spots, bright red and hard like pimples. "I bathe!" she insists. "I bathe twice every day. I even got a scolding the other day for using up too much water." But Sarjit gives her a wary look.

"Get out so I can finish packing," he says before he yanks one of her plaits and makes a sound like a toilet flushing. She pinches his arm and leaves the room, rubbing one of the patches on her skin.

She goes out into the backyard and sits in the moonlight, thinking. In the dark, the houses in the neighbourhood seem to slouch less. Bright fluorescent lights shine from square upstairs windows, revealing pale walls and ceiling fans, rusted iron grilles and wall calendars. She looks over her shoulder at her own house to see what others might see when they peek in. A gate that never stays latched. Patches of grass and dirt and dust. A mother pacing her room nervously, never sleeping, always thinking. A fitful little boy who can't express the pain he is feeling unless he opens his mouth and screams it out. A young man lying on his back in his bed, staring at the ceiling and thinking about theories and equations he will never solve.

And how would she look to a passer-by? A girl crouched in the moonlight, running her hand down her bumpy arm. A girl with long plaits that hang down her back. A girl who is growing up but wants to put the whole world on hold, stop the buildings from rising, stop the night from swallowing the evening sun, stop everything until her family is normal again.

PART II

5

1990

MONSOON SEASON WAS only supposed to arrive at the end of the year but it began in early October and stayed. Heavy clouds hung low in the sky, threatening to burst. Rain fell in slanted sheets and wind ripped through our corridor, knocking over the potted plants. Raindrops rolled off the canvas awnings outside shops, off the leaves that tipped like open hands making offerings. Our shoes had to be kept inside otherwise they would get soaked. Our clothes could no longer be strung on the bamboo poles because the sun was hardly out long enough to dry them. Ma draped them on the chairs and hung some from hangers that she hooked onto a ceiling pipe in our kitchen. In the dark, the ghostly shapes of clothes were all I could see besides God's eyes.

Daddy made a joke to me one day that the monsoon was as unexpected and as unwelcome as Nani-ji and maybe it was learning from her example of barging in and staying. He was very careful when he made this joke; he looked around to see if Ma was within earshot and even though she wasn't, he whispered. Nani-ji was not to be joked about these days. She was often tired. When she did speak, she chose her words carefully and she made sure that everybody listened. She did not like being interrupted. She got older in the same way the sky rapidly darkened in the evenings—every time I looked at her, she seemed to have withered a bit more.

I complained one evening about the flying ants and moths that flew in from outside. They always appeared during the rainy season. Nani-ji told me that their homes had been destroyed by the rain, so they needed the warmth from our lights. I switched off all of the lights if I saw any insects. I was afraid they'd lay eggs in my nose while I was sleeping. Farizah's sister told her it happened to a man in rural Malaysia years ago and he was still coughing up insects.

"You know what I used to do?" Nani-ji said after I whined that there were so many flying ants in the corridor, I felt like they were crawling on my skin. "I used to fill a bucket of water and put it directly under the lamp. The flies are attracted to light first, then warmth. They used to dive right into the water and drown before they even realised it was just a reflection."

I thought that was rather evil of Nani-ji. *Are you listening to this?* I asked God silently, hoping He'd take note. Nani-ji told me to get a bucket.

"Go on, fill it with water. I'll show you."

"No," I said and walked away. When I glanced over my shoulder, she looked worn and sad and I felt a bit sorry for her. I tried to be kinder. "I don't want to kill them," I said gently.

Nani-ji looked too tired to argue. She shuffled into my room and sat on the edge of the mattress. She let out a shaky sigh. "Close the windows," she said. Wind whistled through the flat. I reached over the bed to shut them. Nani-ji rubbed her arms to warm them. Next to her on the mattress was a small velvet pouch fastened with golden strings. She untied the strings and emptied the contents onto the bed. It was Ma's jewellery.

"You gave those to Ma for her wedding," I told Nani-ji.

"I did," she said. She laid out the long chandelier earrings, the necklace that looked like a string of tears, the solid bangles with intricate patterns engraved into their sides. They sparkled in the dimness of my room.

"Did Ma look pretty on her wedding day?" I asked, holding the earrings to my lobes. They were heavier than I had expected.

Nani-ji shrugged. "Every bride is beautiful on her wedding day. Your mother was no exception." She took the earrings back from me and lay them out on the mattress again. "Your mother could have married anybody. Had she been more decent, she could have married somebody with more money and I wouldn't have had to give her my jewellery for her wedding."

This made me mad. I thought about the wedding portrait that hung on the wall of Ma's room and how Daddy beamed in the picture, holding her hand tightly as if she might disappear if he didn't. Nani-ji was saying that Ma should never have married Daddy.

I pushed myself off the bed and shrugged. "It's just jewellery," I scoffed.

Nani-ji looked up sharply. "*Just* jewellery?"

"It's not a big deal. Ma says your jewellery is old and outdated anyway. When she gets it back, she plans on melting it all down and changing it." The words rushed out of my mouth so quickly, I didn't have time to think. I told myself that it was okay to tell Nani-ji what Ma had said; I wasn't lying. But I felt uneasy, especially when Nani-ji scooped up the jewellery and funnelled it back into the pouch. "Changing it," she repeated softly to herself before she pursed her lips. She pulled the gold strings tightly together so the mouth of the pouch puckered.

I left the room and looked at God and shut my eyes. Could He turn back time? I wanted to go back five minutes and bite my lip when Nani-ji had insulted Daddy. *Help*, I said frantically. *I've done something terribly wrong.* If He were listening, He did not look like it. His stare was vacant, as if busy thinking about something else.

• • •

The rains did not last all day; they came in bouts. In the gaps between, snails inched out of the wet soil, stray cats roamed cautiously from the sheltered void decks and the boys spilt out of their flats, anxious to get a good game in before the older boys claimed the space. Roadside didn't come round to our flat because he was frightened of Nani-ji, but he saw me getting off the school bus one afternoon and told me to join them.

"Will you let me play?" I asked. I demonstrated how I could remove my new kara. Roadside nodded. I went back to the flat and searched for Ma. She was in her room and wouldn't even notice if I came home and left again. Nani-ji was asleep. I changed quickly and went back outside. The ground was wet and fat raindrops were still rolling off the leaves on the trees. Late afternoon sunlight, golden and dappled between branches, shone on the neighbourhood.

"I'm going to be goalie!" I called.

Kaypoh turned around. "Too late. You can go over there," he said. He pointed at a cluster of boys standing around the designated goal—a wide space between a pair of sandals.

I shook my head. "I'm the goalie today."

"Who says so?" Kaypoh challenged.

I pointed at Roadside. Kaypoh grinned. "Ah, I see," he said. "Like that." Roadside shifted uncomfortably. I didn't understand what Kaypoh meant but when I looked at Roadside for an explanation, he avoided my gaze.

The basketball court was next to a large canal that ran through the neighbourhood. It was usually empty, but after the day's rain, a shallow stream of water ran through it. Each time the ball rolled close to the canal, a boy would run to save it while the others yelled excitedly. The boy who saved the ball was a hero for the moment and he returned to applause.

I wanted to save the ball from the canal too, but every time it rolled off the court, a faster boy like Malik or Wei Hao would race ahead of me and get all the glory. I still gave chase. Once, I got really close before Kaypoh swooped in and kicked it back toward the court.

"That's not fair," I said.

Kaypoh shrugged. "You're too slow."

"You're a show-off," I shot back. I noticed Roadside standing nearby.

"You're a—" Kaypoh began, but Roadside interrupted him. "Eh, it's going to rain again soon. Let's get back to the game."

Kaypoh glared at me and stalked back to the court. The game continued. I stayed at my post and kept my eyes trained on the ball. My feet shuffled to the game's rhythm, and when the boys began advancing towards me, I was ready to block the goal. Malik had the ball. He stared past my shoulders and drew his leg to score when Kaypoh darted out behind him and punted the ball hard. It flew way past the goal post and landed in the high branches of a tree.

The other boys gathered round and looked up at the tree. I smirked at Kaypoh. "What kind of goal is that?" I taunted. Malik and Wei Hao chuckled.

Kaypoh didn't seem bothered. He shrugged and wiped the

sweat off his forehead with his T-shirt. Then he said, "Go and get it."

I looked up at the tree. The ball was wedged between in the crook of a thick branch that bent like an elbow. I glanced at Kaypoh.

"How to get up there? Can't you just shake the tree?" I asked.

Kaypoh shrugged. "You want so badly to catch the ball. That's the goalie's job, right?" Now he was the one smirking.

I looked up again. On a dry day, it would be possible for me to scramble up the trunk, pressing my feet against the little nubs that stuck out from its sides before reaching a sturdy branch. But the rain had made the trunk slippery and I would surely slip.

"I'll fall," I said.

"Then maybe your boyfriend can save you," Kaypoh said. "Can or not, Roadside?"

My heart caught in my throat. Was that what everyone thought? "He's not my boyfriend," I said, glancing at Roadside for confirmation. "Tell them," I urged.

"Kaypoh, you better watch your big mouth," Roadside warned. "Don't go around saying stupid things like that. It's not true."

"Of course not, lah," Malik said. "He's only joking. Where got Chinese boys go out with Indian girls? Crazy, right?" Wei Hao and Samuel laughed. I joined in even though I didn't think it was that funny.

The boys became occupied with finding things on the ground to throw at the ball to loosen it. Deven offered his sneaker. It became its own game, trying to get the ball out of the tree. By the time it finally bounced out onto the ground, it had started raining again.

When I got home, I scowled at God sitting comfortably in

His frame. Nobody ever challenged Him or told Him to sit on the side of the courts. Even He seemed to be laughing at me. I thought about what Ma had said when she was telling me her story. "We feared God so much, we didn't even think to blame him for the things that went wrong." I realised that I feared God much more when I didn't see Him all the time. Now that He lived in our flat, I was beginning to grow weary of Him. He didn't leap out of the frame to punish me when I was rude. He just sat and watched, a bemused expression clouding His face. He had the opposite effect on Ma. She had twitched nervously throughout her story, glancing at Him as if seeking approval. She had ended where Pra-ji was going to arrange a marriage for her older brother because she was tired, she claimed, but the way she kept her eyes on God told me she was afraid to go on.

That night, I tossed and turned. I couldn't get to sleep because I was hurt by what Malik had said. I told myself that I should have climbed the tree and avoided being insulted. A low wind whistled through the windows before the familiar patter of rain began. The room was humid, the air in short supply as if Nani-ji was taking it all up with each loud gasp. I climbed onto the bed gingerly to crack open the window. Nani-ji's arms and legs stuck out stiffly from her body. A towel folded into a triangle lay at the bridge of her nose. She soaked it in warm water and mint oil before she slept every night.

I still couldn't sleep. All I could hear was the rain. Maybe it was all I wanted to listen to. I got up and walked out into the living room and sat on the floor in front of God.

"What's your favourite colour?" I asked. No response. "Do you have any friends?" Still nothing. I tossed every question I could think of, hoping that one would strike Him. "Why can't I cut my hair? Why do I have to cover my head when I go to your house?"

"Pin?"

I jumped. It was only Daddy. He squinted at me.

"I can't sleep," I informed him.

"Who were you talking to?"

I looked at God shyly and just shrugged at Daddy. "Nobody," I said. I hoped that my words would sting God. *You're not important,* I wanted to tell Him. But His expression did not change. He was good at staying still when Daddy was around.

"Go back to sleep," he told me. "You have school tomorrow—you won't be able to wake up."

"I can't sleep," I insisted.

"You have to try," Daddy said gently. He hooked his hands under my arms and lifted me up but I hung limply like a dead weight. "Go on," he said, steering me back into my room.

But I still couldn't sleep. Nani-ji rolled over and mumbled something in her sleep. The wind made ghostly sounds through the gaps in our windows. I sat up straight on my mattress. My eyes were heavy but I did not want to close them. Suddenly, I knew what I had to do to get God to pay attention. I crept back out of my room and went into the kitchen. Ma kept a pair of scissors in the bottom drawer close to the sink. I walked out into the living room with the scissors, looked straight at God, and slipped a lock of my hair into the open mouth of the blades.

Say something, I challenged. But He shrugged. I pressed the scissors against my hair and heard a crunching noise before the loose strands sprinkled down the back of my neck. I gave another snip. God just watched expectantly. Nothing seemed to surprise Him. *I don't believe in you,* I said to Him. *If you were real, you'd try to stop me. You'd do something.* And He still didn't move.

• • •

Ma no longer cooked. The refrigerator shelves and cabinets were bare. Under the sink, there was a bag of flour and a hot plate on the stove. A few onions, some garlic and ginger sat in a small bowl next to the salt and pepper bottles. Next to them were jars of chilli powder, curry powder, coriander and turmeric. Besides these, the kitchen was a hollow shell.

I did not count making roti as cooking because Ma did not enjoy it. She dragged herself into the kitchen twice a day and stared blankly at the flat dough as it bloated and smoked on the stove. Her dhal was bland no matter how much chilli powder she put into it, because she did not care about this food. There were no messages in roti and dhal, only memories of how little she'd had to eat as a child.

I ate my lunch at school nowadays. I queued up with the other girls in the tuck shop and paid for fried bee hoon, chicken rice, fishball noodle soup and nasi briyani, which the Malay Auntie only cooked on Wednesday. The nasi briyani was always too salty but the Auntie could not taste it. She was fasting for Hari Raya and she cooked everything without tasting it first. She always apologised when she handed over the plate of steaming yellow rice and curry chicken. "Sorry, girl. Maybe today more salt, ah? Auntie cannot taste," she said.

Farizah was also fasting, so I made it a point to eat quickly even though she said I didn't have to. "You're not the one who's fasting. I am," she said.

"Aren't you hungry?"

She shrugged. "You get used to it," she said. I thought about my hair and felt guilty. I was supposed to grow out my hair and just get used to it. I told Farizah about it and showed her the end of my braid that I had snipped off. The hair was jagged and uneven. Farizah's eyes widened. She looked impressed.

"Does your mother know?"

"No," I said. Ma didn't notice anything these days.

"Does your grandmother know?"

"No," I said.

"Why did you do it?"

I thought of telling Farizah about how I wanted to challenge God, but realised that if I said it out loud, it would sound silly, like I was talking about an imaginary friend. "I was feeling hot," I said. Farizah laughed. She pointed at her legs, covered by her long socks. "I'm feeling hot too, but if I pull these down, my father will rotan me."

"But if you did it in school, your father wouldn't know," I said. "Who is going to tell him?"

Farizah's eyes darted around her like she was considering this. "Nobody," she said slowly. "But I just can't. I always cover my legs." She tugged at her socks to make them a bit higher as if our conversation was somehow making them slip down to expose her skin. "Hurry up and finish eating. We can play cards or something," she said in a quiet voice. She did not look at me. Later, while we were playing, I asked her if she was angry, but she said, "No."

"You sure?"

"Yeah." Then the bell rang, and she gathered her cards and raced to the class queue ahead of me.

I promised myself that I would not cut my hair any more. It was an experiment to see what God would do, and it had failed because he had displayed no reaction. As I stepped onto the school bus at the end of the day, I pulled my plait around my shoulder and stroked the bristly ends. The girls were playing the Question Game again but I didn't join in.

As the bus approached my stop, I pulled the straps of my bag over my shoulders and made my way to the front. I noticed that Bus Uncle was asleep, but he still gripped the railing. His knuckles were tense and white. I watched him and tried to imagine him as a young boy in Singapore, but could not see past the creases and folds of his skin. Some people just looked like they had been born old.

Suddenly, the bus braked hard, the bus driver swearing under his breath. My arms shot forward to protect myself as I fell onto Bus Uncle, my hands pressing against his rough face. He jumped awake and shouted something at the bus driver, then grabbed my elbow. I tried to pull away but he was surprisingly strong. He brought me so close that our faces were practically touching. His breath smelled sour, like stale cigarettes and fish. The bus stopped. I could see my block, blurry through the afternoon drizzle.

"Mungalee," he breathed like he was still dreaming. "Go. Go home. Dirty Mungalee." The words were like blades. I turned to see if the other girls had noticed but the few left on the bus were too busy playing the Question Game. I yanked my arm away from Bus Uncle. I wanted to say something terrible to him but I knew I'd get into trouble. He just smirked at me and said the word again, stretching it out this time. "Mung-a-lee."

I raised my foot and stomped down hard on his. I dug in my heel, then flew down the steps of the bus and ran to my block. My heart beat loudly in my ears. I could hear Bus Uncle calling out still, yelling it now, "Mungalee! Mungalee!" But I was not sure if he was really shouting or if it was just in my head.

When I got home, I looked at God squarely in the eyes again. He moved this time. He shifted back in the frame, sensing my anger. "Why did you let that happen?" I asked Him. Why was Bus Uncle allowed to humiliate me? Why did the bus stop like that and cause me to topple onto him? Why did I step on his foot? I was furious with Him. I ran back to the kitchen, took out the scissors and chopped off another bit of hair. God looked taken aback this time.

I'll keep doing it, I warned him. *I'm not afraid of anything.* But if He could read my mind, He would know what I was really feeling.

• • •

"You need to follow the doctor's instructions," Ma was telling Nani-ji. "Or your breathing problems are never going to get better."

"Rubbish," Nani-ji said. "Since when did you become such an expert?"

"I'm not very educated, but I know a few things about taking care of you," Ma replied haughtily. "Take your medication and you'll be fine."

A puff of air escaped Nani-ji's tightly pursed lips. "Fine? I will not be fine. I am old."

"You're making yourself older," Ma said.

"Pin!" Nani-ji called. "Pin, come into the kitchen."

I tucked my plait into the back of my T-shirt in case Nani-ji noticed, but she didn't even look at me. She looked at Ma as she spoke to me. "Tell your mother to stop bossing me around, eh? Do you boss your mother around like this? I tell you, your manners are better than hers."

Ma threw her hands in the air and said, "I give up." She shook her head wearily at me. "When I'm old, Pin, don't take me in or take care of me if I'm going to be half as annoying as this woman."

Nani-ji coughed so hard, her entire body rattled. Ma tried not to react, but I saw her eyes—she was panicking. "What's wrong?" she asked when Nani-ji finally stopped.

"Nothing. Nothing is wrong with me. I'm not dying."

"I never said you were. But you'll be in serious trouble if you don't start taking the doctor's advice seriously. These sorts of infections are common killers."

"I know exactly how I will die," Nani-ji said. "It's written in my palm."

Ma's face turned to stone. She got up from the table and occupied herself with clearing it. "Pin, help me tidy up here," she said in English. Nani-ji gave me a questioning look but I pretended not to see. Ma's shoulders were suddenly very tense. Nani-ji settled back into her chair and started to look intensely at her palms.

"He could see the future, you know," she told me.

"Who?" I asked. I glanced at Ma, who shot Nani-ji a dirty look. It did not seem to bother Nani-ji though. She was smiling as though recalling a sweet dream.

"A wise man who lived in our neighbourhood. He passed away a few years ago. We called him Pra-ji because he was like everybody's big brother. He was blessed—he could look into your eyes and tell you what God wanted you to know."

Ma's mouth was a straight line and her arms became rigid. "Pin, I don't want you hearing this. Leave the kitchen," she said quietly in English. I stood, frozen. Nani-ji's eyes darted back and forth between Ma and me. She did not know English, but she could read Ma's tone.

I put the teacups in the sink and rushed to my room. I expected to hear shouts ringing out—Ma telling Nani-ji never to mention Pra-ji again, Nani-ji telling Ma that she was disrespectful. But there was a dreadful silence, like something had entered our flat and sucked all of the noise out of it. And after listening to the silence for a few moments, I decided that this was much worse, and I wished they would start arguing again.

• • •

Bus Uncle did not complain to the school about me. He did not even look at me when I got on the bus the next day. He pretended I didn't exist. I figured that God might have had something to do with this; perhaps shutting up Bus Uncle was God's way of helping me. We were almost even then, although I was still upset about what Bus Uncle had said, and God couldn't erase the feeling of shame that sank in my stomach every time I heard Bus Uncle's taunts in my mind.

Nobody noticed how my hair was short and long in different places. Ma did not do my hair in the mornings. She did not wake up for breakfast like she used to. I braided my own hair, which was messy at first, but Farizah had taught me how to tuck in all of the stray strands. She was a good accomplice because her sister was in Secondary School and she sneaked out to meet with her boyfriend on weekends. But she did not approve of what I did. "If your mother catches you, you'll get a caning for sure," she said, shuddering as if she were the one being punished.

"My mother doesn't know. And she doesn't beat," I informed

her. The consequences of Ma finding out did not concern me these days. I was testing God. I didn't dare say it out loud yet, but I wasn't sure if I believed in Him at all.

"Just don't tell her I helped you," Farizah said, pulling back my hair. "Don't you dare."

"Deal," I said.

. . .

Nothing bad came from cutting my hair. I realised this a few days after I had started doing it. It didn't matter if I did that or if I prayed or if I ate temple food. God paid attention when it suited him; He ignored me when it didn't.

I started snipping off chunks of my hair without having any reason, just to see what God would do, and nothing happened. Lightning did not strike our flat, I did not get hit by a speeding car on my way to school—nothing. This lasted for a week. Then one night, Nani-ji began to gasp loudly in her sleep and before I realised she was starting to die, I knew that God was paying me back a lump sum of punishments for my little batches of sins.

. . .

When it was night-time, it was hard to see the stars from where we lived, because the buildings opposite swallowed the sky. One by one, the lights in other flats went out like candle flames. Deepavali was coming soon. There were a few Indian families in our block who framed their doorways with colourful lights that blinked long after they were asleep. One of our neighbours down the hall had hung a string of silvery paper flames around their gate. One of the paper flames was torn off by the wind one day and somebody came and slipped it under our door. It wasn't our holiday though. Sikhs have a holiday called Vesakhi, but I didn't think it was all that special because nobody got off school or work on that day. I kept the paper flame in my room between my school textbooks. It was ripped in the corners but ever since Nani-ji had been hospitalised, I had a hard time throwing anything away. To get to the garbage bin, I had to pass God in the living room and I couldn't bear to look at His face, *I told you so* dancing in His eyes, making the corners of His mouth twitch. He could barely contain His glee. I felt it every morning when I rushed past Him to get to the door.

Daddy poked his head into my room. "How are you, Pin?" he asked.

"Okay," I said.

"How was school?"

I shrugged. "Boring. Miss Yoon didn't come to school today."

Daddy raised an eyebrow. "Things have changed. When I was in school, if a teacher didn't come to school, we had fun."

"We got an old man relief teacher. Like an uncle." I said.

Daddy nodded sympathetically. "I see," he said. I noticed he was wearing his work uniform—the starched greyish-blue shirt, a pair of navy blue pants. The pants were not properly ironed. There were wrinkles near his ankles. He followed my eyes and looked embarrassed. "Yeah, I know. I'm not very good at ironing," he said. "Your Ma usually does all of these things, you know? But she's so busy." We both looked down when he said, "busy". Ma practically lived in the hospital now. I had not seen her in three days, and only heard her hoarse voice over the telephone. One night, I picked up my phone extension when she called. "Pin, please pass the phone to your father."

"Okay," I said. I called out for Daddy, who picked up the extension in the living room. I lingered on the line and decided only to hang up when either one of them told me to, but as soon as Daddy's voice came on, Ma's stern voice broke down into sniffles and sobs, and neither of them noticed that I was still listening. "My mother is dying," she wailed. "And she's going to die thinking I caused Bilu's death."

Daddy tried to console Ma. "Now is the time to put aside all of your petty differences, the two of you. Just forget about the whole incident—your mother is not going to change her mind."

"She thinks I went to Pra-ji's house that day and I…"

"I know what she thinks. I know what Pra-ji said. But you know the truth, don't you? And if you just explain it all to Pin, she'll know too. That's the important thing. Forget about what your mother wants to believe."

Ma sniffled, then she said she had to go. Daddy hung up the phone and came into my room. I quickly put down the receiver and pretended to be looking for something on my desk. "Have you had your dinner?" Daddy asked me. It was what Miss Yoon would call a silly question. Of course I hadn't eaten my dinner. We relied solely on hawker food these days. We didn't even enter the kitchen unless we were passing through it to get to the toilet or the washing machine.

"No," I said.

"Hungry?"

"Not really. You?"

"Not really." Daddy stepped out of the room, then came back, his eyebrows furrowed in concentration as if he was remembering that I was supposed to eat, whether I was hungry or not. "You have to have something for dinner. I can go down and buy you a packet of food. What do you want?"

It had been raining all day. Clouds slid over the moon like a blanket and the wind sighed against our windows. Monsoon weather always called for something mild and soothing, like hot dumplings in chicken soup or glass noodles with stir-fried vegetables. But I was feeling guilty and I wanted to eat something doused in red chilli to cover up the queasiness in my stomach. "Nasi biryani," I said.

Daddy chuckled. "I thought you said you weren't hungry." Nasi biryani was very filling. One chicken thigh covered in curry paste and basmati rice was enough to keep a person from eating for the rest of the day. The man who ran the Indian stall downstairs was generous with his papadums and yoghurt as well. I thought of saving the food for two or three days because Daddy had almost forgotten about dinner tonight.

"I'll come with you," I said, scrambling to get up.

"No, Pin. You finish your homework. I'll just take a few minutes."

I frowned. Outside, it began to pour again. It was better to be indoors during the monsoon season but I did not like being alone in the flat with God. It was during these times that I could hear Him clicking His tongue inside his mouth like the tick-tock of hands on a clock. If I closed my eyes and stood with my back facing His portrait, I still saw Him shaking His head in disappointment. If I continued to shut my eyes, I saw Nani-ji wheezing and convulsing in my room, her eyes bulging out as she gasped for Ma to take her to the hospital. "I'll go, I'll go," she kept saying, clawing at the sheets. I felt her breath lingering in the still air of my room. I smelled her musky clothes and the minty smell of minyak kapak medicated oil that she dabbed on her temples for headaches. I always waited for my mind to go blank and for Nani-ji to exit my thoughts but stubbornly, she stayed. She was there even after I opened my eyes.

6

"WE ARE NOT allowed to celebrate anything now," Ma told me gravely as she stood tiptoe on a wooden stool and reached up to unhook the curtains from the window. "Do you understand? So stop asking me what we're doing for Deepavali this year. It's not even our holiday anyway." I listened, but my heart was making too much noise as it beat frantically in my chest. Ma could fall now. She could slip off the stool and break her neck, and God would just shake his head and remind me that it was all my fault.

Ma was at home because the doctors at the hospital had told her to go home and rest. I overheard Daddy telling her to go to bed, but she stayed awake and close to the phone. She did not enter the kitchen. In the afternoon, she began cleaning the flat as if preparing for a visitor. "Is somebody coming over?" I asked cautiously.

"Can't I keep my home clean?" Ma snapped. I tried to avoid her for the rest of the day but it was a challenge. Our flat was small and it was a Saturday. I had finished my homework and all of my revisions already. Ma jumped off the stool, leaving the curtains half unhooked and dangling slanted from the windows. She went outside to water the plants. Then she came back inside again and began spraying Windex on the glass top of the coffee table. Her arms and legs were all raw patches now, and in some spots there were small dots of blood where she had scratched too hard.

I opened the fridge. There was a plastic container with a small stick of butter, a water pitcher, a carrot and an eggplant in the vegetable rack, and a few small bottles of ground spices. I spotted a loaf of bread on one shelf and checked to see if it was mouldy, relieved to discover that it wasn't. I took out the butter and switched on the toaster. We had learnt in science class that humans could go for days with just water, so I could do just fine on bread and butter until Daddy came home with some food from the hawker centre. I wondered about Ma. How did she go all day without eating? She was getting thinner. I saw for the first time today that her bangle could almost slip off her wrist if she shook it a little.

Then I had an idea. I opened the closet door again and pulled out a packet of sugar. Tiny black ants scrambled away as I unwound the rubber band that was tied over the mouth of the packet. I spread the butter over the bread, then sprinkled sugar over it. Then I sprinkled a bit more. I wasn't sure how to turn on the stove but I had seen Ma do it tonnes of times. I pushed then twisted the knob and heard the short clicks before the flames appeared with a gasp.

"Pin? What are you doing?" Ma called from the living room.

"Making lunch," I replied. "Sugarbread."

"Making what?"

"Sugarbread," I repeated. Ma was not the only person around here who could make up recipes. I placed the bread on the pan and pressed it down with a fork, watching as smoke curled up from the browning edges. Ma did not say anything after that. She continued cleaning. "Do you want some?" I asked. There was a pause and again, I panicked, fearing that Ma had fainted from hunger. I could not push these horrible thoughts from my mind. God was bound to punish me again soon.

"Yeah, leave one for me." Ma's voice brought me some relief.

I made three slices and there was only one slice of bread left in the packet. I placed it on the table to remind Ma of our food shortage in the flat and it worked. "Is this all we have in the house? Butter, bread and sugar?" she asked me. I nodded.

"I've been very busy with your grandmother," she said defensively.

I pushed the plate of sugarbread towards Ma as a peace offering before we began an argument. "Try it," I said. The kitchen smelled like smoke and caramel. I had made sure to turn off the stove and soak the pan so the crusty bits of burnt sugar wouldn't cling to the surface.

"Who taught you to make this?" Ma asked. She gave the bread a wary look.

"Nobody. I thought of it on my own."

Ma took a bite and chewed. She looked like she was thinking or concentrating on something. "Nice," she finally said.

I took a slice of my own and bit down on it. It was sweet and crunchy. I took another bite. Although I didn't dare say it out loud, this was better than any dish Ma had ever cooked because I had invented it. I had made it on my own. I felt smart and satisfied, like I had done something right for once, even if it was a small thing like making sugarbread. After I finished my slice, I offered Ma the last one. "Let's split it," she said, tearing the bread in half. When she was done, she said, "You know, my younger brother Bilu would have loved this. He loved anything sweet. There was a point when the only way to get him to eat was to give him something with sugar on it." She smiled and shook her head. I stopped chewing and waited for her to continue, but then she dusted the crumbs off her hands and took the plates to the sink without uttering another word.

• • •

I was trying very hard to get on God's good side. I stopped cutting my hair and I began doing good deeds again. I hoped that He was watching when I returned school library books to their correct places on the shelves instead of just cramming them in with the encyclopaedias like the other girls did. I wanted His eyes on me all the time now. I wanted Him to see me holding doors open for my teachers, picking up rubbish, feeding the crusts of my bread to the birds downstairs.

But it wasn't enough for Him. Ma stayed at the hospital for two days straight. She called home to say that she couldn't leave Nani-ji's side. I asked if I could visit and Ma said, "No, Pin. There are lots of sick people here. You'll have bad dreams."

At school, Farizah asked me why I had grown so quiet during recess lately and when I told her that my grandmother was sick, her eyes widened.

"I'll ask my parents to pray for her," she assured me.

I did not know how to pray but it was a good idea. God might stop taking out his anger on Nani-ji if I spoke directly to Him in the language He knew best. I knew a few scattered words and phrases that I'd picked up from all of Nani-ji's routine evening prayers, but none of them made much sense to me. I was afraid of offending God even more than I already had.

Then one afternoon after school, I went to Ma's room and got a gutka, a Sikh prayer book, from her dresser drawer. She had three of them, and each one was wrapped in a handkerchief. The oldest one had a tattered cover and pages that spilt out the minute I tried to turn them. I tucked them back in and picked out the newer edition. The prayers were all written in Punjabi script that curled and hung from a long bar across the page. Some of the alphabet looked like teapots, snails, squatting men and wide-branched trees. At the temple, these letters were responsible for all of the low chanting, the steady hums that came out of the old ladies' mouths. I traced my finger over them, half-expecting to feel them rise and squirm under my touch.

At the back of the newer book, there was an English translation of all of the prayers. *God is everywhere and in everyone. He is the Truth—Immortal, Creator, Without-Fear, Without-Enmity, Unborn and Self-Created.* I didn't quite understand this bit but I kept on reading. I looked at God in His portrait and tried to read to Him. He looked disinterested. I kept on reading and the more pages I turned, the less I looked at God. I began to notice that the Sikh prayers were very similar to the Christian hymns we'd learnt at school. The Gods were different and the people were different, but we were saying the same thing. I shut the book and looked at God. I noticed His eyes roaming from mine to the space above my head. A breeze entered the flat and cooled the top of my head—my bare head.

"I forgot," I said, flattening my palms out over my head. "I'm so sorry!" I ran into Ma's room to get a scarf. Now I'd have to start all over. Nani-ji always said there was no use in trying to pray to God if you couldn't show Him basic respect. I figured He'd seen me speaking but couldn't hear me unless my head was covered and my feet were tucked away from his view.

While I was searching Ma's closet for a scarf, I heard the

doorbell ring. I went out to the living room and looked through the peephole. Fat Auntie's face stretched out so she looked even wider than usual. "What does she want?" I muttered to myself, forgetting for a moment about my plan to score points with God.

"Hello, Pin," Fat Auntie said as I opened the gate with the spare key.

"Hello," I said. We greeted each other with the same sideways hug she exchanged with Ma. "Ma's not here."

"I know. I just came to pick up some of your grandmother's things."

"Nani-ji took everything to the hospital with her," I told Fat Auntie. She pushed past me impatiently and entered my room. Suddenly, I longed for Ma to be there. She didn't care how big Fat Auntie was or how much older she was. She'd tell her off for just barging in like that.

It turned out that I was wrong about Nani-ji bringing everything to the hospital with her. Fat Auntie went straight for the closet and knew exactly which shelf to search. "What are you looking for?" I asked innocently, but I had a feeling I knew what Nani-ji had instructed her to take. Fat Auntie dug and muttered until she retrieved the small velvet pouch. It jingled lightly as she opened it and inspected each piece of jewellery inside. "All here," she said smugly. I hoped God was watching. I hoped He could read my mind and see how hard it was for me to keep from grabbing the jewellery back from Fat Auntie's sausage fingers and putting it back where it belonged. She had no right to take things like that, whether Nani-ji had told her to or not.

"It's my mother's jewellery," I informed her. "Why are you taking it?"

"It was your grandmother's jewellery first," Fat Auntie replied.

"And she doesn't think your mother deserves to keep it." She spun clumsily on her heels and trotted out of my room. I followed her.

"So who gets it?" I asked.

Fat Auntie shrugged. "That's really up to your Nani," she said. She made a solemn face and dipped her head to God, tugging her shawl over her head. When she placed the jewellery pouch into her purse and snapped it shut, I felt my good senses coming back and with them a rush of dread. Nani-ji had already made up her mind about where the jewellery was going. Fat Auntie had just come to collect it.

•   •   •

Sugarbread was dinner for two nights in a row. Daddy asked me if I wanted food from the hawker centre, but I waved him away. "I like this better," I told him. I made him a slice.

"Very nice," he said. "Not very nutritious though. Let me go down and buy you some Point-Point Rice. Do you want crabsticks? Some spicy rendang?" I shook my head. I didn't want to trouble him or anybody. It was part of my plan to get on God's good side and I had to work harder at it because of Fat Auntie's visit.

I wasn't going to reveal to Daddy that Fat Auntie had come over and taken Ma's jewellery, but it slipped out. Daddy mentioned that he saw Fat Auntie at the hospital and that she looked like she had gained a few more kilos, if that were possible. "She's as big as a truck, Pin," he marvelled. "We'll have to start calling her Fatter Auntie."

I giggled and told him that she had nearly knocked over our television when she entered the living room. It wasn't true but it was a funny image.

Daddy snorted and took a big bite out of his sugarbread. The grains of sugar tumbled from his mouth and scattered onto the table. He pressed his thumb into each grain and placed them neatly on his plate. Then he looked up. "Wait—when was Fat Auntie here?"

I took a large gulp of my unchewed bread by accident and began to choke. Daddy leant over and patted my back awkwardly but his eyes still demanded an answer. "When?" he asked.

"Just once."

"When?"

"Tuesday. In the afternoon. I guess she knew Ma would be gone."

"What did she want?"

"She went to my room and she took Ma's jewellery from the closet," I said. "Nani-ji says it's not for Ma to keep. She doesn't deserve it."

Daddy groaned and buried his head in his hands. "Oh, that's very bad," he said when he finally looked up. The fluorescent light buzzed above us and small flying ants flickered around the bulb. "She took all of it?"

I nodded guiltily. It felt as if I had stolen from Ma even though Fat Auntie was the real thief. Suddenly, that familiar rush of anger that used to surge through my body every time I thought of Nani-ji taking up space in our flat returned. She was in the hospital, she was ill and attached to tubes and machines, but she was still causing trouble. Then I remembered that God was observing my behaviour, and I took a deep breath and calmed down. I took another bite of the sugarbread. It filled my mouth with sweetness and made me forget Nani-ji for a moment. When

I was finished, I made two more slices.

"Could you buy more bread on your way home?" I asked Daddy as he left for his evening shift. He looked over his shoulder doubtfully. "I still don't think you should be eating sugar on toast for dinner," he said. I noticed that his voice was weighed with sadness and I knew it had nothing to do with what I was eating. He was still thinking about the jewellery, about how he would have to explain it to Ma. "Do me a favour and keep it a secret, okay?" he said. "Your Ma will have a fit when she finds out your grandmother has given it to your Auntie. It's a very sensitive issue."

"Why did she do it?" I asked Daddy, hoping that he would sit down, remove his shoes and tell me the rest of Ma's story. There was still so much that I didn't know and Ma was prone to talking only when the mood struck her. I knew I was supposed to be patient, but I was making so many mistakes with God that maybe it was better that I found out now. But Daddy would not say a word. He gave me an apologetic look, then left the flat without saying goodbye. And I was left alone with God on the wall and the burning caramel smell wafting from the kitchen to fill the space between us.

• • •

The next day, I was instructed not to go to school. I almost jumped for joy because it was a Friday, and on Fridays we had a double-period art lesson and a shortened recess. Then I remembered we were not supposed to be celebrating. Daddy told me that my responsibility at home was to answer phones because people would be calling to ask about Nani-ji. I was to sombrely tell them that she was "leaving this world" as Daddy put it. "It's only a matter of hours," Daddy told me, stroking my hair. "Her lungs are not functioning properly." He looked genuinely sad, not like he was pretending for anybody's benefit.

I tried to cry. I squeezed my eyes shut and tried to press out the tears. When it didn't work, I went to the kitchen and stood close to the rack where we used to keep the onions when the shelves were well stocked. I thought that when the tears started flowing, the sadness would come too. But there was nothing. I realised with guilt that I just wanted the day to be over. I wanted Nani-ji to go quickly so our lives would return to the way they were before she had come to stay.

I know it's wrong, I mentally told God as I passed Him in the living room. His glare was hot on my skin. I covered my head with my hands and said I was sorry about twenty times before I noticed His expression soften. His eyes transformed from stones to puddles of water and His lips began to curve at the corners. I really was sorry, but I could not help feeling the way I did about Nani-ji. Every time I tried to feel sad for her, her unforgiving face and bony fingers returned to my thoughts. In my mind, she was always pointing an accusing finger at me and Ma. Then I thought of what she must have been like when she was Ma's age and Ma was a little girl. From Ma's story, it sounded like Nani-ji hadn't changed much since then. The only time I ever saw her looking truly happy was when she talked about Pra-ji, the man whom Ma despised so much, like all of her problems had magically slipped off her shoulders and disappeared into the ground below her feet.

I didn't think many people would call to ask about Nani-ji but I was wrong. The phone rang all afternoon as news spread that she was not recovering. Most of the callers were old women—I could tell from their croaky voices and the quiver in their speech. "God bless you, beti," one of them said endearingly. I thanked her and looked at God to check if He had heard.

Between calls, I made my lunch and clumsily swept the kitchen floor. Daddy called home twice to check on me. Ma called home once. Her voice was faint and she didn't say much. "Pin, if you want something for dinner, ask your Daddy to buy a packet of rice," she said.

"I'll be fine," I assured her firmly.

Daddy came home in the early evening and he looked very distracted. His eyes searched the walls and the space above my head and they never rested on one thing. "What's wrong?" I asked him.

"Nothing," he said. He shook his head too hard. It looked like he was trying to shake something out of his skull. Then he sat down and took a piece of paper out of his shirt pocket. Before I saw it, I recognised what it was. "A really good number, Pin," Daddy said. A smile spread across his face. "I think it's a winning one."

I exchanged a glance with God and was secretly pleased for this opportunity to put Daddy in his place. I could prove myself to God now. "You shouldn't gamble at a time like this."

"I know, but Pin," Daddy whined. He sounded like a little boy. I put my hands on my hips for added effect and said, "No," very firmly. I was good at this. Even though she wouldn't like it, I was good at being like Ma.

Daddy told me the story of how he got the numbers. He swore it was different from how he had obtained the others. While he was doing his shift that day, a man entered the hotel and asked for directions to a bank nearby. Daddy guided him outside and pointed him down the street. As the man was thanking Daddy, a fruit truck backed out of its spot and nearly knocked them both down. Daddy shouted out to warn him and he jumped back onto the pavement. Crates spilt and watermelons, bananas and longans tumbled onto the road. Daddy demonstrated for me how the man still had his hand pressed to his heaving chest when he asked Daddy for his name.

"I asked him why he wanted to know my name. He said he wanted to tell the hotel that they had exceptional staff. It turns out he's a very distinguished guest. It means I might get a raise, Pin!" Daddy said. His grin stretched from one ear to the other.

He had written down the licence plate number of the truck, the number of fruits that had spilt out, the number of the street, the date and the exact time he had seen it on the hotel's clock when he had walked back in. He pointed to the paper and explained each number to me. "I have to buy the numbers today before the shops close," he said, looking out of the window. The sky was getting darker. Dense clouds gathered above the buildings and hid the setting sun from our view. I got excited hearing his voice. For a moment, I forgot that I didn't believe in the lottery.

"You can't go," I said. "If you buy tickets, I'll tell Ma."

Daddy was taken aback. "Come on, Pin. It's just this once. I'm definitely going to win," he reasoned. I shook my head. "I'll buy you whatever you want for dinner."

"No," I said but I felt myself relenting. It wasn't the food. It was the hope in his voice. I, too, thought he might win. I looked at God again. Surely something good was lying in store for us, and maybe this was it.

"You can come with me," Daddy said. He must have already known that I would say yes because when he went back to the door, I noticed that he still had his shoes on.

The plan was to buy the lottery tickets, then walk to

McDonald's where we would have dinner together. Ma did not approve of fast food and she never allowed me to eat anything at McDonald's. "How can anybody eat something that's packaged like that?" she asked me one time when we passed the restaurant. People unwrapped burgers from colourful wrappers and sank their teeth into the soft buns. "It's food. It's not a meal," she said. "I hope I've taught you that there's a difference. Like a house and a home."

As Daddy and I crossed the basketball court, I heard a familiar shout. "Girl!" Deven hollered, running towards me. "Oi!" He stopped when Daddy turned around. "Oh, hello, Uncle," Deven mumbled.

"Hi, boy," Daddy said. "You're Pin's football friend, I see." He nodded at the ball tucked under Deven's arm.

"Yes, Uncle," he said. Then he turned to me. "How come you never join us any more?"

I look over his shoulder and saw Kaypoh on the court. Behind him, Roadside was shuffling around the ball. "Just busy," I mumbled. I couldn't give the real reason in front of Daddy—that I didn't want to be called Roadside's girlfriend. Worse than that, I didn't want the boys laughing at the thought that Roadside might have an Indian girlfriend.

"We need a goalie," Deven said.

"She can join you boys today," Daddy said. I looked at him in surprise. He laughed. "I'll go and buy your dinner, Pin, and I'll run my errands. You stay and play with your friends. You deserve to be having some fun too. It'll take your mind off things."

He probably thought I was acting so strange because I was upset about Nani-ji, but I was more concerned about what God was planning for me. I had felt His stare on my back when we left the flat. "Okay," I said. Daddy tipped his head and jingled the keys of the flat at me. "Only for about a half-hour though, Pin. I'll walk back this way, then we can go back upstairs together. We only have one pair of keys between the two of us and I don't want your Ma calling and getting worried." Being caught was what he was more afraid of, I knew.

"You're not wearing proper shoes," Deven said. "Can you play barefoot?"

"Yes," I said.

The other boys were gathered on the courts already. They threw their shirts and wallets into a pile. I felt guilty about removing my kara so I sent God a hasty apology. I laid it down carefully near the boys' valuables—watches, Walkmen, loose bills held together with a paper clip.

"I'm the goalie," I called. Kaypoh's eyes narrowed when he saw me. Roadside spoke up.

"Okay, but the goalie is in charge of getting the ball if it gets kicked out of the court. Don't be a chicken like last time," he warned.

"I'm not a chicken," I told Roadside. He shrugged and stalked off.

"Let's play," Kaypoh shouted at the boys and they all spread out across the court.

Ankles and feet shot out and darted across the court as if they were separate from the bodies to which they belonged. I kept my eyes on the ball. I darted quickly from one end of the goal post to the other in quick movements as the boys from the other team came closer. The boys on my team were too good to be beaten. Every time the ball came close, they jumped in and kicked it back to the other side, sending the other team running in the opposite direction. I was supposed to be happy for my team, but I really wanted the ball to come spinning my way so that I could throw my body across the goal like the World Cup goalies on television. A goalkeeper for a weak team could save the day, and how could God punish me after seeing that?

But it became clear to me pretty early that the boys had tricked me again. I was only the goalie for this side because the team was so good they didn't really need somebody to defend the goal post. If they really thought I was good enough, they would have put me on the other side. The goalkeeper for the other side wiped the sweat off his brow with the back of his hand as Roadside kicked the ball past his head.

"Goal!" they all shouted, giving each other high-fives.

It started to drizzle. Dark clouds moved quickly over the sky. Ang Mo Kio was smaller and full of shadows during monsoon season. Falling leaves and twigs stirred on the ground until they finally settled. I saw a large snail inching along the edge of the court, his body slick and bloated.

"Girl! Stop daydreaming!" Kaypoh shouted. I quickly shifted my gaze from the snail to the ball. The game had started again. The ball rolled towards me and I pitched myself forward to protect the goal post. Then Roadside darted in and with a flick of his ankle, he sent the ball sailing away from the post. The boys on my team relaxed and praised Roadside until they realised that the ball was still rolling and an old uncle was riding by on his bicycle. Roadside called out to warn him. "Sorry, Uncle! Ball!"

The uncle swerved slightly to avoid hitting the ball but his tyre knocked it off the court. He kept going, muttering under his breath and glaring at all of us. "Raining—all of you will get sick!" he shouted. Nobody paid attention to him because our eyes were fixed on the ball, which was still rolling. Some boys began to chase after it, but it was too late. The ball rolled straight into the canal. Everybody groaned in unison.

"Girl," Kaypoh said. He nodded towards the canal. "Go."

I hesitated. The rain was really starting to pour down and it was beginning to pool in the canal. The boys danced around and shook their hair at each other, spraying the air with water. I stayed close to the goal. I knew there was nothing they could do to me if I didn't want to go into the canal.

"Go on," Roadside said.

"It looks dangerous," I said.

Roadside sighed. "Come on, Girl. We talked about this. You're the goalie and the goalie is in charge of getting the ball."

Girl? Roadside had never called me that. I didn't understand why he was being so rude to me. It was as if he wanted to be more like Kaypoh.

"You were the one who kicked it," I told him.

Roadside moved closer to me and under his breath, he said, "Come on, Pin. I'll help you if anything happens. If you don't do your job, you can't play with us any more." Loudly, he repeated this. "You can't play with us."

"Okay, fine," I said. I walked reluctantly to the canal. It wasn't so bad. There was some water but I could see the football floating slowly towards the other end of Avenue 10. That was where the McDonald's was, where Daddy was probably waiting in the queue now.

There was an iron ladder propped on one side of the canal and it was easy to lower myself in. The boys cheered as I went in and for a moment, I felt brave and proud. Then I heard the water below me. It was moving a little bit faster now. I clung to the last rung of the ladder and tested the water with my feet. It was cold, but it wasn't too deep. I took in a deep breath and told myself to be calm.

Roadside shouted encouragement from the top of the canal. "I can see it! Just reach to your right." I held on to the last rung of the ladder and planted both feet on the bottom of the canal. The city looked very far away from this deep end of the ground. I saw wheels and feet, but not the cars and the people attached to them. Buildings looked even taller and the sky seemed to stretch for miles. The rain kept pouring and I knew I had to be quick, or the water would start to rise.

I reached for the ball but a small current shot it forward and I had to stretch further to get it. I couldn't reach. My fingertips barely grazed the ball. Then more water began to rush into the canal from the pipes on its sides, and it swept the ball further away. I let go of the ladder and waded towards the ball. The water was just below my knees and I had plenty of time before it rose. It looked like the rain was about to stop anyway.

I caught the ball before it drifted away again and tucked it under my arm. As I turned, I felt something crawl over my foot. I remembered seeing a snake in a dry canal once when Daddy and I were walking along a bridge near Bishan Park. I would have mistaken it for a small tree branch if Daddy hadn't told me to stop and watch its movements.

I kicked and shrieked and stumbled, feeling the water seep into my shorts. When I looked up, the boys were still looking into the canal. "Throw the ball up here, Girl! Why are you sitting?" I pushed myself up and rushed back quickly to the ladder. *It was just a loose branch. A wet pile of leaves,* I told myself.

I had to throw the ball back up to Roadside because I couldn't climb up the ladder without the use of both of my hands. I tossed it up once but it fell back on me. "Try again!" he shouted. "And hurry up." He sounded anxious. I threw the ball as high as I could, aiming for the road. I hoped it would bounce clear across to the other side and get squashed by a speeding car for all the trouble it was causing me.

Then I heard a dreadful gushing sound. From two pipes on the high walls on either side of me, muddy water shot out and pushed me down on the seat of my pants again. At first the boys laughed, but when they heard my strangled screams, they began arguing with each other. "You go in and help her." "No, it's too deep." "You go in." At first, I heard their shouts mingling with traffic and the patter of rain against the trees and every sound of the neighbourhood. Then the water went over my head, and I could hear nothing.

The water carried me forward and my lungs felt like they were about to burst. I waved my arms around, looking for something to hold on to, but all around me were just smooth, tall walls. Everything went dark for an instant and I thought I had drowned but then I realised I was just being pushed under the bridge by the rushing water.

This was when I saw God. I saw him just like the first time Ma told me that God was everywhere. There He was in the high branches of the trees, there were His eyes staring out of the muddy water. He peered over the bridge and sat with coarse feet dangling over the sides of the high walls. *Help,* I pleaded with Him as more water seeped into my nose. My throat burned. *Please help.*

The water didn't stop rushing and the rain became heavier but as I was being pushed forward, I felt something cold and hard against my ankle and I quickly hooked my leg around it. It was another ladder, on the other side of the canal. I couldn't believe that the water had carried me so far. I pulled myself forward and held tightly onto the rungs above me. I waited until I had stopped coughing, then I climbed out of the canal. There was nobody around. The boys had scattered. Roadside was gone. Daddy was nowhere in sight even though he was due to come walking down this path and see me sitting on the pavement in the rain, soaked to the bone and shivering from a near-death experience. Even God was gone. If He was around though, I knew what He would say. He would look at my short hair and my bare wrist and he would count every evil thought I'd had about Nani-ji and every dishonest thing I'd ever done. He'd raise an eyebrow at me and say, *Now we're even.*

•   •   •

There was water still in my ears when I entered the flat. I tipped my head to one side to shake it out and didn't notice Daddy rushing towards me. "Where were you?" he demanded to know. "And what happened? I walked through the basketball court but all of you were gone. Were you playing in the drains?"

I gave Daddy the short version of what had happened. I didn't tell him how the boys made me go into the canal. I didn't want him to tell Ma. She would probably confront the boys and embarrass me. It didn't matter anyway. I was never going to play football with them again.

"I just went into the canal to get the ball and I fell a few times. That's all." I looked past Daddy's shoulder as I said it. He didn't catch my lie. He was thinking about something.

"Your Ma just called," he said gently. "Nani-ji has passed away."

I sank into the rattan chair in the living room. Daddy didn't bother to tell me that the water from my clothes was soaking through the seat covers. They were old and faded anyway, with brownish prints of wide flowers and curling stems. Passed away, he'd said politely, like she had just gone from one room to another. If I had drowned in the canal a few minutes ago, would they have said the same about me? Would the newspapers have printed a story about a stupid girl who had jumped in to save a ball to impress the boys? Was that all it was, passing away?

"She died?" I asked Daddy, just to confirm. He nodded and put his hand on my shoulder.

"You're shivering, Pin. You should take a shower and get into some dry clothes. We'll need to go to the temple this evening. There will be prayers tomorrow morning, then the funeral…"

There was a low buzzing in my ears, like the sound of the flying ants flicking against the fluorescent lights. It grew louder and absorbed Daddy's words. Nani-ji was dead. Nani-ji was gone. There were nights when she had slept that I noticed how stiffly her fingers were curled like the edges of dry leaves. I imagined her in a hospital bed now with her eyes closed, her fingers flat on the mattress, her legs stretched out ahead of her. Then I saw Ma sitting by Nani-ji's side, smoothing out her hair, speaking to her for the last time. She was whispering something but I couldn't hear it—the buzzing noise in my ears blocked out everything else. Ma's face was drained of colour and her skin was covered in fiery red patches.

Daddy put his arms around me when I began to cry. "Oh Pin. I know. I know, Pin." But he didn't. He didn't know anything. I was relieved to be sad, finally, and a part of me was crying for Nani-ji. When I thought hard enough, when I recalled the few moments we had when Nani-ji wasn't meddling in Ma's business or giving me her disapproving scowls, I felt a short, sudden jolt reminding me that I would never see her again. But I was crying because I almost drowned that afternoon, because I didn't want to spend the rest of my life eating sugarbread for lunch and dinner, because I didn't think Daddy would ever win the lottery, because Fat Auntie had taken Ma's jewellery. I was crying because I felt stupid for thinking that things would go back to normal in our flat. Things had never been normal.

"I know you're sad. But it was your grandmother's time," Daddy whispered into my dirty hair.

I didn't say anything. I was tired and fed-up, not sad. The only person who could see into my mind and know the difference was God, but He was strangely silent.

7

THE FUNERAL STARTED and ended at the temple, with the crematorium in between so we could see Nani-ji one last time. I had expected a brown lacquered coffin, but she was in a white container that looked rather flimsy. She was dressed in white, as always, and there were flowers strewn all over her. It looked like she had just fallen asleep in a garden. All day, my head rang with prayers, mournful songs and chants. At the crematorium, there were more prayers, and that was when the crying got even louder. Fat Auntie was the loudest crier. She wailed and shrieked. At one point, she even clutched Mama-ji's shirt collar and sobbed so loudly into his chest, the priest stopped and stared. Ma was calmer. Daddy explained that she had done most of her crying when she was letting Nani-ji go and now there was very little left. She shut her eyes for long periods of time and blinked rapidly when she opened them, looking out of the narrow doorway of her eyelids.

I noticed Mama-ji looking at Ma as they followed Nani-ji's coffin into the crematorium. Even when Fat Auntie grabbed his shirt and leant against him, he distractedly patted her on the back and continued to look at Ma. She only looked back at him once and when she did, his eyes quickly darted away and fell on me, then it was my turn to look away.

It was odd to see the sun shining on such a sombre day. All

around me, the corners of people's lips were turned down. Daddy stared at his hands during the entire funeral. When I got tired of looking at Nani-ji for the last time (it wasn't really Nani-ji anyway, just the shell of her), I stared at the people gathered around the white box, trying to figure out who they were. I recognised some of them from the temple—the lady who always wore polka dots, the woman with the full head of silver hair, the tall man with the mole on his cheek so flat and round it looked like a ten-cent coin. If Nani-ji were alive, she probably wouldn't want all of these people crowding around her, taking up space and making so much noise. I almost expected her to sit up and tell everybody to stop moaning and go home, since they were causing a disturbance.

God was not at the funeral. His name was mentioned several times in the prayers and He was praised and pleaded with to take good care of Nani-ji's spirit, but I did not see Him among the mourners.

After the crematorium, there were more prayers in the temple and food—simple food because mourning meant blandness, food that tasted like the emptiness the deceased had left behind. Daddy had plain water with his roti instead of the steaming hot milky tea he loved. Ma just ate a bowl of sour yoghurt. "I'm still not hungry," she said. I took the rice and covered it with dhal, but left out the yoghurt and the desserts to show God how much I was grieving. Every spoonful was dry, like eating mashed-up paper.

When we got home in the evening, Ma instructed me to take a shower because I had been in the crematorium and God-knows-what was in the air there. I scrubbed my arms and legs and the back of my neck very hard in the shower, thinking about the invisible particles of dead strangers clinging to my skin. I spent so much time in the bathroom that the sky had turned dark by the time I stepped out. Wrapped in a towel, I tiptoed past God, avoiding His gaze. My room had been empty for a week now but it suddenly felt bigger. It finally belonged to me again. I changed into my pyjamas and lay down on the bed. The sheets were warm from the day's heat. A light breeze rustled the leaves of the potted plants outside. Thunder rumbled in the distance but the air was still thick with heat.

Ma did not step into my room. She stood in the doorway and looked in as if she needed permission to enter. "It looks different now," she said softly. She attempted a smile but it came out crooked. I was afraid she would start crying but after taking in a shaky breath, she looked fine. "What shall we eat for dinner?" she asked.

"I'm not hungry," I told her and I was being honest. The funeral had taken away my appetite. "I'll just toast some bread later."

"Okay," Ma said. She turned like she was about to leave the room, then she turned back. "Did you greet your Mama-ji today? Did you say 'Sat sri akal' to him?"

"Yes," I said. "In the morning, when he and Fat Auntie came in." Not greeting an elder with "sat sri akal" was very rude, so I said it automatically to any Punjabi adult I encountered, whether I knew them or not. It saved me from getting into trouble.

"I saw him looking at you during the funeral."

"He was looking at you first," I told Ma. "And then me."

"He was probably thinking that we looked alike. A few people mentioned it today, you know," Ma said. She walked into my room and sat down on my bed. "They said that you were starting to look just like me."

Immediately, I stretched out my arms and looked to see if my skin had suddenly changed. But it was still clear. Maybe it was possible that I could look like Ma but not have her skin condition. Maybe then it was also possible that I could be some things that Ma was—beautiful, confident, elegant, funny and bold—and not be all of the bad things that Nani-ji had tried to warn me about.

Ma narrowed her eyes. "I know what you're thinking," she said. All of the questions that were forming in my mind quickly dived into corners where Ma would not find them. We sat in silence for a long time. I let my mind drift off to other things. I thought about school and how much I dreaded being in Primary Five next year. I hoped for a good teacher, somebody like Miss Yoon, who smiled even when she was scolding us.

"Last time," Ma began. She paused. With those two words, she had my full attention. People in Singapore said "last time" when they referred to the old days in Singapore. "Last time, the river was clogged with dirt." "Last time, we used to buy ice kacang from the street vendor." "Last time, you could buy a plate of noodles for just ten cents." I had heard Daddy and my teachers and Mrs D'Cruz say these things. They always seemed to be comparing now to another time. As I watched Ma come closer to telling me the truth, I realised that this was exactly what she was doing.

8

1970

PAK-PAK-PAK-pak-pak.

The flat soles of Jini's worn sandals thunder against the concrete as she weaves through parked cars and bicycles lying on their sides, which look as if they are taking a nap in the afternoon heat. She is racing faster than ever before but nobody is watching. For the first time, she prefers it this way. She usually likes an audience. She enjoys the gazes and the breaths of awe from the children in the neighbourhood as she dashes by. *She's so fast for a girl!* some say. Others say she runs faster than any boy they've ever seen. When they say this, they sound slightly suspicious.

Jini started running three years ago, when she found out her father had left them for good. Anger flooded her heart and coursed through her veins. She had many evil thoughts about her father then and the more they entered her mind, the worse her skin became. Rashes appeared on her stomach and disappeared just as suddenly. Small bumps spotted her ankles. Luckily, her mother makes her wear long pants because she thinks shorts are indecent. "Running around half-naked is what you're doing. I don't want people talking and saying, 'Look at Harjinder Singh's daughter, becoming loose because he's not around.'" Her mother was happy this morning to see her putting on a loose cotton blouse with long sleeves. She doesn't know about the rashes;

even Sarjit hasn't commented on them in weeks, but that's not unusual. He doesn't say much to her these days.

She is not supposed to be running outside but her mother is at the temple and she will not come home until evening. She cleans houses for a living now, taking the bus out of the kampong and away from their gossiping neighbours to the homes of the British officers on the naval base. They pay her little because she does not speak English and sometimes she doesn't understand their instructions. But when she speaks of them at home, she always emphasises how kind they are. "Such creamy skin they have," she tells Jini as they cook. "Their houses have three or four levels, and large bookcases." She brought home a few picture books for Jini once, but Jini thought they were too babyish. Her mother raised an eyebrow and told her not to complain. "At least I'm bringing you books," she said. "You're lucky I'm keeping you in school. The money for fees and books could be used on food and clothes. After your O-Levels, you're going to have to start working."

This is why Jini runs. Because there are things she will not and cannot accept. Running makes her feel like she can escape her mother's instructions, her thoughts about her father, the growing itching feeling she has all over her body from the inexplicable rashes.

"Oi, Jini!" a voice calls out. She slows down and glances behind her shoulder. Don't stop, don't stop. That is her rule—to never stop for anybody or anything while she is running. Unless of course it is Bilu, then she has to slow down and take him home. He still has a habit of chasing her when she leaves for school in the morning and when she comes outside for her afternoon runs. He doesn't cling to Sarjit any more because Sarjit ignores him.

"What?" Jini asks, slowing down; she is genuinely tired

and her calf muscles are burning. The voice is from a familiar neighbourhood boy. He walks towards her with quick strides, a football tucked under his arm. He is not wearing a shirt and sweat is trickling down his bony chest, pooling in his navel. She looks away.

"You run very fast."

"I know."

"What are you running from?" A few more boys join him. She looks around nervously. Although she can't see anybody in the neighbourhood, she is sure there are pairs of eyes on her, observing, waiting.

"You," she says nonchalantly, spinning back around on her heels. She can run a little more if it means getting away from them.

"Or are you running to somebody?" one of them calls out. The rest burst out laughing and scatter away as a white car trundles down the bumpy road, the horn blaring loudly.

"Shut up!" she yells at the boys. The car slows down and the driver honks his horn again. She doesn't bother to look; it can't be anyone she knows. She continues to run until she is tired again, then she walks home, panting all the way. As she unlatches the house gate, she feels light, as if she has stomped out every bit of misery that her heart has collected. She pulls up her sleeves and the cuffs of her pants and scans her arms and legs quickly. It looks as though the rashes have gone away and the swelling has also gone down. She smiles with relief and enters her house.

• • •

"I saw you running," her sister-in-law says accusingly. "The neighbours are talking about you."

"Is it a crime?" Jini asks with mock innocence.

"Don't be rude to me," Bhabi-ji says, wagging a finger. "I am older than you."

Jini shrugs her indifference and reaches to tickle Bilu, who is in a good mood. He giggles. Drool spills down his chin and collects in his collarbone. "Slimy-slimy-boy," she sings into his ear. He opens his mouth to receive her words like a baby bird. She makes farting noises with her hands and he shrieks with laughter.

"Quiet!" Bhabi-ji shouts. "Jini, don't get him excited."

"I'm just making him happy," she protests. "He's stuck in the house all day." *With you, the poor thing,* she thinks.

"What do you want me to do? Parade him around for everyone to see? You know, he tried to follow you out today. He saw you dashing past the house when you were running and he tried to follow after you."

"He hasn't done that in years," Jini says. "He was probably just excited today."

"Regardless, I want you staying at home after school from now on. No more running around. Your mother is not going to like it when people hear about it. Then she'll blame me."

"I'm not doing anything wrong!" Jini protests loudly. This excites Bilu. "Wrong-wrong-wrong-wrong-wrong," he repeats like a siren, until the word has lost its meaning. This is what she loves about him. He can take the seriousness out of anything. "Wrong-wrong-wrong-wrong-wrong-wrong-wrong—"

"*Enough!*" They all freeze. It is Sarjit, standing in the kitchen entrance, glowering at Jini and Bilu. He does not dare give the same look to his wife because she is bigger and more powerful than he is. Ever since he married her, he's been colder towards

Jini and more stern with Bilu, treating him like a guest who has overstayed his welcome. This is why Bilu shies away from him; he may not know how to behave like the rest of them but he knows when people don't want him around.

Jini fights back words of anger because she is not allowed to show disrespect for her sister-in-law, who is ten years older than she. She is even older than Sarjit, who married her as soon as he was discharged from the army. The wedding happened quickly. Jini's mother did not want to attract too much attention to their family because of her missing husband. She was also partly embarrassed because Pra-ji had been right about this girl from Ipoh. She was not good-looking. She was rather overweight and she always looked like she was about to complain about something. She was unfriendly and sighed a lot during the wedding, as if she couldn't wait for the whole ceremony to be over so she could go home and take a nap. She was bossy with Jini and often tried to discipline her because Mother was gone all the time. She was uncomfortable around Bilu—in the first few months, she spoke to him without ever making direct eye contact. Now she just lets Jini handle him but she takes credit whenever Mother comments that he is behaving well, which annoys Jini. Bilu is only calm because Jini sings and reads to him, and secretly lets him follow her out to the shop sometimes after making him promise to behave himself and hold her hand the entire time.

Her mother returns from the temple with more roti, dhal and yoghurt wrapped in plastic bags tied up by their ends so that they look like fat bulbs. She places them in the kitchen and asks Bhabi-ji to please serve the food. "Help her, Jini," she says before retreating to her bedroom.

"Aren't you going to eat?" Jini calls out.

"I ate at the temple," her mother replies. She eats at the temple every evening now after praying.

They eat dinner quietly. Sarjit reads the newspaper and doesn't pay attention to anyone. Jini makes faces at Bilu, who giggles, then sprays his food across the table.

"Stop it," Bhabi-ji says to Bilu. "I'm warning you now." It is her job to feed him during dinner because he makes such a mess with his own fingers. He still cannot break the bread and scoop up the dhal without spilling everything onto the table. Sometimes when he eats, he keeps his jaw slack and refuses to chew so the food just dribbles down his chin. If he's giggling, there's a chance he might be distracted enough to allow Bhabi-ji to feed him. But she doesn't see it that way. Now she notices Jini making faces and she pushes herself away from the table. "That's it," she says. "I've had enough of your disrespect." She storms into Mother's room. Jini hears her talking in a low, angry voice and a feeling of dread settles in the pit of her stomach.

Her mother comes out of her room, rubbing her hair away from her eyes. She looks strangely alert. She raises a hand and slaps Jini across the cheek. "Did I hear from your sister-in-law that you've been running around outside talking to neighbourhood boys? Playing with them? What kind of daughter am I raising?"

"I wasn't playing with them!" Jini shouts at her Bhabi. She receives another slap for the volume of her voice. Sarjit sighs, folds up his newspaper and storms into his room. "I was running." Jini says quietly.

"Running? Running for what?"

"For exercise." Tears are gushing down her cheeks now.

"Exercise? Rubbish. I don't want you going outside like that any more. No wonder Auntie Lakhbeer was giving me looks at the temple. I had no idea that my daughter was the cause of so much trouble. Isn't it bad enough that your bastard of a father has left us?"

Jini and Bhabi-ji both stare at her, shocked. She has never used such a word to describe her husband. Even she looks mildly startled, as if somebody else said it.

That evening, Jini helps wash the dishes silently, without looking at the smug expression on her sister-in-law's face. She can't stand her. She wishes her brother had married somebody nicer. She knows that her mother wishes for the same thing, but Bhabi-ji is family now and it has never been up to them to choose who is in their family. Pra-ji had said so quietly to her mother when he introduced Sarjit to his future wife at a small matchmaking ceremony. He was nice enough to hold part of the ceremony at his house. He wouldn't even accept any money from Jini's mother, but she insisted on paying him, so he took the money and told her he would give it to the temple. Jini remembers the look on her mother's face when she saw Bhabi-ji's flat nose, the shadow over her upper lip, her wide hips and chunky arms. "She's a nice girl," Jini's mother had said, even though she hadn't properly met her yet. It was as though she had been trying to convince herself.

Bhabi-ji knows that Jini's mother is disappointed, which is why she does everything to please her. If Jini's mother told her to run around the house in the rain wearing nothing but a bedsheet and a plastic bag on her head, she'd do it twice. She has told on Jini before—a few weeks ago, she revealed to Mother that Jini had said a Chinese curse word under her breath when she accidentally cut her finger while chopping onions. Her mother was angry that Jini knew any Chinese word, vulgar or otherwise. Other languages were strictly forbidden in the house. "There's no such thing as 'Singaporean'. You're Indian, Malay or Chinese. If you all mix, you will forget your traditions." Jini had never seen her mother so adamant before, but now that their father was gone, her mother blamed this new country for seducing and weakening him, and eventually chasing him away. Mother gave Bhabi-ji full permission to rub chilli on Jini's lips if she ever heard her utter a word in another language in the house again.

As they wash the dishes now, Jini remembers to keep her arms covered because she can feel the rashes returning. The urge to scratch has gotten worse since dinner and she wants to scrub her entire body until her skin peels off and a new layer is revealed. If Bhabi-ji sees her marks, she'll surely use it to cause trouble, to take the attention away from herself so nobody notices her own faults. For once, Jini is grateful for the dim lighting in their kitchen, for the pale moonlight that makes it difficult to distinguish a mark on the skin from a mere shadow. With her sister-in-law, she will always have to dodge in the shadows and depend on tricks of the light.

•   •   •

The first time Jini discovered how fast she could run, she was in school and they were doing a 100-metre sprint during PE. Her teacher was so impressed that he asked her to stay back after school and compete with some of the older boys. One of them was a curly-haired boy who smiled more than he spoke. People sometimes called him Blackie but he just grinned right back at them. He had dark skin and his hair sprang from his head in so many directions that he had to be Tamil. This was what Jini thought, so she was surprised when he spoke to her in Punjabi after school one day.

"How come you can run so fast?" he asked her.

"You're Punjabi?" she asked.

"Yeah. I don't look like it?"

"No," she said. "Honestly, you don't. Your hair."

He laughed. "Punjabis don't have curly hair?"

"Yes…I mean they do. My brother does. But your hair is short. Your parents let you cut your hair?"

"Yeah. They're not very religious. And it's hard to keep this kind of hair long. It gets very messy. So they've always cut my hair."

Jini shook her head. "My mother would kill me. She would pull me out of school and make me go to the temple every day for the rest of my life."

"My parents don't go to the temple very much. We prefer to pray at home."

Who on earth did that? She didn't speak to him much after that but she saw him around school. He never said hello to her, for which she was grateful, because she didn't want people teasing them and making up stories. But she saw him in the neighbourhood playing football with the other boys a few times and if their eyes met, he tipped his head slightly and flashed a quick smile in her direction. She was grateful for his discreetness.

Since her mother found out about her running outside, she can now only run during PE lessons in school. Her teacher, Mr Goh, has urged her to join the track team. "There are races and marathons. I could train you to run really well. You have it in you already." But every time he brings it up, she refuses. "My parents," she simply says. He nods and gives her an understanding smile. "I know," he says. Plenty of Punjabi kids go to this school and they often have to plead to do things differently. Some girls sit out PE classes or wear track pants even on the hottest days because their parents won't let them wear the required shorts. There are boys who have admitted they have never been swimming because it's too much trouble to wash their hair afterwards, yet Mr Goh tries to persuade Jini to join the team. "I don't want you to get into trouble at home," he says gently. "But maybe your parents just don't like the idea. When you start doing well, they might be more accepting."

"I don't know," she says. "I'll think about it."

The next day, she borrows a pair of shorts and a T-shirt from a Chinese classmate. She'll have to figure out how to wash it at home without anybody noticing, but there are more important things on her mind now. Her legs are covered in scabs. They range from wide circles to long red lines where she must have scratched her skin in her sleep. She decides to run out onto the field and pretend the scabs don't exist. She uses them as motivation to run faster—if she slows down, people will get a chance to see her dirty skin. If she moves quickly enough to become a blur, nobody will see her. This is another reason she loves running—she can be invisible.

On the track, Mr Goh shouts words of encouragement and soon the passers-by are slowing down to watch. Jini speeds up so they don't recognise her. She knows her mother will find out eventually because there isn't a Punjabi person who can keep a secret in their neighbourhood, but for now, all she wants to do is run. She thinks about Sarjit in his silence, how he barely speaks to her now that his wife dominates everything. She runs it off. Her father in India, enjoying his life, while she is only a faded speck in his memory. She runs faster. Her mother's anger, her sister-in-law's bitterness, the staleness it all brings into their wilting house. She can feel herself breaking her own record speed and when she finally slows down, it is like she is walking on air above everything and everybody else.

"I'm impressed," Mr Goh tells her. He pats her on the back and tells her to come back the next day.

Jini washes the borrowed clothes under the tap in the back of the school building. The brittle stubble of grass pricks at her feet as she squats and scrubs the dirt out with her knuckles. Then she rubs water on her arms and legs, willing the scabs to disappear.

As she leaves the school gates, she has to think of a lie to tell her sister-in-law when she gets home. She was asked to stay back for extra lessons. There was an accident on the road and she had to walk home by a longer route. A sudden car honk interrupts her thoughts. She turns around to see the same white car she saw the last time she ran outside. With her hand shielding her eyes from the midday sun, she strains to see who is inside. A window rolls down, and it is Pra-ji.

"Sat sri akal, Jini," he calls out. She walks over to the car, eyeing the glistening paint. It's very grand. "Sat sri akal," she says, clasping her hands together in respect.

"How are you? Just returning from school?"

"Yes. I had extra lessons."

Pra-ji gives her a thin smile. "I see. Want me to drive you home? I'm going to the temple."

She climbs into his car. It smells fresh and new, like damp earth after a long monsoon. He doesn't say much on the short trip back to her house but when they are approaching, he asks her when her birthday is.

"Already passed. 15 May."

"May. I see. And you are sixteen?"

She blushes. People think she is older because of her height and her body, which is clearly developing now. Her breasts are becoming more obvious, even under this pleated pinafore.

"Fourteen," she says.

"Your O-Level exams are in two years! What do you plan on doing after that?"

Jini shrugs. "I'll have to work, I guess."

Pra-ji nods slowly, and there is a long silence in the car. She realises that they are outside her house now. She thanks him and runs inside, preparing a lie in her mind.

●   ●   ●

Jini is only allowed to leave the house nowadays if she's running errands for her mother or her sister-in-law. She used to dread going to Shop Uncle's provision shop down the street but now she goes eagerly, happy to be outside. Her mother always tells her to come back quickly. "No talking and playing outside," she says. Bhabi-ji echoes Jini's mother's words if she's not around. Today, Jini has been asked to buy a bag of sugar. They've run out and they're having Pra-ji over for tea.

In the shop, the shelves are lined with different brands of sugar. Shop Uncle is pounding away furiously at a calculator and scribbling in a blue ledger. "Girl, what you want? Hurry up. Don't stand there."

"I need sugar," she says.

"Sugar. There—got so many bags."

"The cheapest one," she says, scanning the row. The prices are not written on the bags.

Shop Uncle's scowl softens. "How much you have?" he asks.

Jini hesitates but Shop Uncle looks sincere. He pushes aside his ledger. "How much?" he asks. She unfurls her fingers to reveal the coins she's been clutching. Once Shop Uncle sees her money, he'll say there's nothing for her here. *Cheap Indian*, she remembers him calling her, and her face burns.

But Shop Uncle doesn't say anything. He steps away from the counter and returns with a bag of sugar and a plastic bag. He tears the top of the sugar bag and pours it into the plastic bag, pausing every now and then to weigh it in his hands and glance at Jini's coins. "This is enough," he concludes, taking some coins from Jini and leaving the rest in her palm.

She opens her mouth to thank him but he waves her away. "You want to come back and buy things like that also can," he says. "Next time you bring your own bag." Jini nods.

Storm clouds are beginning to form in the sky and a sharp flash of lightning in the distance of the kampong sends children scattering through the streets, shouting, "Electric! Electric!" The sky is ash-coloured. Raindrops tap her face, gently at first, then they begin to hit harder, like small bullets. She runs back to the house without looking where she's going and slams right into Pra-ji, who is standing at the gate.

"Sat sri akal," she says quickly by way of apology. He greets her back and steers her into the house. In the dining room, Bilu is sitting on the floor and refuses to make eye contact with anybody. His face is wet with tears.

"He tried to follow you again," Bhabi-ji says accusingly. "I had to hold him back by his T-shirt and it ripped in the back. He's getting too strong."

"Too strong?" Jini asks her. She doesn't like the way Bhabi-ji says things like that. She always seems to be implying that Bilu is too much to handle, that they should send him away. She notices Pra-ji looking at her curiously.

"Come and help me in the kitchen with the tea," Bhabi-ji says.

"Actually, I want to talk to Jini," Pra-ji says. "You don't mind?"

Bhabi-ji looks at Jini suspiciously and says, "No, not at all." She disappears into the kitchen but bangs the pots and pans loudly to show her discontent.

"Mother's working in Bukit Timah today. She might be stuck somewhere now because of the rain," Jini tells Pra-ji. He doesn't seem to be listening.

"How are you, Jini?" he asks her after a moment's silence.

"Good," she says, forcing a wide smile onto her face.

"You're doing well in school?"

It hurts her to admit it. Her marks are decent and she is the fastest runner. You can do anything, Mr Goh told her the other day. She decided against telling him that he was wrong.

"I'm okay in school," she says modestly, playing with her thumbs.

"You're a fast runner," he tells her. She separates her hands and looks down guiltily.

"You saw me?" she asks. "Please—"

Pra-ji laughs. "Don't worry, Jini. I didn't come here to get you into trouble. I know that your mother doesn't approve."

Jini feels like she might die of embarrassment. Pra-ji has seen her in her running shorts! "She doesn't know," Jini says, her voice barely louder than a whisper.

Pra-ji raises an eyebrow. "So you've been disobeying her?"

Jini nods. From head to toe, she is flushed with shame. Her skin is burning.

"I just really like to run," she tells him quietly. "It makes me feel better."

"Things have been very difficult for you," Pra-ji says with a nod. "I understand."

"I know it's wrong to lie to my mother," Jini says. "But please don't tell her?"

Bilu makes a guttural groaning sound that startles them both. Jini pulls him up from the floor and makes him sit on the chair, but he just slides back down and crawls around under the table.

"I won't tell," Pra-ji repeats, keeping one eye on Bilu under the table, who is running his finger in slow circles over the floor. "I do want you to know, however, that God punishes us for disrespecting our parents. I was worried about you the other day when I saw you after school, so I pleaded with Guru-ji to be merciful. And He revealed something rather disturbing about you." His gaze shifts from her eyes to her arms. Jini feels her heart stop for a moment and her throat gets tighter. But Pra-ji does not look angry, only concerned. "Let me see," he says.

Reluctantly, Jini rolls back her sleeves and shows Pra-ji the redness on her skin. "It's on my legs too," she says. She fears she might start crying, and when Bhabi-ji comes out with the tea, she'll demand to know what's going on.

"This is worse than I imagined," Pra-ji says. "Do you know what this is?"

"No," Jini says although she can already guess.

"This is how God punishes you for lying and having dirty thoughts. Do you know what dirty thoughts are, Jini?"

She has to think about this. The anger she felt at her father in the beginning has since subsided but when she thinks about him now, it becomes real and fresh again. The image of her father lying dead somewhere is the dirtiest thought she has ever had. She nods reluctantly, shame burning her face.

Pra-ji closes his eyes and presses down her head with his hand, the way God is always poised to do in the portrait that is hanging on their living room wall. She sees Him there so often that she barely notices Him and lately, with all of her horrid thoughts and lies, she's been ignoring him completely. "You must change or your skin will worsen. For every filthy thought you have, God will give you filthy skin. Do you know my maid, Rani? Do you know what she did?"

Jini nods. She has seen the girl at the temple a few times. She walks with a limp and she avoids everybody's eyes. There have been lots of stories about Rani. Her parents disowned her after they found out she had plans to run away with her Malay boyfriend. She boldly told them she would convert to Islam and marry him to get away from them. They beat her and kicked her out of their house. Pra-ji had tried to intervene, but they wanted nothing to do with her, so he took her in as his servant.

"She used to be able to walk just fine. Then shortly after she was sent to live with me, she complained that something was wrong with her foot. Something mysterious—she had pains in her legs and her left foot went limp after a while. She wanted to see a doctor but I asked her, 'What's the point?' This was God's doing, I was sure of it. I spoke to her and I found out she was still in touch with the Malay boy. While running errands at the shops, she made short trips to his home. I scolded her and told her it was obvious that God was punishing her. He wanted her to stop sneaking around. God is doing the same thing to you, Jini. He uses illness and deformities to teach us lessons."

Jini looks down at Bilu. Surely, this can't be entirely true.

What did Bilu do to deserve being like this? Pra-ji seems to read the doubt in her eyes.

"If you want, you can go see a doctor. He'll give you medicine and make everything go away for a while. But God will present himself in other ways. You have to change."

It never occurred to her to see a doctor. When she has a cold, she doesn't even tell her mother because she knows the response. "What am I supposed to do?" It is what any mother in their neighbourhood would say. Going to the doctor for a cold would be a frivolous expense, money that could be spent on food or electric bills. Once, when she was very little, she coughed so hard she thought her lungs were going to explode. Her mother had given her hot tea and rubbed her chest with mint oil until she fell asleep. These are the only remedies they possess at home. The other remedy, a less expensive one, is faith.

Bhabi-ji comes out with a tray of teacups and pakoras that she has deep-fried. Jini wonders where she got the pakora mix from, because the last time she was in the kitchen, the cabinets were bare. She looks out the window. Her mother is probably stuck in somebody's house now, praying for the rain to stop. She hates to keep anybody—particularly Pra-ji—waiting.

That night, while Jini is sitting in bed, she makes herself stop thinking about her father. She rehearses a speech for Mr Goh to let him know that she cannot run any more because she has to listen to her mother. She even vows to be more helpful to her sister-in-law, to stop complaining about kitchen work, to pay less attention in school and accept her fate. In a few years she will be working and she will be married off. Then God will be pleased with her again for doing all of the right things.

• • •

Her mother has the afternoon off and she's using it to rest at home before going to the temple in the evening. Bhabi-ji is outside in the yard hanging clothes to dry. The glaring sunlight makes the edges of everything sharper. Jini can hardly stand to look outside without shielding her eyes first. She wishes for the comfort of rain and cool air. Moods change and soften with the rainy weather. The stray dogs outside stop their loud barking and lie in the tangled shadows of the trees. Neighbourhood gossip becomes less vicious. She can hear her sister-in-law exchanging secrets with the neighbours now.

"And I heard she's finally marrying him."

"Her parents approve?"

"Not at first, but now they're accepting it."

"Did you heard about Manmohan Singh's son? He's got a motorcycle."

"Really?"

"Rides it everywhere like he's king of the world. He'll get into an accident one day, and then he'll know."

"Children never listen."

"That's true."

Jini feels like her sister-in-law is talking about her when she says that children never listen. Her mother can hear it too. They are both in the kitchen. Jini has become an expert at making a plump ball of dough out of the wheat flour.

"I should teach you how to roll it out into a flat pancake. You still don't know," her mother says. She sprinkles some flour on the countertop, then breaks off a small ball of dough. With the heel of her hand, she flattens it, then smoothens it out with her palm. Jini searches the cupboard for the rolling pin and hands it to her mother.

"This is important," Mother says. "Are you watching? It's not as easy as it looks. You roll it out but you have to keep your wrists relaxed and your grip on the handles shouldn't be so firm."

Jini takes the rolling pin from her and presses it down on the dough. The dough clings to the pin. She peels it off and tries again. It still clings and this time, she keeps running the pin over it. When she's finished, what she has on the counter barely resembles a piece of roti. It is not a circle or oval shape and some edges are much thinner than others.

"I can't do it," she says simply.

"Then try again," her mother says, rolling the dough back up into a ball. How easily it is transformed into its original shape again, like it never changed in the first place.

Jini is conscious of the scars on her arms as she rolls the dough over and over again to try to make a successful roti. Luckily, she is wearing long sleeves and there are fewer scars on her hands, which she can pass off as scratches. "Bilu did this to me," she tells her mother. "He scratched me." It's not entirely untrue. Bilu has been very angry lately and he's been threatening to bite and scratch everybody who comes near him.

"I don't know what to do with him," her mother says, shaking her head. "He barely eats any more."

"I think you should try sugar," Jini says. "He likes when I add sugar to his food."

"Sugar is not good," her mother says. "He has to start eating like other children." She takes the rolling pin away from Jini. "You're not doing it properly," she scolds. "Look at your roti. Flat in the middle, thick on the edges. Do it again."

Jini knows that she can repeat the motion a hundred times, but she still won't get it. Ordinarily, she'd find an excuse to leave the kitchen, but she has been practising being good lately and so far, it is working. The scars have faded. Last night, they flared up again, but she decided it was because the weather was so humid and the sweat had aggravated her skin. She finds reasons for everything her skin does now. If the scabs are milder, she prides herself for having done only good things that day and thinking only clean thoughts. If they act up despite her good intentions, she blames the weather or mosquitoes, or searches her mind for any bad thoughts that may be hidden. She always finds something.

Her exasperated mother finally takes the rolling pin away from Jini and tells her to help her sister-in-law with the clothes. "I'll finish this," she says. "And then I have to bathe Bilu." Bilu is outside in the yard, playing in the dirt. Jini has a feeling it won't be easy for her mother today. He is too content to want to come inside.

She is snapping the clothes pegs onto the line silently on the end of the yard furthest from her sister-in-law when she hears somebody calling her name from one side of the fence.

"Jini. Psst. Jini!" She turns to see the curly-haired boy peeping through the fence, waving at her. She looks behind her. Bhabi-ji is busy talking to the neighbours. She can see her mother through the kitchen window, but she looks preoccupied with the cooking.

"What do you want?" she asks him.

"How come I never see you running any more?"

"I can't run," she says.

"You can!"

"No, I mean my mother doesn't let me."

"Oh," the boy says, frowning. He looks as if trying to come

up with a solution for this, but after a while he gives up. Jini feels a twinge of sadness. For a moment, she hopes he has something encouraging to say. Then his expression brightens.

"Want to see a magic trick?" he asks her. "I know all kinds." He takes out a coin from behind her ear but she could see it in his sleeve the whole time. He closes his hands into tight fists and asks her to guess which one is holding the coin. She guesses wrongly both times because neither hand is holding it.

"That's quite good," she says. Then she sees her mother coming out into the yard. "I have to go," she says suddenly. She runs back into the kitchen and begins to clean her hands in the sink, scrubbing between her fingers. This is a ritual she has created for every time she might be caught doing something her mother, Pra-ji or God might not approve of. Her mother comes back into the kitchen. "Jini," she says sternly, turning off the tap. "Who were you talking to?"

"He's from my school. Just a classmate. He was asking me something about maths."

"He's not somebody you should be speaking to," her mother says. Jini realises that her mother is too tired to be angry. She lowers herself onto a chair.

"Why? What did he do?" Jini asks.

"He didn't do anything but his family…they are different from ours. They are lower caste. They have darker skin and they're not very religious," her mother says. So that's why she's never seen him at the temple. "We're Jat. They are not. When Pra-ji was looking for girls for Sarjit to marry, he considered a pretty girl from their caste but I said no. I'd rather have a fat girl from the right caste than a pretty one from their side."

Her mother reads her expression. "I know you think it's silly," she says quietly. "But we have little, Jini. We came here with almost nothing and twenty years later, we have even less. Who we are is all we have." She trudges out into the backyard to pick up Bilu, whose face and limbs are caked with dirt. He begins to squirm and opens his mouth to scream. Jini has never felt so strongly that her mother is wrong. She may be from a higher caste but surely that's not all she is. She turns on the tap and begins to wash her hands again.

• • •

They are in the temple courtyard and people are crowding around Pra-ji with their questions. Jini recognises the father of the boy who has bought the motorcycle, the one her sister-in-law was gossiping about. "Can you speak to Guru-ji and ask him to make my son stop?" the man pleads. Pra-ji nods and says yes, he can. He can do anything, and this is why people don't want to leave. Even when their questions have been answered, they remain in the courtyard until food is served inside. Jini and her mother are standing among them, waiting to get his attention. Around her, Jini hears the women talk about their success with Pra-ji.

"My son was having an asthma attack. He was wheezing all night and I was so worried. I asked for Pra-ji's help and he spoke to Guru-ji. Now look at my son—healthy as can be!"

"I was worried about money the other day because our roof was leaking and we didn't have enough to pay the man to fix it. I told Pra-ji, and within days, my husband was given a small raise at work, just enough to get the leak patched up."

Jini's mother always waits for the others to leave so she is the last one waiting to speak to Pra-ji. He smiles and nods at her, greeting the two of them with his hands clasped tightly. "Hello,

Jini," he says, pressing down on her head. She notices him looking her up and down again, probably looking to see if she has scars. "How are you?"

"Fine, thank you," she says.

"Pra-ji, my son is not eating."

"Sarjit? Or Bilu?"

"Oh no, Sarjit is eating fine. Bilu. He refuses to eat temple food and we have to cook everything at home for him and put sugar in it. Now he's even refusing that. What should I do?"

"Let me speak to Guru-ji and I will come back to you," he says in his calm voice. "I am sure he can give us some guidance."

Jini's mind drifts away. She looks at the dome of the temple building, illuminated in the shimmering sunlight. It looks almost regal. There are shoes scattered everywhere on the ground and children are playing "What's the time, Mr Wolf?" on the sun-dried grass. Another group of children huddle around a small bush that sprouts tiny red flowers in the shape of stars. The stems of these flowers have a tiny drop of nectar on their ends and the children are roughly picking them off. The scratchy fabric of their Punjabi suits flare and trail behind them as they spin, run and flail afterwards, screaming wildly at each other. Sometimes she wishes she could hurry up and grow older because she's caught at an age where games like Mr Wolf are too childish, but cooking is something she still cannot grasp, and she is still too young to speak to boys. Her mother and Pra-ji are speaking in hushed tones now.

Then Jini sees her, a girl wearing a plain blue Punjabi suit, with a salwaar that may be too small for her because she can see her ankles jutting out. There is something strange about her that Jini can't figure out at first, then she realises it's the way the girl is walking. She is limping, dragging one foot behind her as she makes her way across the courtyard to the road. Wrapped around her wrists are the handles of plastic bags of food. A woman nearby comments to another that the girl has some nerve, coming to the temple and eating their food. "After what she did with that Malay boy." Jini realises that this is the girl Pra-ji had spoken to her about. Thoughts begin to flood her mind about what the girl must have done to deserve her lame foot. She pictures her climbing out of her window, running to the boy who was a mere shadow in the darkness of her yard, kissing him passionately.

Immediately, Jini remembers her rashes and begins to scratch at one on her shin. It burns angrily with her thoughts and she tries to soothe it, but the more she scratches, the more it itches. She tears her eyes away from the girl who is hobbling up the road now, the plastic bags bumping against her thighs. She looks back at her mother in time to see her pulling out her purse and putting two fresh ten-dollar notes in Pra-ji's hands.

"I really appreciate your help," she says to him. He nods and quietly puts the money in his pocket. "Come, Jini. Let's go and eat," she says. Jini turns to follow her mother, thinking about the money. She knows that Pra-ji takes fees from people sometimes, especially now that so many people ask him for help, but he always promises to donate most of the money to the temple. Twenty dollars is too much money to give away at one go; even Jini knows that.

As she walks away, Pra-ji taps her lightly on the elbow. "How is your skin?" he asks.

"Okay," she lies. His eyes trail down to her shin. He must have seen her scratching while he was speaking to her mother.

"I can help you," he says. She would accept his help if she had the money, but she can't afford it, so she says, "No, thank you."

"Okay. But you come to me if you change your mind."

"I don't want everybody to know," Jini says, thinking about how the women were gossiping about that girl just now.

"They won't know. I won't say a thing, Jini. You're like a daughter to me. We can speak in my house. I can talk to Guru-ji while you're right there and we can cure you."

Jini nods, looking down at her feet. She sees her mother wiping her feet on the mat and entering the langar hall slowly, and she feels a pang of sadness. "Okay," she tells Pra-ji. "I'll come to see you one of these days."

A smile spreads across his lips. He pats her head. "Good girl," he says softly. She lets him touch her hair, press his palm down on her head, then she goes to the hall to join her mother. As she eats, she can barely taste the food. Perhaps she is too used to the sugar she's been sprinkling in everything at home. Or maybe she is too excited about the idea of being cured once and for all. But as she continues to eat, she realises what is numbing her taste buds, making her unable to enjoy God's food. She is thinking about the limping girl, imagining how long the journey back from the temple must be with the weight of that foot slowly dragging behind her.

PART III

9

1991

ON THE FIRST day of school in January, we met our new teacher, Mrs Parasuram. She was older than Miss Yoon and wore a sari. Her grey-streaked hair was tied up in a tight bun and she wore deep pink nail polish that was chipped on nearly every toe.

"Today's Chapel service is entitled 'A New Year, A Renewed Faith'," Mrs D'Cruz announced at assembly. She paused to give some time to the Muslim girls to trail out of the hall. I was supposed to join them, but I didn't have Ma's note with me. Miss Yoon had kept it. I glanced at Mrs Parasuram. She had thin, unforgiving lips, and she looked like the type of teacher who would scold me if I just got up and left with Farizah and the other girls.

We were late getting back to our classrooms because it was a long service with new hymns to learn. When Mrs Parasuram arranged us according to her seating plan, it was clear that she had gotten some suggestions from Miss Yoon over the holidays. All of the girls who were friends were spaced out across the classroom in different corners. Farizah was in the front row on the far left side of the room near the windows while I was two rows from the back. It would be difficult to pass notes without getting caught. I looked around as Mrs Parasuram assigned each girl to her seat. The spaces around me were soon filled with unhappy faces, everyone grumbling under their breath.

Behind me, Abigail Goh whispered to her seating partner, "I don't like this teacher. I could smell her oily hair when I walked past her. She doesn't shower, or what? That's why she's so black." The girl next to her giggled into her hands. I felt the hard jab of her words even though she wasn't talking about me.

The seat next to mine remained empty. Mrs Parasuram's mouth was set in a grimace so when she started talking to me, I thought I was in trouble for not having a partner. "A new girl will be joining the class. She can sit next to you," she said.

A murmur went through the room. From which class was this mysterious new girl transferring? And why did Pin get to sit next to her? The only reason a student went from one class to another in primary school was that she had either done very well or very poorly for her exams. In either case, having a new classmate was exciting.

Mrs Parasuram tapped her attendance book and began to read out names. She pronounced the Chinese names wrongly. The x's were shhhs and the q's were chhhs. "Chew Shia?" she called out. Qiu Xia blushed and everybody giggled. Some girls tried to correct Mrs Parasuram but she went on pronouncing the names the way she saw fit.

Abigail said, "Do you know her first name? It's a Hindu name."

"What is it?" the girl next to her asked.

"Ayo-yoooo!"Abigail said in a high-pitched voice before the two of them broke into fits of laughter. I spun around, furious.

"You think you're so great, Abigail Goh?" I taunted. "You think you're better than everyone and can make fun of Indians? You want to know what I think of you?" I dared her. My face was warm and my voice was shaking. There were many ugly words that I had learnt from the neighbourhood boys: yellow-skinned;

slanty eyes; pig eater. My mind raced to think of an original insult but my thoughts were interrupted by the sharp sound of a ruler rapping against my desk.

"What on earth is going on here?" Mrs Parasuram demanded to know.

Abigail didn't say anything. The entire class was looking at us. I shrugged.

"Please do not interrupt my lessons to cause a disturbance. I want to see you during recess," Mrs Parasuram said.

I turned back to face the blackboard, humiliated. I didn't listen to Mrs Parasuram for the rest of the lesson. How could I when she had allowed Abigail to get away scot-free? Abigail had told Farizah last year that Muslims didn't eat pork because they were descendants of pigs themselves. "If you don't believe me, you can ask my father," she had said proudly. I waited for Farizah to retort, but Farizah just shrugged and said, "Your father doesn't know anything." She told me later that her religion taught forgiveness. I didn't know how anybody could forgive someone like Abigail Goh with her smugness and her cutting insults. Now it was the first day of school and Mrs Parasuram probably thought that I was a troublemaker. I noticed her looking at her seating chart a few times before she wrote out our timetable on the board. She was probably considering giving the honour of sitting next to the new girl to somebody else who didn't cause a scene on the first day.

As Mrs Parasuram continued to explain to the class what she expected from us in Primary Five, a woman knocked on the door and called, "Excuse me!" Her voice was so certain that it was like she was commanding the entire room. She wore high heels and a pair of sunglasses on her head, which pushed back a high pile of permed curls.

Nobody noticed the girl next to her until Mrs Parasuram said, "Ah, yes. You must be Kristen! The new girl." Kristen's pinafore skirt was a bit too long for her and her ponytail was tied too high and tight. She kept her arms stiffly at her sides and didn't protest when Mrs Parasuram walked her away from her mother to the empty seat next to mine. "This is Parveen," Mrs Parasuram said. "She will be your seating partner. She will help you settle in."

Kristen nodded and gave me a quivering smile. Everybody was staring. Mrs Parasuram picked up where she had left off and had to stop a few times to tell the class to pay attention. "Girls, keep your eyes on me," she insisted. But nobody could. At every chance they got, the class craned their necks and tipped their heads to get a better view of the new girl. Even I looked at her a few times out of the corner of my eye. From her bag, she unloaded a pink pencil box, the kind that had secret compartments and mirrors. She pushed it to the far edge of her desk and let her crossed arms rest on the desk.

The recess bell rang while Mrs Parasuram was checking to see if we had all of the required books for the year. "Parveen, please stay behind," she reminded me. The girls queued up single file and disappeared down the stairs, their footsteps becoming more rapid as they got closer to the courtyard.

Mrs Parasuram smoothened the wrinkles on her sari before sitting down at her desk. I expected a scolding as loud as her long wooden ruler had rapped on the surface of my desk. She looked like the type of teacher who banged things to scare you into thinking she might hit you.

"Pull up a chair, Parveen," she said. I did as she told. "Now tell me. What happened just now?"

"Abigail was making fun of you."

"What did Abigail say?"

"She said you were…she was being racist."

Mrs Parasuram did not look surprised at all. "What exactly did Abigail say, Parveen?"

It took me a while to tell her and when I did, I couldn't look her in the eye. "She said you were…black. And she could smell coconut oil and you don't bathe."

"And?"

"That was all. She says things like that all the time."

"About you?"

"About lots of people. Last year, she said that Muslims were pigs."

Mrs Parasuram's face was a mask. Nothing I said seemed to bother or surprise her. Behind her, the ticking hands on the clock reminded me that precious recess minutes were being taken away. It was 9.10am. Zero-nine-one-zero. I memorised the numbers for Daddy's lottery.

Finally she spoke. "Parveen, I know you may disagree with me but there are far worse things than being called such names. Do you know that there are countries in the world where people are killed for the colour of their skin? You will always run into people like Abigail. But you made yourself look like the bigger fool just now when you shouted back."

"But—" I began, then shut my mouth. I didn't know what to say. I thought I had done a good thing by telling Abigail off, and I wished that Mrs Parasuram hadn't interrupted our conversation so I could have called her all the names I wanted. I knew it wasn't the right thing to do, but who really cared? She needed to be taught a lesson.

"But nothing, Parveen. You can't change the way people

think, but you can prevent yourself from being bothered by their stupidity. Is that clear?"

I nodded vigorously, my eyes fixed on the clock. "Yes," I said, but it was not clear. I thought she was plain wrong, and I could have told her so, but then I'd have to listen to another lecture and my recess would go down the drain. Mrs Parasuram told me to conduct myself like a lady, then dismissed me. I walked slowly out of the classroom with my head hung low to show my remorse, then broke into a run as soon as I turned the corner.

Mrs Parasuram's words echoed in my mind for the rest of the day. *There are far worse things...* If I'd had the guts to challenge her, I would have requested a list of all the things that were worse than being called a Mungalee, a dirty Indian who used too much coconut oil, or a Blackie. To me, there was nothing worse.

•   •   •

"Don't rub your eyes! Drink some water," Ma said. She was chopping onions and they made my eyes sting. I opened the fridge door and searched the side racks for the old two-litre Coke bottle we used as a water pitcher. The shelves were full again. Eggs and jam bottles rattled as the door swung. The vegetable drawer overflowed with leaves and fat stalks.

"I'm making fried rice," she said. "With prawns, peas and carrots. Could you pass me a chilli?"

"Red or green?"

"Red. Always red with this kind of rice," she said. I opened the vegetable drawer and pulled out a package wrapped in newspaper and bound tightly with rubber bands. There were three more newspaper packages, all containing various spices bought from the market and it was a lucky guess that I had got it right. Ma split the chilli with her fingernail, scooped out most of the seeds and pushed them aside, which meant that she wanted the chilli for flavour, not to challenge us. If she kept all of the seeds in, she was trying to see how much we could take.

"What time is Daddy coming home?" I asked. Ma's back was turned to me. When she was cooking, there was always a delay before she replied because her mind was so focused on adding the right ingredients at the right time. Any distractions she had while cooking surfaced once the meal was already cooked. Mushy potatoes; soggy spinach leaves; dry, chewy chicken.

"He will be back in the evening," Ma said. "How was school?"

"Okay."

"Just okay? What did you do?"

"Nothing."

Sesame oil bubbled in a pan on the stove. Ma pushed the onions off her chopping board and into the pan. They sizzled. Drinking the water made my eyes hurt a bit less, but they were still teary.

"Nothing? Just nothing?" Ma said.

"It was the first day! We really didn't do much. We went through the school rules about uniforms, socks and hair," I said. I touched my ponytail. Ma had sent me to the hairdresser two days ago. She said my hair was too unruly to be kept long. I agreed with her. God would have to understand. He didn't have much say these days anyway. A few days after Nani-ji's funeral, I woke up to find Ma dragging a chair to the wall where God sat. He gripped the edges of the frame and ducked his head into his shoulders as she pulled him off the wall and placed him back in the storeroom. A square of paint in a paler shade remained on the wall where the portrait had been.

Ma stirred the onions, spreading them across the pan so they didn't clump together. There was time for her to turn around briefly. "Okay, then what is your new teacher's name?"

"Mrs Parasuram."

"Indian?"

"Yes."

"Young or old?"

"Old. Like maybe not a grandmother but still old."

"Is she nice?"

"She's okay."

Ma turned around and began making slits in the sides of the prawns. They were silver and curled with long whiskers. She removed the whiskers, then pulled out a thin black string from each prawn. "That's the waste," she informed me.

"That's yucky," I told her.

Ma threw the prawns into the pan and turned around again. "It's rude to call food yucky, do you know that?"

"Why?" I thought of all of the times we saw signs at the hawker centre with pictures of fried chicken feet and fish head curry. They didn't look very appetising, and there wasn't anything wrong in saying so. I was just being honest.

"It's like you're saying that you don't appreciate that you have food to eat every day."

After God had been put away, the meals in our flat began to explain Ma's emotions again. Tofu stir-fried in oyster sauce for contentment; crisp deep-fried brinjal slices with fish curry to stifle her anger; glass noodles with shredded cabbage and carrot soup for sadness.

I slipped off the kitchen stool and went to my room to start on my homework. When I passed the storeroom, I walked as close to the opposite wall as possible. God was probably furious about being imprisoned there. If I listened closely at night, I thought I heard a faint knocking sound coming from the storeroom, coaxing me to open the door and help Him back onto the wall again.

At Chapel that morning, Mrs D'Cruz had spoken about learning to love God and trust in His word. She told us that we should treat our friends and family with the same respect and trust that we treated God. I thought about God sitting in the depths of our storeroom and I liked the idea of putting all of the people I didn't like in there as well. Fat Auntie would be the first, then Bus Uncle. Abigail would join them as well. I would send Mama-ji there just because Ma didn't like him.

• • •

We missed English the next day and the day after because it was the beginning of the year and Mrs Parasuram told us she had a lot of administrative work to handle. She collected fees, checked our uniforms and went through the school rules while we sat in our seats, bored stiff. I kept the book of tickets Daddy had drawn on and flipped through it during the lessons. Sometimes I gave Kristen advice. "In this school, you have to stand up when the teacher asks you to give an answer. And remember to wear your belt all the time or you will look like a pregnant girl."

In the corner of the tuck shop, Kristen slowly unwrapped a sandwich. "She moved here from another country," Farizah said.

"How do you know?" I asked.

"She rides my school bus in the morning and I heard her mother talking to the driver." We both stared at Kristen, who didn't seem to have a clue that we were talking about her. "Where did she come from?" I asked. Farizah shrugged.

I reported this to the girls on my school bus who were also intrigued by Kristen, even the ones who weren't in my class. "She came from another country," I told them.

"How do you know? She doesn't talk to anyone," a girl said. Some of the others cast irritated looks in her direction for being so sceptical.

"I sit next to her," I said proudly. "So I know." The truth was, Kristen had not said a single thing to me. It seemed that she deliberately kept her lips tightly pursed. She never had any questions and only offered a small smile and mouthed "okay" or "thank you" when I gave her tips on what to do.

There was a new Bus Auntie in charge and we all listened to her because she smiled and helped us onto the bus with the pull of her strong arm. She never allowed the bus driver to move off until she saw that we were safely in our void decks when we were dropped off. She told us to call her Auntie Honey even though the name on the fees notice said "Lau Siew Hock". Honey was her Christian name, she informed us. She wore a big jade cross around her neck and hummed under her breath. We could make as much noise as we wanted, but that was also a very Primary Four thing to do. The previous year, the Primary Five girls had sat closer to the front of the bus and talked about their favourite American pop stars and film actors, and snickered meanly about the girls they didn't like. We did the same, making sure to hide our pick-up-sticks deep down in our bags so nobody could see that we would still play games if we were allowed to.

• • •

Kristen finally spoke up on the day that Mrs Parasuram handed back our first compositions for the year. Mine came back with a few red marks, but there was also a comment written at the bottom: "Parveen, good grammar and spelling. Your handwriting is good as well. But in the future, please write the truth." My face burned. We had been instructed to write about our school holidays and I had written about going skiing in Los Angeles. It wasn't true, but it was far more exciting than my holidays had actually been.

"She knows because it's always warm in Los Angeles. You can't go skiing there," Kristen said. I thought she might be making fun of me but there was a kind note to her voice. She must have peered at my paper when I was looking at it. "Have you ever been there?" she asked.

I shook my head. "Have you?"

"Yeah. I lived in Chicago for two years," she said.

"What was it like?"

"It was nice, but much colder than it is here," she said. "I didn't really get much of a vacation though, because we were preparing to move back here." As her voice got louder, the girls sitting around us turned back to look and whispered. She could speak! Kristen noticed and blushed. She took an eraser from her pink pencil box and began to play with it.

"I've never been out of Singapore. Except to Johor Bahru. And Kuala Lumpur, but I was very young," I confessed. Everybody knew that Malaysia didn't count. To really leave the country, you had to fly.

"What did you do over the holidays then?"

"Nothing. We couldn't have fun because my grandmother died."

"Oh," Kristen said. "I'm sorry."

"It's okay," I said. The others were turning back to look at us. From the front, Farizah cast me a curious look. I sent one back, which meant that I promised to tell her everything during recess. Then it occurred to me that Kristen would be sitting alone again. "You can sit with us for recess if you want," I said. I was nonchalant in case she said no.

Kristen beamed. "Okay," she said. Mrs Parasuram tapped on her desk with her ruler. "Girls, stop talking," she said sternly. I rolled my eyes at Kristen once Mrs Parasuram's back was turned towards us again. She covered her mouth with her hands to stifle a giggle.

Farizah ended up having to stay back during recess to do make-up work because she had been absent the day before. I hardly noticed she wasn't there as I talked to Kristen, who was suddenly very chatty. She told me more about herself. "I lived in America for two years. My father's company decided to transfer him back here. I was born in Singapore." She had a slight accent so I could hear the letter R in her words.

"Do you miss your friends?" I asked her.

Kristen nodded. "My parents told me I'd make new ones," she said nervously. I gave her my warmest smile and she returned it.

"Which school did you go to here before you moved to America?" I asked her.

"St Mary's, the one in Bukit Timah. But my mother went to this school so she wanted me to come here too," Kristen said. Of course Kristen was not a Bursary Girl. She was one of the girls whose mothers had gone to First Christian. She lived in Bukit Timah, probably on landed property. It didn't matter—it never mattered to me with the other girls, but for some reason Kristen was the kind of person that I wanted to impress.

"It's a good school," I told Kristen. And then I told a lie. "My mother was a student here too."

"Cool," Kristen said. "Maybe they knew each other." But thankfully, she did not ask when Ma had gone to First Christian and I quickly changed the subject. For a moment, I wanted to tell Kristen that what I had said wasn't true. But as she continued with her stories about America, her friends and her new house here in Singapore, I kept my mouth shut.

• • •

I watched the shadows of neighbours bobbing past my window. The family next door had visitors who all left in a group, a cluster of heads and arms floating past. The ceiling fan swirled above me, stirring a breeze through the room that usually soothed me to sleep. Tonight, the air was too still and no matter how fast the fan was spinning, I could not sleep. The door of the flat opened and I heard Daddy leaving for his night shift. His was a tall shadow with broad shoulders. "Bye bye!" I called into the window.

"Go to sleep, Pin," he said. He tapped his goodnight on the window and continued down the corridor. I watched for shadows, but there were fewer as it got later. The night was suddenly very quiet. I lay back in my bed and shut my eyes to force myself to get tired. My mind began to wander instead, making me feel more awake. Over the week, I had sat with Kristen at the tuck shop every day during recess. The other girls were welcome to join us, but I secretly preferred that they didn't. They stayed at their own tables and watched us, occasionally whispering when they thought I didn't notice.

It was only on the school bus that the other girls crowded

around me to ask questions about Kristen. "She knows how to roller blade. She has an older brother," I announced. Abigail rolled her eyes and pretended not to listen. I knew it bothered her that Kristen sat with me for recess. When Auntie Honey told us to sit down, we hurried back to our seats and two girls I didn't know very well pushed to sit with me.

At home, the floor tiles were cold against my bare feet as I walked into the kitchen to get a glass of water. The next day was Saturday—homework day. Mrs Parasuram gave us homework for everything, even art, and she made us write out our spelling corrections ten times instead of five like the other teachers did. When we complained softly amongst ourselves, she paid no attention but we hoped that she heard. Today, she had given us a lecture on how we needed to start bucking up because the PSLE was next year and preparation started now. "I expect this class to excel in everything, even the subjects that you don't think matter. Being a good student isn't just about getting good marks for your graded subjects," she said, her eyes surveying the room. I looked away. I knew she was addressing the whole class, but I had a feeling she was specifically talking to me. Miss Yoon must have shown her my disappointing art folio from last year.

I was walking back to my room when I noticed a shadow that I could not recognise. I stood in the hallway of the flat waiting for the neighbour to return to his or her own flat so I could figure out who it was. "Go on," I whispered. But the shadow remained, hanging like a fog outside our window. I gave the storeroom a furtive glance, wishing that God could be out there to protect me. I ran back to my room and leapt into bed, yanking the curtains across the window so the shadow couldn't look into my room. Seeing the shadow outside kept me even more awake than I had been before and I didn't drift off to sleep until early morning light began to seep into the room, making all shadows seem like something out of my imagination.

Ma left early for the market the next morning. "I'm only picking up a few things so I don't need you to come with me, Pin. We have enough in the fridge to last for the whole week. I just need to buy more chicken," she said as she closed the door behind her. Just to make sure she was telling the truth, I went into the kitchen to check our fridge. It was nice to see that we did in fact have a lot of food.

I saw Daddy sitting in the living room reading the newspaper and I asked him if he believed in ghosts. I sat myself down on the arm of his chair and held on to his shoulders to keep myself from slipping off.

"May I ask why you're so interested all of a sudden in ghosts?"

I kept quiet for a moment to think of what to say. It seemed silly to tell him the truth—that the shadow in the window was Nani-ji's ghost, especially since I'd seen it once before she died. But I had heard of near-death experiences, when a person's spirit left their body and lingered to watch. Farizah swore that the spirit of her great-uncle still came back to his old house to sit in his old chair and read the newspaper. "You can see the chair rocking slowly at night and it feels cold just where he would be sitting." It seemed like something Nani-ji would do, peering through our windows into our flat.

"Because my friend saw a ghost in the school toilets the other day, that's why I want to know," I finally said. This was true, although it wasn't my reason. One of my classmates whose mother went to our school said that a nun's ghost haunted the toilets. It was why we always went there in pairs and held in our pee if the lights were broken.

"I don't believe in ghosts and neither should you. You'll scare yourself silly for nothing," Daddy said with a frown. He looked disappointed, and I knew what I had to do to make him smile again.

"Three-five-nine-nine," I said. They were numbers from Kristen's address, which she had printed in my autograph book that afternoon. "What if you win?"

"I'll buy you something really nice," he promised as always. I grinned at him. I didn't care any more that I didn't believe in the lottery. I was going to school every day, Ma was going to the market, Daddy was working his shifts at the hotel and God was sitting in the storeroom. Everything was back to the way it had been before Nani-ji came along and it was about time. I looked out of the window, expecting to see the shadow again but there was nobody in the corridor. It was probably nothing, I told myself, just some trick of light outside in the dark. It was daytime now anyway and I couldn't even think about ghosts without scoffing at myself for being a scared baby.

Monday morning at school, Mrs Parasuram reminded all of us that it was the last Monday of the month. Girls whose parents could afford to pay the full fees at First Christian didn't pay attention when Mrs Parasuram made the announcement. But for Bursary Girls, the last Monday of the month meant that we had to queue in the canteen during recess and get the special forms for our parents to sign. "Please don't forget," she said. Farizah twisted in her seat and mouthed something to me while pointing outside. I knew she was telling me to meet her in our usual spot in the tuck shop near the drinks stall so we could queue up together. I nodded at her and widened my eyes to warn her that Mrs Parasuram was dangerously close to her desk. Farizah got the message and whipped back around.

"What forms? Do I have to get one?" Kristen asked me.

"Financial forms," I said. "For the girls who are getting help from the school with their fees."

Kristen giggled. "Help? With the school fees? It doesn't cost that much to go here, does it?"

I was surprised at myself for what I did next. I laughed along with Kristen and shrugged. "Yeah, it doesn't cost that much at all." Inside, I felt the pinch of my words.

To make things worse, Mrs Parasuram told us to take out our social studies textbooks. We covered a chapter on Singapore in the 1960s and I thought of Ma as a girl, surveying the bare cupboards in her dimly lit kitchen. Her words echoed in my mind: *Don't become like me, Pin.* I forced the heavy feeling of guilt out of my stomach by telling myself that pretending to be somebody else was better. After all, wasn't this what Ma wanted for me?

•   •   •

I came home from school that afternoon to find Ma searching frantically through my room. She had turned over the mattress on the bed and all of the drawers were open. Even the curtains were tied at each end of the window as if whatever she was looking for might have been wedged in the window grilles. My first thought was that the shadow I had seen outside was a thief but then it dawned on me that Ma was looking for her jewellery.

"Pin! You're home. Oh, thank goodness. I need you to help me find something."

"Your gold?"

"Yes!" Ma said. She stopped moving around the room. I saw that her eyes were darting all over the place and stray hairs had sprung from her head, making it look like she had just gotten out of bed. "Your Nani-ji took it for a while when she was staying here and I just realised that she never gave it back. I don't know how I could have missed it but I guess I was just so busy…" Her voice trailed off. She sat down on the chair and surveyed the room. "Do you have any idea where it is?"

"Fat Auntie took it."

Ma's eyes were closed and she was rubbing her temples but at the mention of Fat Auntie's name, they flew open. "She did what?"

"Fat Auntie came over one day while you were at the hospital with Nani-ji…and she took all of the jewellery."

There was a tremor in Ma's hand as she brought it to her lips. "That's my jewellery, not hers," she said. She sounded like a child fighting over a toy.

"She's probably just keeping it for you," I offered. Ma shook her head and waved my suggestion away like it was a cloud of dust. Even I knew it wasn't true. Why would Fat Auntie do such a nice thing for Ma?

"It's mine," Ma said. She marched over to the phone and made a call. I followed her outside, nervousness making my stomach churn. "Hello, Bhabi-ji. It's me," she said. She used the term of respect for sister-in-law but her voice was still curt. "Oh, I'm doing fine. And you…? Good. I actually can't speak for very long. But I just noticed that my wedding jewellery has been taken from my house and I was wondering if you knew…yes. Yes, Pin told me you came over. No, she just told me. I assumed the jewellery was always in her room where Mother had left it. I can come over tomorrow to pick it up. I was thinking of renting a safe deposit box in town so I can keep it there."

This was when Ma's face changed. Her eyes widened and became full of fire. I braced myself for a shout. Her lips became thinner and every word shot out of her mouth like a bullet. "It's *my* jewellery. I wore it on my wedding day and I intend to keep it. What I do with it is none of your business, is it? No, *no*, I don't care what my mother told you, I don't care what she thought. I want my gold back and I'm coming over *tomorrow* to get it." The slamming of the receiver shook the flat like a clap of lightning. "Can you believe that woman?" Ma said into the air. "After all these years, she's still going on about it." She marched over to the storeroom and kicked the door. I flinched in shock—she might as well have given God a kick because He was in there.

Ma smoothened out a wrinkle in the cotton blouse she was wearing. It was light blue, the colour of the afternoon sky and it looked strange on somebody who looked as worn out as she did—too bright and cheery. She ran her fingers through her hair, flattening the wisps that had come undone.

"Hungry?" she asked quietly.

"Yes."

She left the mess in the room and went into the kitchen. I followed her. I watched her take out ingredients from the fridge. Flat noodles; broccoli; garlic cloves; black spicy sauce; minced pork and onions. We were going to be in the kitchen for a while. She peeled the flaky skin off the onions first and only spoke to instruct me to cover my eyes so I wouldn't start crying. Then, as she chopped rapidly, the onions crunching under the blade of her knife, she told me everything.

10

1970

JINI STANDS AMONG the dusty rows of gunnysacks and tinned food. A woman's operatic wail crackles through a radio on the highest shelf behind the counter where Shop Uncle keeps Tiger Balm, Axe oil and small bottles of colourful pills. One row down, there are jars containing roots of plants and odd spices suspended in a thick liquid that resembles glue. Shop Uncle's abacus beads click rapidly. He pauses and notices Jini. "Girl, what you want?" he asks.

"Just deciding."

Shop Uncle returns to his calculations. Jini doesn't have to look at the coins in her hands to know what she can afford. There is just enough for a tin of powdered milk, a small bag of salt and some canned sardines.

The abacus beads stop clicking. Shop Uncle shuffles to the back. While his back is turned, Jini briefly considers stealing the sardines. She could fit two cans in each pocket and have enough money left over to buy some polish for her shoes. But the thought of stealing makes her stomach churn. She couldn't do that to Shop Uncle, who has kindly continued to sell her sugar and cooking oil in small portions.

Jini selects her groceries and approaches the counter. "Hello, Uncle," she calls. He emerges from the back of the shop. She unfolds a few bills and places them in front of him. As Shop Uncle counts the money, Jini hopes he will offer a discount. Every saved cent now counts. He mutters to himself and puts her items in a bag. Then he pauses and sniffs the air. Jini takes a step away from the counter, shame burning her face. He has caught a whiff of her shoes. When Shop Uncle has packed her groceries, she grabs the bag and walks briskly towards the door.

"Girl," Shop Uncle calls. "Come back."

Jini turns around. "I have to go. My mother—"

Shop Uncle steps out from behind the counter. "Girl," he says. "Your shoes."

Jini peers at her feet as if it's the first time she's looking at them but of course, she has known all day. This morning, while rushing to school, she stepped in a muddy patch. She scraped her soles against the grass to clean them only to discover that she had actually stepped in dog droppings. Although she did her best to clean her shoes with leaves, a foul-smelling streak remained on the canvas sides. It was her bad luck that the school inspector was present at assembly, checking the tidiness of the students. He had singled her out in front of everybody and said, "This is disgraceful."

Jini keeps her gaze lowered while Shop Uncle clicks his tongue and shakes his head. He must think that she is filthy, that she doesn't bathe. Finally, she breaks the silence. "Uncle, maybe I can buy some shoe polish? About twenty cents worth?"

Shop Uncle shakes his head again and walks away. Jini's face burns. How embarrassing to have to ask, to practically be a beggar. Shop Uncle returns with a can of bleach. "You must clean your shoes with this," he says. The can looks heavy and too costly for Jini. She has some savings but they're being put towards fees to see

Pra-ji about her skin problem. She shakes her head at Shop Uncle and steps out of the shop. Moments later, she hears Shop Uncle calling out. "Girl, wait," he says. "I can give you some." He waves an empty Coke bottle at her.

"How much is it?" Jini asks, but he waves her away and turns his face slightly so he doesn't have to smell her shoes. "Thank you," she says, watching him fill the bottle. "Thank you so much."

•   •   •

Neighbourhood noises drift through the open windows, along with smoke from the kitchens and a light breeze that makes the loose hairs from Jini's plait dance around her shoulders. She is alone in the house with Bilu. Sarjit is at work, her sister-in-law is at the temple and her mother is working on the other side of town again. It's the perfect day to go to Pra-ji's house, but she has to make sure Bilu doesn't follow her. When she's the only person at home, he can barely stand to be away from her. He is sitting in the kitchen now, squatting among tin cans of kerosene and an old gunnysack they use for rubbish, watching her.

"I'm making you lunch," she tells him. "You have to eat."

He shakes his head. She ignores him. Lunch takes a long time to prepare because the itching of her arms and legs distracts her. After she scratches, she has to wash her hands. She wishes her sister-in-law were around to deal with Bilu but Bhabi-ji has been going to the temple every afternoon, probably just to escape from him. He doesn't mind when she leaves because he doesn't like her. When she ties his hair in the morning, he bites and screams. "It's so embarrassing. The neighbours think I'm torturing him," Jini heard her telling Sarjit one night. Jini was furious to hear Sarjit agreeing with her. "Just go to the temple during the day then. I know how difficult he is." She wanted to tell her mother about what they'd said but she had a feeling that her mother already knew.

Jini only knows how to make dhal and roti, so she pours the lentils in a bowl and starts to sort through them, looking for stones. She finds three and tosses them out the window. Bilu's eyes follow them.

"Don't go outside," she instructs, as she notices him rising slowly from his corner. She's afraid that he might race into the road one day and get hit by a car. His movements are unpredictable like that and she finds herself consumed by worry now that it's harder to stop him.

To take her mind off her worries, Jini focuses on cooking. She turns on the stove and puts a pot of water on it. She washes the lentils and pours them into the pot, then covers the pot with a lid. She opens the cupboards and rummages through them for spices to add. There is a container full of cardamom, some coriander leaves and a few small tins of powders—red, yellow, brown, orange. She could do what her mother does and just start adding and mixing. She doesn't know what each spice is, or what they taste like, but the colours have to have some meaning. Red for anger, love. Yellow for a hot afternoon. Brown for relaxing, forgetting. Orange for excitement.

"Sugar?" Bilu asks her.

"No. No sugar."

"Sugar," he insists.

"Mother said no more sugar for you. We don't have enough for tea because I keep putting it in all of your food. One day your teeth will fall out," she tells him. He seems unfazed by this. He pops a thumb in his mouth and begins to suck on it.

Jini is about to tell Bilu to take his dirty hand out of his mouth, that nine-year-olds don't suck their thumbs, when she hears her gate creaking. She glances out the window to see a shadow. Before she can call for help, she recognises the person walking into her yard. The curly-haired boy makes cautious steps towards the back door. When he catches her eye, he waves. She runs out into the yard and shouts, "Get out!" She hopes the neighbours hear her. "You can't come here!"

The boy looks confused. "Why?"

"Your kind isn't allowed around my house."

The boy looks surprised, like a strong gust of wind has just pushed him back. But he recovers quickly. "Okay," he says. His voice is a tiny whisper, but Jini can read the movement of his lips. "Okay." He turns and runs out of the yard into the street. She stands there for a long time with her hands on her hips, feeling so guilty that she is frozen to the ground. But this is what the neighbours and her mother want. They would be proud of her. She wishes the boy hadn't come over. She has been avoiding him for some time now. Each time he waves, she ducks away. Each time she sees him walking up the road, she turns around and goes in the opposite direction. *You can't afford to get into any trouble,* she reminds herself.

When she returns, too much water has boiled and the lentils are stuck to the bottom of the pot, burnt. "Wasted!" Jini cries as she turns off the stove and scrapes away the burnt dhal. Bilu would never eat this. His nose is already wrinkled in disgust. She looks at him and sighs. The dough for roti has already been made, but he'd never eat it plain. She takes out the rolling pin and makes two uneven rotis, lumpy in the middle, but Bilu wouldn't know the difference. Then she throws them onto a hot plate and watches them bloat with steam and turn a nice golden brown. Bilu gets up to watch.

"Sugar?" he asks.

"Yeah, okay, sugar," Jini says. She turns off the fire and puts both pieces of roti on a plate. She takes the sugar from the container she has hidden at the back of the cupboard and pours it onto the hot roti. It melts instantly into the dark pockets on the bread. She hands the plate to Bilu and makes two more for herself, sprinkling a generous amount of sugar over the bread. She needs something sweet to forget what she just said and did to that poor boy outside. The sugar cancels out the sour taste in her mouth, the bitterness of her words.

"Don't tell anybody," Jini says. "Mother will kill me."

But Bilu doesn't know the meaning of secrets. Jini realises then that this is why she loves him so much.

• • •

It is early evening when Jini sneaks out of the house.

She leaves Bilu in the living room with a plate of sugary roti. He has been eating it every day for a week now. Thank goodness her mother has hardly been home this whole week between her work and the temple, or she'd surely be furious that they've used up all of the sugar. Wrapped in a handkerchief in one of Jini's pockets is a pile of notes and coins for Pra-ji. Jini counted $10.65. This will be enough for one session with Pra-ji—her problems might require more, then she'll have to save up for another few months to keep paying him for his help. Jini closes the door behind her, leaving it unlocked in case there's a fire and Bilu has to get out. Just two months ago, in a house on the other side of the island, a little girl had died in a house fire when her mother left her alone at home with the door locked. Jini shudders to think of Bilu trapped in a burning house. She vows to hurry home from Pra-ji's place.

"Where are you going?" Two voices in unison startle Jini. The sisters who live next door are peering over the fence, watching her tiptoe across the lawn.

"The shops," she lies.

"You're dressed too nicely to go to the shops," Jasbir Kaur says bluntly. She exchanges a glance with her sister, Amanpreet.

"Not the nearby shops. The shops in town. My mother wants me to buy something from there," Jini says. She looks past the two girls as she talks. The girls are not satisfied but at least they leave her alone. They wander away, whispering to each other and glancing at the house. Jini thinks she hears one of them saying Bilu's name and now she wonders if she should go back to the house. *He'll be fine. He eats slowly and when he finishes, he usually falls asleep on the spot.* If her mother comes home to find him sitting there alone, she can always lie and tell her she had to go back to school to collect some things.

Last week at the temple, Pra-ji told Mother that he spoke to God and found out that their father had another family in India. A wife and twin baby boys. Her mother's knees buckled a bit and Jini had to hold her shoulders to make sure she didn't collapse right there in front of all of the temple women, who were watching. They always watch when Mother has something to ask Pra-ji, which is why she waits for them to leave before she speaks.

After that, she told Pra-ji she did not want to know any more.

"What is the point? I'll only become more upset. Thank you for your help, but I don't have any more questions." Pra-ji did not look pleased. He tried to convince her that speaking to God was the only way to relieve her sadness. "You can ask about your health, when you will get grandchildren from Sarjit and his wife, or about Jini." He looked pointedly at Jini when he said this, making her blush.

Mother was suddenly alert. "What would I want to know about Jini?"

Pra-ji did not betray her. "Nothing right now. But if you ever have any questions, maybe about who she should marry in the future, then please come and speak to me."

"I already know her future," her mother said. "She is leaving school after the O-Levels, then she'll work to help us. Later on, she'll marry some boy, somebody who is hopefully better off than us."

"Yes, Jini is a very pretty girl," Pra-ji said. "I'm sure finding somebody, despite her lack of education, will not be a problem. Sometimes these boys don't want a girl who is too highly educated. She'll be troublesome, they say." Something about this statement made Jini nervous but she ignored the feeling. It was probably just the way he said it. It was as if he was sure he knew everything about her.

The road behind her is clear except for three young boys who are crouched on the pavement, turning over a dead snail. They yelp and jump away, then slowly approach again, nudging each other and calling their friends to look.

As Jini leaves the kampong, she feels as if a heavy cloak is sliding off her shoulders. She has an urge to run to Pra-ji's house, but somebody might notice her. She walks a bit faster than she usually does, though. A woman wearing a sarong chides her husband, who stares solemnly at his sandals. In the distance, a radio plays an English song and a group of teenage girls try to harmonise their voices with it. Slowly, the rows of cramped houses open up for more space and soon, she is walking in the spaces between larger, neater houses. These are made with proper brick and have painted roofs and coloured shutters—blue; green; yellow. It is like walking through a toy store. Even the ground feels different—steadier—under her feet. Pra-ji's house is at the end of the street, a bungalow surrounded by a bright garden. There is a small pond in the front yard and little flowers line the edges. She presses the doorbell.

The servant girl runs out, her limp foot dragging behind her. "You don't have to hurry," Jini tells her. "Please." The girl just stares at Jini and opens the gate.

"Can I ask you why you're here?" Rani asks.

Jini opens her mouth to speak but she catches herself. She barely knows this girl. "Something private," she says.

"Your mother should be here with you," Rani says. "Does she know where you are?"

Who does this girl think she is, asking about her mother? She is just about to tell the girl not to say a thing to anybody when Pra-ji comes out of the house. "Rani!" he says sharply. The girl jumps and runs back into the house. "Get a drink of water for Jini and for myself. And don't poke around. This is none of your business." Jini smiles with relief.

"Come in," Pra-ji says. "She's very nosy. What did she say to you?"

"Nothing—she just wanted to know why I was here."

"I'll speak to her later."

"Pra-ji, what if she tells my mother? My mother doesn't know I came to see you."

"Don't worry," Pra-ji assures her. "Your mother will not find out."

Pra-ji's house is very ornate. A large wooden chest sits in the corner of the living room, near the stairs. A curtain made of carved wooden beads hangs from the kitchen doorway. Elaborate picture frames line the coffee table, which is also intricately carved with a scene of villagers climbing a steep mountain. There are two Persian carpets woven with images of tigers and elephants. Pictures of God are everywhere, so Jini can't look at any of the walls without seeing Him. She focuses instead on all of Pra-ji's decorations.

"Where did you buy all of these things?" she asks him.

"I didn't buy them. They were gifts. I help all kinds of people. Sometimes I tell fortunes for foreigners. I read their palms. They ask me about their money, about their families back in England, what to do. Mostly I just tell them about themselves. I read people very accurately," he tells her. When he says this, he scans her body as if he can look past her clothes and see the scars on her skin. "Show me your hand," he says.

She reaches out her hand and he takes it, stroking the lines on her palm. "You have struggled," he says. "You are still struggling. Correct?"

"Yes," she says but there is nothing remarkable in his knowing that. The entire community knows that her family has struggled.

"You and your sister-in-law don't get along," he continues.

"Yes," she admits.

"You must start to respect her. She is older than you are."

Jini tells him about how Bhabi-ji escapes to the temple each afternoon and how she does not take care of Bilu.

"Do you like taking care of your little brother?" he asks her.

"I don't like it when he's giving me trouble but somebody has to help him."

"Maybe your sister-in-law has too many other duties," Pra-ji tells her. Her hand is still in his.

"She just has to cook and clean. It's not a big deal," Jini scoffs, thinking of all the times she and her mother took care of the house before Bhabi-ji came along. It seems like they managed better without her.

"I'm talking about other duties, Jini," Pra-ji says carefully. "A wife has a duty to make her husband happy."

Jini thinks of how quiet Sarjit has become since marrying his wife and she wonders if he is happy. She notices that Pra-ji is staring at her again and it makes her uncomfortable. She wants to look at God, just to make sure she is doing the right thing by being here, but she is still afraid to look Him in the eye. Still, she is nervous all of a sudden and she doesn't know why.

"I'm thirsty," she says. Pra-ji lets go of her hands and calls Rani to hurry up with the water. "How long must it take for you to serve my guest?" he shouts. It surprises Jini that he can be so stern. She has only seen him speak gently, in a voice that people use to coax their babies to sleep. She thinks about Bilu. She remembers with a small ache that she forgot to leave a drink for him. It is a hot evening and he must be thirsty. She scolds herself silently for this oversight and hopes that he fell asleep after eating his food.

Rani comes out with the drinks and sets them down on the coffee table. Her gaze lingers on Jini and she looks as if she wants to say something, but when Pra-ji asks her why she is still standing there, she hurries back into the kitchen. Pra-ji takes Jini's other hand.

"It looks like you will have a long life. A good life ahead of you," he says, inspecting one of the lines on her hand. "Don't worry about your studies. You will have plenty of time to catch up with those things later on."

"Really?"

"Really," he says. "For now, we must work on your soul. What kinds of things have you been thinking about, Jini?"

"I think about my father. I'm so angry at him," she confesses. She is surprised to feel tears pouring down her face. "Because of him, things are difficult for our family. Sometimes I wish I could see him suffer the way he's making my mother suffer now. And sometimes…sometimes I can't believe that God would let something like this happen." She begins to sob into her hand. She pulls the other one away from Pra-ji's lap. Then she remembers the money in her pocket.

"Oh. This is for you," she says, taking out the handkerchief. Pra-ji takes the money with both hands and puts it aside. "It's almost eleven dollars."

"Never mind how much money it is, dear. Even the smallest amount will do. I just want to help you. Tell me more." He counts the money and puts it his pocket. Jini feels her heart sink. A part of her had hoped that he would return her money, knowing her family's situation. "Go on. What are you waiting for?" Pra-ji asks.

She tells him about how indifferent Sarjit has become, how her mother's back has been giving her trouble. She tells him she feels guilty for turning the boy away from her yard this morning. "Is it true we shouldn't mix with people from their caste?" she asks.

"It's better not to. It's not just a matter of caste. Their ideas are different. They don't respect religion. That boy you're talking about—have you ever seen him at the temple?"

"He doesn't go. He doesn't even look Sikh. He has short hair."

"He cuts his hair! See what I mean? They are not like us."

Jini nods. There was a look in the boy's eyes as he turned away and went back down the road, which still makes her sad. Pra-ji is watching her. "You're a very sweet girl, Jini. You care about people almost too much."

"Is this bad?" she asks him.

"No. But you should let go. Don't think about what your father has done. God will catch up with him—you can be sure of that. Nobody can run away from those watchful eyes." He points at the wall behind him and Jini is forced to look at God for the first time in months. He watches her with His hand raised, ready to pass his judgment.

"I want to see these scars," Pra-ji tells Jini. Obediently, she pulls up her sleeves. He draws her arms to him and puts them on his lap. She feels strange having her arms across his thighs like that but he is really looking at them, like a doctor. He circles the scabs with his thumbs and she wriggles uncomfortably.

"They are very itchy," she says.

"When do they become itchy?" he asks.

"When I'm thinking of something bad," she says immediately. But this is not always true. Sometimes, when her mind is clear and only filled with the purest thoughts, her scabs begin to itch and burn. She can't explain this. But she wants Pra-ji's help, so she tells him what he expects to hear.

"I can help you," he tells her. His voice has lowered. "I'm going to close my eyes now and I want you to do the same. We're going to commune with God."

Jini's hands go to her head. "Can I have something to cover

my head? If we're going to pray—"

"No need," Pra-ji says. There is a note of impatience in his voice. Again, Jini feels uneasy. Pra-ji is fidgeting, biting the corners of his lips. He looks like he is trying to suppress an unfriendly smile. "This is different from temple praying. At the temple, we cover our heads to respect God's home. This is my home, so I am in charge." He laughs. Jini feels a sense of discomfort. The whole world is supposed to be God's home.

Pra-ji asks her to close her eyes and he begins to chant softly. Jini listens and concentrates hard on the scabs going away, disappearing altogether. She thinks about her father and tries not to be hateful towards him. She vows to be nicer to her sister-in-law, to return the money to Shop Uncle, to help her mother more.

"Open your eyes," Pra-ji says. "I have another question for you." Jini does as she is told. "What other thoughts have you had, besides the ones you told me about?"

Jini racks her brain to think of anything else she's pictured in her mind. Pra-ji comes closer to her so his lips are almost touching her cheek as he whispers into her ear. "How about boys?"

"Boys?" she asks.

"That boy from the low caste family. Do you like him?"

Jini shifts uncomfortably. Suddenly, it feels very warm in Pra-ji's spacious living room. She takes a few gulps of water. "He is just a schoolmate."

"Not your boyfriend?" he asks her. He is gazing at her chest. She tries to stop breathing so hard.

"No. No, he's not like that. I don't have a boyfriend. I don't even talk to any boys. My mother would kill me," she says.

Pra-ji looks sceptical. He strokes her hair, pulls it away from her face and tucks it behind her ears. "There's nothing wrong, as long as you don't tell anybody," he whispers. Jini feels her whole body tense up. Then, Pra-ji resumes his straight posture and begins to chant again. "Close your eyes again, Jini," he instructs.

She closes her eyes but she feels unsafe. In her own mind, she starts her own prayer: *God, please help me. I think I've made a mistake.* Please help me out of here. She could just run, but then what would Pra-ji say to people? They would believe him, not her, even if she ran through the streets telling people that he is an indecent man, that he tried to talk to her about boyfriends. Or maybe this is how he helps. *God, help me,* she urges. But her head is uncovered. Can he even hear her?

Then she feels something, a cold hand, drifting up her blouse and onto her stomach. "I just want to feel your skin," Pra-ji says. "I want to know how bad it has gotten." She stays still, frozen to the spot. Then Pra-ji brings his hands up. They are cupping her breasts now, squeezing them. With a sudden force, he pushes her down on the floor and presses down on her face with his, his body grinding against hers.

"No!" she screams but her voice is louder in her head. With her mouth pressed down by his shoulders, it is just a muffled noise. He is pulling at her pants now, tugging them down, forcing her legs apart. "Stop it!" she pleads, kicking at the air. "Help!"

Then she sees the glass of water on the coffee table. Pra-ji has one of her arms pinned down but he cannot control the other one as he struggles to spread her legs. She reaches for the glass and throws the water on his back. For an instant, he stops, startled. She uses this to get a wider swing and she smashes the glass against the side of his head. Blood and water trickle down his face and down her wrist. He lets out a strangled cry.

"You little whore!" he shouts, holding a hand to the gash on his face. Blood pours freely through the spaces between his fingers. "Who the hell do you think you are? You come here asking for my help; you have no father; your family has the worst reputation in the whole community and you dare to attack me?"

"You bastard!" she spits. She doesn't care if it's a bad word. She doesn't care if the scabs remain on her body and spread to her face and itch for the rest of her life. She will never become a follower of God if this is what followers do. She sees His portrait all over the house now, His eyes accusing her. "You son of a bitch! *You filthy dog!*" She screams and screams these insults over and over again until she realises that she is out of the house, she has been running since she got free. Her hand is bleeding and throbbing with pain. There is a cut on her palm. Her heart is racing. She runs past the big houses, now looming and casting long shadows from the evening sun. She runs all the way back to her neighbourhood, a trail of blood dotting the pavement behind her.

• • •

It is when Jini arrives at the top of the street, where the narrow road goes down a slope to lead to her house, that she notices the crowd. At first she thinks it might be a wedding, but it is a weekday evening, and weddings are only on Sundays. Besides, the air feels damp and heavy with something dreadful. She looks up at the sky, but there are few clouds, only a quickly descending sun. She wonders sometimes why the sun takes so long to appear in the morning but it manages to race away in the evening as if it has better places to be.

She stops running once she gets to her street because she doesn't want anybody to see her. She puts her bleeding hand behind her back. Her mother will come home, then Jini will calmly tell her what Pra-ji did. Her brother will be furious with Pra-ji, he'll tell him off one day at the temple and everyone will know what a fraud he is, what a disgusting man. As for her skin, she will live with it. When she starts working, she'll go to see a doctor and maybe he'll be able to explain what's wrong. Maybe the kind of soap she uses is too harsh or she has some kind of allergy. These excuses have come to mind before but she was so dependent on God that she thought it had to have something to do with Him. She can't believe how foolish she was. Once again, shame fills the pit of her stomach, but she has a plan now and that is important. Yet her heart cannot stop racing. What is going on at her street?

A woman comes running up to her, the thin batik fabric of her nightgown flapping wildly at her ankles. It is Auntie Gurpreet, the mother of the girls next door. "Where have you been?" she cries. Past Auntie Gurpreet's shoulders, Jini sees that the door to her house is wide open. "Bilu?" she whispers. Dread spreads like a fire through her body. The crowd parts for her and lets her run into her home. Bilu is nowhere to be seen but there is a smaller crowd of people in the kitchen. They are not people from the community—they are wearing uniforms and they are lifting a large opaque bag. *Where is Bilu?* Jini wonders again. Of course he is not hurt. She did everything to keep him safe. She only left him for a short time.

But then she sees it: the Coke bottle. Last night, she poured some of the bleach into a tub and soaked her shoes in it. She hid the bottle afterwards with the rest of the cleaning supplies and it was still three quarters full. Now it is nearly empty. She thinks of how Bilu eats—how he gulps everything down so quickly she's afraid he'll choke. He would have thought it was water.

Somebody in a uniform is asking Jini a question. Did she hear him screaming? Where was she? The neighbours rushed in to help. They had heard him and called for help. They broke into the house and tried to pick him up, but he was impossible to control and in a terrible amount of pain. Every time Jini tries to open her mouth, a thick and sour taste prevents her from uttering a word. She wants to crouch near Bilu—who she now realises is inside the large bag—to speak to him and tell him he will be okay, that she is so sorry for leaving him, but something keeps her at a distance and she doesn't realise what it is, until she notices the entire community staring at her. There are stares from the crowd and more stares from the windows, illuminated in the dimness of evening. She keeps standing there, silent, under their gazes. She knows right then that this is where she will remain for the rest of her life.

PART IV

11

1991

MA'S FACE WAS wet with tears when she finished her story. "When people began to ask questions about where my mother and I were when Bilu died, I had to tell them that I had been at Pra-ji's house. But he denied it. He said I was never there. He was afraid that I would tell people what he had done, so he just pretended that it never happened. Then the rumours started."

"What kind of rumours?" I asked.

"People said that I was probably in town meeting with men, since I couldn't account for my whereabouts. Pra-ji added fuel to the rumours; I'm sure of it. If he convinced people that I was that kind of girl, nobody would listen to my side of things."

I thought of the servant girl. "Do you think that's what happened to Rani?"

Ma nodded. "That's why she wanted to know where my mother was. I thought she was being nosy, but she was just trying to warn me. I can't imagine what her life was like living with that beast." She shuddered. Ma swept the back of her hand across her cheeks. The tears left a shiny path on her skin. "Your Auntie thinks I don't deserve to have my jewellery returned because of what happened that day. She says my mistake cost them everything, and the jewellery was just on loan from Nani-ji anyway."

We sat there for a long time in silence. Ma craned her neck

to look at the clock outside and sprang from her chair when she realised it was time to start cooking dinner. She paced the kitchen for a minute before she opened the door of the fridge. The details of her story began to flood my mind. I could see her now as she was when she was 15, scared and confused. I remembered how anger had choked her voice that day we left the temple. She couldn't just let Fat Auntie get away with taking her jewellery. There had to be some way to get it back.

"Maybe Fat Auntie will listen to your side of things if you call her on a good day," I suggested.

Ma shook her head. "In all the years I've known your Fat Auntie, I've never seen her on a good day. I don't think she's capable of being generous." I opened my mouth to protest but Ma silenced me. "That's enough, Pin," she said sternly, and I had to drop the subject. I watched closely as she pulled out the ingredients for dinner. Anise seeds; cardamom and red chilli powder; meat and potatoes; rice and crunchy long beans. Ma was still thinking. She could not forget so easily.

• • •

Chinese New Year was in two weeks and the city was lit in red. Bloated lanterns hung from the streetlights and fabric dragons danced as the light February breeze rippled through their spines. Daddy and I sat down on Saturday morning at the hawker centre to draw the neighbourhood, but I couldn't do it. To draw Singapore during Chinese New Year, you needed red, pink and gold. You had to include the music—high-pitched and punctuated with clashing cymbals and echoing drums—that blasted from the convenience stores on the path opposite the hawker centre.

"I can't do it," I told Daddy, pushing my paper back to him. He was too busy concentrating to look up. He didn't believe in colour when he drew and claimed that all the colours he needed were shades of black, white and grey.

"Done," he said. "Nice?"

I nodded, even though the scene looked a bit depressing to me. He had drawn the block across the street, where lanterns of different shapes and sizes dangled in the corridors. "You can keep it and colour it in if you want," he said.

"Thanks," I mumbled, folding up the drawing.

"You're thinking about something," Daddy noted. "Tell?"

"Nothing," I said.

"Have any more ghosts been bothering you?"

"No." The figure at the window had not come back and I was convinced that it had all just been my imagination. At night, the lanterns in our corridor sometimes swayed with the wind and made odd shadows on the opposite walls.

"How's school going?" Daddy asked.

"It's okay."

"Mrs Paraswati, right?"

"Parasuram."

"Is she a good teacher?"

I made a face. "She gives too much homework," I complained.

"Every teacher gives too much homework. It's better for you though. Think about how smart you'll be at the end of the year. Even smarter than the girls in the other classes who don't have Mrs Parasurna."

"Parasuram!" I was exasperated. Daddy was terrible with names.

"That's what I said."

"I have a new friend at school. Kristen. Her birthday's on the same day as Chinese New Year this year and she told me she's having a party. She just moved here from America."

"That's nice," Daddy said. "I've always wanted to go there. When I win the lottery, we'll go."

"*If* you win," I corrected him. "You don't know if you ever will."

"*When*," Daddy said firmly. He started drawing again, pressing his pen hard down into the paper. There was a small child at the next table with his mother feeding him spoonfuls of rice porridge. He clapped, wiggled about and sometimes turned his head when his mother tried to slip the spoon into his mouth. The porridge was all over his cheeks and on the collar of his T-shirt. Daddy attempted to draw him. His bold strokes did not quite match the boy's thin head of straight hair or his small nose, eyes and mouth. But it was early in the day when Daddy was most confident. I decided to stop arguing that he was wrong.

Kristen handed out her invitations the following Monday. The chatter in our classroom was so loud that Mrs Parasuram had to threaten to take marks off our weekly spelling and dictation test before we settled down. Nobody wanted to score poorly for spelling and dictation. That week, there were words like "pandemonium" and "dilapidated". Elaine Lee and I had quizzed each other on the bus until I was sure even Auntie Honey knew the words by heart, even though her English was not nearly good enough.

Kristen wrote me a note on the edge of her science exercise book. "Remember to wear red!" I gave her a quick, confident nod but my mind raced. Did I own anything red? I had pink clothes, but they were all either too childish or not formal enough for a party.

During recess, a group of girls gathered around our table to talk about the party. When Farizah got up to buy a drink, Kristen's eyes followed her. She waited until Farizah was out of earshot, then she told the other girls that she hoped we could all wear similar cheongsams. "It doesn't have to be the exact same one," she said generously. "But my mom says we'd all look really nice in a photograph together if we all wore short red cheongsams with black shoes."

I looked at Farizah now, who was queuing at the drinks stall. Every girl in the class had been invited, including her. "I don't think Farizah can wear a short dress."

"But Sofia Rahman is also Muslim and she says she'll do it," Kristen said.

"Yeah, but Farizah is…different. She'll probably wear a long skirt or she'll wear pants."

"Maybe I shouldn't have invited her then," Kristen said. I looked at the other girls for sympathy but they were smirking as well. Not many people understood Farizah and even fewer wanted to try.

"She probably won't come anyway," I said quickly. "She won't eat from plates that have touched pork." This was true. Back when we were in Primary Three, there had been a birthday party at Alison Chu's house and she had invited the whole class. The potato curry puffs, peanut pancakes and keropok had all been served on Alison's mother's best porcelain platters. Farizah had refused to eat anything. She had said that it was a sin for her to eat from a plate that had ever touched pork. There were two other Muslim girls at the party and they had argued that it was okay. "The food is halal," they had assured her. "It doesn't matter if the plate has touched pork as long as the food itself didn't touch pork." Farizah had quietly refused.

"That's weird," Kristen said. She made an ugly face that made the other girls laugh. I joined in; my laugh sounded forced and I felt the girls' eyes on me, testing to see if I was on their side or not. Farizah wasn't around anyway. I decided that she was weird sometimes and instantly, the laugh became lighter.

"But you're definitely coming to my party though, right?" Kristen asked me later as we queued up to go back to class.

"Definitely," I said, giving her my most convincing smile. I didn't want to look different from the other girls and risk being spoken about behind my back, but a red cheongsam would be costly, especially now that most of Singapore was doing their New Year shopping. Ma would definitely consider it a waste of money to buy a dress just for one party—I knew this without even asking her. Daddy would probably say the same thing but in a nicer way.

At Assembly a few days later, Mrs D'Cruz gave yet another talk about God and money. "During the Lunar New Year celebrations, we receive red packets from our relatives in the hopes that they will contain a lot of money. God wants you to prosper, not just in your wallets, but also in your hearts. If you are thankful for your gifts, you will offer them to God. In return, he will make your gifts grow." With that, the school prefects took their cue to distribute red envelopes. They looked a lot like Chinese New Year red packets with gold trim and pictures of delicate branches with pink leaves and plump oranges hanging from them. But close to the seal was the name of our school in gold lettering.

Still stretching her lips into a strained smile, Mrs D'Cruz explained that the school was building a new chapel where the old art building used to be. She said that the construction of the new chapel depended on donation money, then she mentioned the names of a few parents who had already written large cheques. "We don't expect you to donate large amounts, but do think about putting in some of your pocket money for a good cause. Think of how pleased God will be." Around me, all of the other girls glanced at each other and pulled out their purses. I felt a slim two-dollar note in my pocket and knew that if I gave that up, I wouldn't have enough money to buy food with for the rest of the day.

"Aren't you giving?" Kristen asked me. She folded a green five-dollar note into the envelope and pressed the flap to seal it.

"I forgot my money today," I lied. And then it hit me. All of Mrs D'Cruz's talk about God making our money grow gave me an idea.

We went back to class after Assembly and our first lesson was social studies. Mrs Parasuram continued her boring lecture on Sir Stamford Raffles. She passed around a picture of his white statue in town, arms crossed, chin up and legs spaced wide apart as if he was trying to chope the entire island. I raised my hand and asked if I could go to the toilet.

"School will be dismissed in twenty minutes. You can go then," Mrs Parasuram said. Before she could continue with her lesson, my hand shot up in the air and I waved it around.

"Yes, Parveen?" she said. Her voice was exasperated.

"It's urgent," I told her. The class tittered. Deborah Ong had said that just before she had diarrhoea and vomited at the same time back in Primary Two.

"Okay, just go then," Mrs Parasuram said hurriedly. She must have been informed about Deborah Ong.

I dug my hand into my desk and shoved the envelope into my

pocket. The hallways were quiet except for the occasional raised voices from teachers in the other classrooms. I looked around before I passed the toilets, just in case there were prefects lurking near the stairwell. I didn't want anyone to tell on me because I wasn't going to the toilets. I hurried down the stairs and kept close to the walls until I was at the familiar stained-glass windows, then without thinking twice, I slipped into the old chapel.

A blast of cold air greeted my face and neck and legs as I quickly took a seat on the first bench I saw. There wasn't a single soul there besides myself. It was darker than I had remembered from the last time I had peeked in. I felt a bit sad for this God, sitting alone in this cold house with no lights. I closed my eyes and immediately my mind conjured up an image of this God. He had long hair that he didn't bother tying up and tucking into a turban.

"Hello," I said. My throat was dry and it came out as a croak. I cleared my throat and tried again. It was a whisper this time.

Hello. This God's voice was gentler, almost a girl's voice. He sounded like the man from the Public Utilities Board who called our house to gently remind us to pay the electric bill.

"What should I call you?" I asked. I was more confident this time.

Anything you want, child, He replied. A few nicknames came to mind but I decided to put off calling him anything until I had to.

"I'm Pin," I said.

I know.

"Do you know my last name?"

Kaur. You're Sikh.

"So is it okay for me to be here?" I asked earnestly.

He chuckled, not meanly, but it still made me nervous. It reminded me of when Ma had paused during the telling of her story to smile to herself. It was not a happy smile—it was a smile that she used to keep her lips from quivering with anger and saying words she'd regret. It was a smile that she thought would protect me from seeing something bad, but it still scared me. I was afraid that the smile would confuse her and keep her from telling me the truth. In the same way, I was afraid now that God would not be honest with me.

It's absolutely fine, He replied. I only realised then that I had been holding my breath while waiting for His answer. A long sigh escaped from my lips and filled the air around me with warmth. I wiggled my way down to the centre of the bench and shut my eyes again, concentrating on what this God looked like. His eyes, I finally decided, were not unlike my God's eyes—watery and drooping a bit at the corners, like He had just watched a sad movie. His mouth was turned down in the same way. He was skinnier than my God and I thought this might have something to do with the different food they ate. My God lived on greasy fried bread soaked in thick spiced gravies, yellowed vegetables and lumpy yoghurt, so it was no wonder He filled all the space in His picture frame. I vaguely remembered Mrs D'Cruz saying something about bread, and wine and a large farewell feast but besides that, I don't think this God must have eaten very much. I could see the thin ladder of His ribs through his tanned skin.

When I opened my eyes, I noticed how long I had been away from class and I got worried. "I have to go back or my teacher will get angry," I said. I almost told Him that she thought I was in the toilet but if He were a proper God, He probably wouldn't approve of lying. I fished out the envelope and quickly folded the two-dollar note into it. I licked the seal, pressed it firmly with my thumb and slipped the envelope into the collections box.

"Help," I said simply, and I meant that I needed His help for everything. I didn't feel comfortable talking to my own God because He was still in the storeroom and I was afraid He was still upset. If this God could help my money to grow like Mrs D'Cruz had promised He would, maybe there would be money for me to buy a red or pink dress for Kristen's party and some left over to give her an ang pow. Maybe Daddy would win the lottery and the bills would be easier to pay and he could take on fewer shifts or get an easier job in town. Maybe he could even buy better and more expensive jewellery for Ma one day so she'd forget all about what Fat Auntie and Nani-ji had taken away from her.

I scrambled out of the chapel into the heat of the late afternoon sun. I held my breath as I rushed back to my seat, worried that Mrs Parasuram would demand to know where I had gone for so long. But she barely paused or noticed as I entered the classroom. She was too occupied with telling stories of how Singapore had transformed from a swamp to a bustling metropolis. Her eyes blazed with excitement, as if she could see the country transforming right before her.

• • •

Something happened the next day that made me believe in that new God. It started at recess, when I found a one-dollar coin on the floor under my table in the tuck shop. "Look!" I cried when I caught a glimpse of the gold colour. "I chope it first."

Kristen ducked down to look as well. "Wow," she said. "I've never found a one-dollar coin before. It's always the one-cent coins on the ground."

I put the coin on the table and we both examined it. There was nothing fake about it—it wasn't one of those chocolate coins wrapped in gold foil. In kindergarten, a boy I knew had tried to convince me that the foil was made of real gold, but I didn't believe him.

I quickly put the coin in my pocket and Kristen went back to sipping her iced winter melon tea. "You're not going to share it?" she asked in her smiley way that meant she wouldn't be angry if I said no. I felt guilty anyway.

"I can't," I said, but I could not bring myself to explain. "Sorry," I mumbled, rising from the table. Kristen paired her chopsticks together and began twisting her thin bee hoon noodles around. A puff of steam rushed forth and quickly brought beads of sweat to the space between her nose and her top lip.

The warning bell rang as I was standing up and Kristen began to eat frantically. Soup splashed onto the table, making us both giggle. In a flash, she seemed to forget about the one-dollar coin and I was glad because I didn't want to have to explain what it was for.

As the day went on, I became less and less sure that the new God had anything to do with the money I had found. After all, it was only one dollar—what could that buy me? I could get a plate of noodles from school or a hot cup of Milo with some change. In her speeches, the principal always said that God gave plenty when people were needy. I was not starving. I only needed a dress. I thought about Ma and Nani-ji counting their last cents to buy onions and salt in their kampong, and I suddenly felt very guilty. But I really wanted to match the other girls at Kristen's party.

During after-recess prayers, I joined in as they said the "Our

Father" prayer. I knew all the words by heart from having had to listen to it all these years, and I kept my head down so nobody would see me and wonder why I was praying to a different God all of a sudden. I prayed hard, my eyes squeezed shut and my hands clasped so hard that they were sticky with sweat afterwards.

He was listening. He had to have been listening because when Daddy got home that evening, he announced that he had some very good news.

"Pin, I won!" He shouted, fumbling with the padlock. It clanged impatiently against the iron bars of the gate, a sound that echoed down the hallway.

"You won what?" I asked.

"4D!" Daddy cried. "A consolation prize, so it's not exactly the real thing, but I still won something!" He flung the gate open and stretched out his arms to pick me up, but I slipped past him into our flat like a burglar. Consolation prizes were three, four or five hundred dollars. The huge prizes were in the thousands. I tried to feel the weight of $300, then I tried to think of the weight of Ma's jewellery. Were they both the same? I wasn't sure. Still, I was excited for Daddy. He had finally won, and it was no coincidence. I thought of the money I had donated to the God at school and pictured it taking root like a tree.

"Your Ma is very happy about it," Daddy said. His voice was not convincing. He reached out for another hug and I returned it sideways. Like a ghost, Ma drifted out of her bedroom wearing her long-sleeved nightgown. "Aren't you glad we've got some extra money to spoil Pin with?" he called out to Ma. I cringed. Spoiling me was probably the last thing Ma would want to do with the lottery money. Ma turned to look at me and gave me a half smile.

"There's some porridge for lunch if you haven't eaten," Ma said.

I nodded. "I'm hungry," I said. Ma's feet sweeping across the floor sounded like the old rotan sapu we kept in the storeroom. When I was very little, I used to raise my feet and watch her beat the dust off the living room carpet with the hard bristles of that broom. I turned to Daddy to ask him what was wrong with her but he was pacing the living room excitedly and rambling about his strategy. "See, Pin, I knew that my numbers didn't work last time because I didn't *feel* it Pin, I didn't *feel* it. But then I bought those tickets and there was something, I don't know, like a light, a warmth, or something. I think I felt it in my heart. And I just knew what I had to do. The numbers just came to me. Sometimes, the numbers just come to you." He paused and tore off a sheet of newspaper to write down his own inspired quote. He shook the scrap at me with determination. "We can do anything, Pin."

I started to get excited for Daddy, thinking that this could be the beginning of bigger prizes in the future. But every time happiness began to swell in my stomach, my eyes wandered towards Ma and the blank expression on her face made me worry. I should not have asked her to recount the whole story that day. It was too much, and now she was miserable, having brought her memories to the present.

Ma put a bowl of porridge on the table and went back into her room without saying anything else. She didn't look sad any more. Her eyes weren't puffy and she wasn't exactly frowning. I stirred the porridge with my spoon to let out the steam and after that, I took a small sip. She had forgotten the pepper and there was very little salt so the chicken broth tasted like nothing. Bloated grains of white rice clung to strips of white chicken. They came apart in strings when I tried to pick them up with my spoon, meaning that Ma had not been paying much attention to the pot when the porridge was boiling. Everything was overcooked and bland. On a good day, Ma would have sprinkled fried shallots on the porridge so there was some crunch to the dish. This should have been a good day because we suddenly had more money. But Ma was indifferent; her food did not lie.

Daddy watched as I took a few sips, then he asked, "How is it, Pin?"

"Not so good," I whispered. My eyes were on Ma's door in case she opened it suddenly. "There's no taste. And I only like porridge with fried shallots."

"Let's get out of here then. Let's go eat somewhere else. Where do you want to go?"

I thought for a while before I answered his question. "There's actually something I really need," I began. I was hesitant. I had asked the new God for money and now that we had it, I was nervous about using it. But then I reminded myself that it would be rude not to use a bit of Daddy's money to buy a Chinese New Year dress because the new God must have gone through a lot of trouble just to get those lottery numbers to be chosen.

I told Daddy about Kristen's party and how I needed a dress. "Of course!" Daddy cried out. "Let's go to Chinatown. Go get ready. And Pin—take your time, you hear me? Because we're not taking the bus or the MRT there. We're taking a *taxi*."

I let out a whoop and ran into my room to change out of my uniform into outside clothes. In the lift, I asked Daddy to show me the money he had won. He opened his wallet just a bit to reveal a few blue notes. $50 notes were blue and although I didn't see them very often, I was disappointed. I thought that the 4D people would have given Daddy a stack of $100 notes or something like that. I had never seen notes in denominations larger than $50.

The taxi sped across the highway until Singapore was just a series of heartbeats. We shot past trees and white blocks of flats, glittering buildings and signs pointing towards the city. We glided into Chinatown as if this was something we did every day. Daddy even told the driver to keep the change of five dollars but when the driver refused, I noticed a look of relief flashing across Daddy's eyes. He pocketed the money and pushed me gently out of the cab.

There were a few places like Chinatown in Singapore that immediately made me remember a past or a place I had never lived in. Little India was like this too—rows of colourful shophouses pushed together; men selling bloated jackfruits on wooden platforms; windows with mannequins wearing glittering wedding saris; pavements stained with dye and smashed fruit skins; the smoke of sandalwood incense so heavy that it clung to my hair. Chinatown was nosier than Little India because we were there during the festive period, and it was also more crowded. Daddy instructed me to hold on to his hand as we made our way through the crowds. Red lanterns hung from every ceiling and every lamp post. Golden statues of Buddha and ferocious dragons grinned at us from store windows. Deep red slabs of bak kwa and rubbery skinned ducks hung from hooks in restaurant windows. We passed the glaring lights of movie theatres, and heard drums and cymbals playing New Year songs. We ate a late lunch at a dim sum restaurant, where we chose from a menu and had our food brought to us by a waitress. I asked Daddy if he was going to leave his job now that he had won the lottery.

"No, Pin," he said with a laugh. "I didn't win nearly enough to quit working!"

"But maybe you can get a better job," I told him.

"I like my job," he said. He took out a piece of paper from his pocket.

"Is that the winning ticket?" I asked, reaching out to grab it from him. He pulled the paper away.

"No." he said. "I left that at home." He began to sketch on the piece of paper. There was so much in Chinatown to draw, but there were too many colours. I looked behind me to see what he might possibly be sketching. There were two tall lanterns swinging in a light breeze, and there was also a row of shophouses with gaping windows revealing the dark insides of homes with television sets and clotheslines draped across the ledges. But Daddy was drawing a girl—me. He was drawing a portrait of me.

"You've grown up so much, Pin. You look a lot like your Ma," he said, examining the picture. I looked at the drawing and didn't think it was very good. My eyebrows were crooked and my nose was wider in real life than in the picture. In Daddy's drawing, I looked stern and unforgiving.

"I know about what happened to Ma," I blurted out. I expected the entire room to freeze—the fans to stop twirling and the waitresses to stop moving between the tables—but nothing happened. Daddy's expression didn't even change.

"I know you know," he finally said. He added a few strokes to thicken my hair in the picture. "I've told you before. Your Ma had a very hard time growing up. People still give her a lot of trouble, so she's not always herself. But she loves you, Pin. She loves both of us very much."

"Why is she so sad today?" I asked.

"She tried calling your Fat Auntie," Daddy said. "She tried to reason with her and your Auntie told her to stop calling."

I did not allow myself to feel angry with Fat Auntie this time. At first I felt rage rise in me, creating a bitter taste in my mouth, but when I looked at my lunch laid out on the table, those feelings melted away. I took a bite of my dumpling. It was pork filling wrapped in soft white dumpling skin made of starch. In the bowl, it was neatly bundled together like a present. The skin slipped off when I tried to pick up the dumpling with my chopstick so all I had was the lump of pork.

"Ma doesn't know how to make this," I told Daddy.

"She does," he said.

"She's never cooked dumplings."

"Maybe there has never been an occasion for dumplings."

I tried to think about what occasion would call for dumplings. They were fairly simple and plain looking, maybe a little oddly-shaped. I tried to pick up the chicken dumpling but it slipped too and this time it bounced across the table and fell onto the floor. I looked around me quickly to see if anybody had noticed but the restaurant was filled with loud chatter and if people weren't busy talking, they were busy eating.

"Sorry," I told Daddy.

"Why are you sorry? It's your food."

I recited Ma's mantra: "Because, 'when you throw away food, you waste money'."

Daddy grinned. "And now you know why Ma has never cooked dumplings at home, Pinny-Pin. She's waiting for you to grow into a graceful woman who won't drop her main dish all over the floor."

After lunch, we crossed the main road and found a row of clothing shops. I liked the first dress I saw and wouldn't even consider anything else. It was a deep red cheongsam with a high neck and a slit up the side. I looked like a lady when I wore it, not a little girl. Ma would usually yank my arm and drag me to every store until she was sure that the dress I liked was the best quality for the cheapest price. Daddy didn't mind. He didn't seem to know much about dresses. In the dressing room, I piled my hair on my head and turned a few times like a fashion model. There were white flowers on the dress, and on the centre of each flower was a small sequin that caught the light and sparkled.

Outside, I could hear Daddy trying to bargain with the shopkeeper. He was not as aggressive as Ma. I could hear his voice wavering the minute he asked the shopkeeper to bring the price down. "I'm a local, you know. Not a foreigner," he reminded the shopkeeper, a squat old woman who wore heavy jade earrings and a matching bangle.

I came out of the dressing room to find Daddy grimly opening his wallet and peeling out two $50 notes to give to the woman. As she wrapped up my dress, I asked Daddy if the dress had really cost that much.

"One hundred," he said softly in Punjabi. "But you like this dress, yeah?"

I nodded. Something did not seem right. Daddy forced a smile on his face but his eyes were downcast. I thought about how he must have spent the whole day consoling Ma after her phone call with Fat Auntie. How badly he always wanted to fix things and make everybody happy for a change. "Daddy?" I asked as we walked out of the store. "Did you really win the lottery?"

"Of course I did, Pinny!" he replied. "Why? Do you think I'm lying to you? I'm just not used to spending a hundred dollars on a small dress."

"I know," I said but I still did not believe him. The new God could not have been so quick in delivering my request, especially since there were people in parts of the world who prayed to him for money all the time and they seemed to need it more. I was stupid to think that he was paying that much attention to me. Who was I, anyway?

As we walked down the street, Daddy waved down a cab but he stopped when he realised there were passengers inside. I pointed to a bus stop. "We can take the 166 from there. It goes straight to the Ang Mo Kio bus interchange."

Daddy shook his head. "It will take too long. Let's just take a cab." He tried to sound like this was something he did every day, but the words came out sounding forced, like he had rehearsed them earlier. I wondered how long he had planned on pretending to win at 4D.

We tried flagging down another cab but the driver pointed to a sign that said "On Call". I saw Daddy looking around and jiggling the change in his pocket. He was searching for a phone to call for a cab. Booking a taxi was even more expensive. "I'm thirsty," I said quickly. "I want some juice or soya bean drink or something."

Daddy pointed at a small street stall and we walked to it. The signs advertised fruit juice blends and iced tea. I ordered a watermelon juice and we both sat down. Then I looked him in the eye and told him why I wanted the dress. I figured that if I told him about Kristen's request and how she had made fun of Farizah, then he'd insist that we return the dress and I would have an excuse not to go to Kristen's party. She couldn't make fun of me if I said that my father didn't let me go.

"This Kristen girl doesn't sound very nice," Daddy said.

"She just moved here," I told him, as if that made up for everything. A doubtful look was etched in Daddy's face. I looked at him expectantly. This was supposed to be his cue to tell the truth. But he simply said, "Pin, you can make your own decisions now. If you want to go to this party, you have a dress. If you don't want to go, then we can return it."

I didn't have to prod Daddy about wining the lottery any more. The truth became quite clear when the hawker arrived at our table with my watermelon juice. "Four-fifty," he said.

"For juice?!" Daddy exclaimed, looking at the glass. I was surprised too. The hawker shrugged, then narrowed his eyes. "My shop is very cheap. You going to pay?" he asked. There was an edge to his voice, like he was ready to fight. I looked around and realised that we were on a street filled with tourists. They milled through the narrow lanes and open stalls selling jade bracelets, small bronze Buddha statues and silk purses. They didn't know how to haggle and they didn't have to.

"Yeah, yeah, okay," Daddy said. He picked up his wallet and leafed through the remaining notes. He still had two $50 notes in there but suddenly, he did not want to part with them. When he finally gave the money to the hawker, he looked nervous. "I know I gave you fifty," he said sternly as the hawker returned to his stall to get change.

I opened my mouth to ask Daddy why he had lied about the lottery, but I knew it would embarrass him. And I knew why. Everybody wants to prove they are right all along, even if the whole world says they're not. I thought about how Farizah insisted on her beliefs, even if they were a bit strange. I thought of the hope in Ma's eyes as she relived her story for me. I thought of how badly I wanted to show the neighbourhood boys that I could be just like them and how I had nearly drowned trying to save that ball to prove I was brave and useful to their team.

I picked up the bag with my new dress in it and pushed it across the table to Daddy. "Can you return it?" I asked him. "I don't want to go to Kristen's party any more."

Daddy rubbed his forehead. "Aiyoh, Pin. You're causing me lots of trouble today," he said. He looked troubled and he took the bag slowly from me. But the relief showed in his eyes, and in the grin that spread across his face and remained throughout our bus journey home.

•   •   •

At school the next day, I wrote a note to Kristen. "Dear Kristen, Sorry I can't attend your Chinese New Year party." I decided not to give her a reason. I tucked the note under her pencil box and asked Mrs Parasuram if I could be excused to go to the toilet.

"Yes," she said. "Please hurry. We have a lot of work to cover today."

I walked briskly to the door, then broke into a run once I turned the corner. I passed the toilets in a flash—I didn't need to go there. I had to go to the chapel again.

A cold blast of air hit my arms and legs. I sat down, shut my eyes and stewed in silence for a minute before I began to talk.

"I think you tried to trick me," I said. "You made Daddy lie about winning the lottery so I'd think we had money. Why?" The words bounced across the walls before they disappeared. It occurred to me that He was probably sick of people asking Him that question. God did not reply.

"You're all the same," I said angrily, and at first I really was furious. But as my words quickly echoed back to me, I heard the truth in what I had said. They were all the same. All of the prayers, all of the teachings—the Gods only looked different, but their intentions were the same. They were always watching and they did some strange things, and sometimes it was hard to believe that they truly existed because they never seemed to appear when you needed them.

I looked down at my knees poking out from under my pinafore skirt. I turned my hands over, examining the lines, the contrast between the lighter skin on my palms and the darker skin on the other side. All the same. Kristen could make fun of Farizah's religion all she wanted. Fat Auntie could criticise Ma for her skin rashes. Abigail Goh could say nasty things about Mrs Parasuram behind her back. They were all the same. When I conjured this God again, I expected Him to nod and bless me for finally figuring it out, but His expression remained blank.

The door creaked as it opened, making me jump out of my thoughts. I turned around to see who it was and when I did, I wished I had hidden under the benches or in a shadow. The colours on Mrs Parasuram's sari stood out brilliantly against the light of the outdoors.

"Just what do you think you're doing here?" she asked sternly. I did not have a reply for her. She shook her head. "Come out right now, Miss Kaur." I scrambled off the bench and walked quickly to the door. Still shaking her head, Mrs Parasuram continued to talk. "Here I was, just walking back to the staff room because I had left your workbooks there and I was thinking to myself, 'I hope that Parveen is okay. This is the second time she's asked to go to the toilet during the lesson when she knows the rules.' And then I saw your shoes outside the chapel and true enough, you were sitting in there, avoiding my class." As I put my shoes back on, I noticed that the rubber in the soles was peeling off and there were brownish-green streaks across the toes from the last time I had padded through the muddy school field during a game of catching. Mrs Parasuram had warned me to clean my shoes and scolded our class for playing games on the grass: "A nice concourse was built for you so you didn't have to run around on the wet field like a bunch of village children," she'd said, directing her gaze at the few of us who had suggested playing catching in the sun. This was probably how she had recognised my shoes outside. She was more observant than I had realised.

"Sorry," I mumbled.

Mrs Parasuram did not look satisfied. "Why are you here?"

"I…I don't know," I stammered. I couldn't think of an excuse that would suit Mrs Parasuram.

"I'm disappointed in you, Pin. Most girls run away from trouble, but you seem to like running into it. I'm going to be watching you closely from now on. You're on very thin ice. I hope you know what that means." She punctuated her sentence with a sharp click of her tongue. "Now put on your shoes and return to class."

My whole body felt like lead as I walked back to class. Kristen was chatting with Abigail Goh when I got to my desk. "Did you read my note?" I asked her, noticing that it was gone.

"Yes," Kristen said icily. "It's just as well. You're no longer invited anyway."

I was confused. Just yesterday, Kristen and I were leafing through each other's autograph books. I had written my signature phrase: "Drink hot coffee, drink hot tea. Burn your lips and remember me!"

I heard a snort and I saw Abigail covering her mouth to stifle her laughter. "You and Farizah are uninvited. No fanatics allowed," she said. She looked pointedly at my kara.

"I have to wear this. It's for my religion. I'm Sikh," I told her, just as I had tirelessly told the prefects, the teachers and the girls on the school bus who had asked. "I'm not a fanatic." I didn't realise how loud my voice was until I noticed a hush fall over the room. Abigail Goh raised an eyebrow.

"Sikhs are disgusting," she informed Kristen. "The men have beards and they wear these funny-looking turbans. They only wash their hair once a week." She wrinkled her nose.

I felt my face grow hot. I couldn't breathe. Everybody in the class was waiting for me to say something. Some girls moved away quietly from the table, distancing themselves from Abigail's mean words. Others stepped in quickly to fill the spaces, observing the expression on my face. I wanted to reach across the table and hit Abigail so hard she wouldn't remember what she had said to me.

Mrs Parasuram breezed back into the room carrying a teetering pile of workbooks. Everybody scattered back to their seats but I remained standing, glaring at Abigail. She looked back at me and I noticed she was getting nervous. She wanted me to say something back to her but I didn't.

"What's going on over there?" Mrs Parasuram called. "Parveen, please sit down."

Her voice brought back the memory of what she'd said to me the first time I had snapped at Abigail: *There are worse things.* I could hear Mrs Parasuram making her way down the aisle. "Parveen, what did I just ask you to do?" She sounded exasperated. I didn't turn around to face her. I still kept staring at Abigail. All of a sudden, I felt very sorry for her. She did not have any real friends. The girls who surrounded her were terrified by her and everybody else secretly hated her. I couldn't imagine anything worse than being Abigail. I told her so. I said it softly, then I said it again for Mrs Parasuram's benefit. "There is nothing worse than being Abigail Goh." Abigail kept her face blank but she twitched nervously in her seat.

Mrs Parasuram cleared her throat. I turned around and sat down in my seat. I thought I'd be asked to stay after class again since I was already in trouble for going to the chapel but Mrs Parasuram didn't say anything. She walked back to the front of the room and continued with the lesson. I tried to do my best to concentrate during the lesson, and didn't drift off and start daydreaming like I did sometimes during science. I raised my hand and answered two questions correctly. When the bell rang for recess and everybody filed out, I glanced at Mrs Parasuram and noticed she was smiling to herself. I realised that it was the first time I'd ever seen her smile.

Mrs Parasuram nodded in the direction of a cluster of girls. I turned around to see Abigail's usual group of followers. As Abigail walked out, they trailed after her, giggling and whispering. I was a little disappointed. I had somehow thought that they would agree with me and finally see what kind of person Abigail was. At the very least Kristen would hang back and say she was sorry. But the only person waiting in the doorway was Farizah. I felt guilty all of a sudden, remembering how I'd laughed along with Kristen when she had made fun of Farizah. If Farizah had been in my place, she would never have done the same thing.

I turned back to Mrs Parasuram and opened my mouth to give her an explanation for what had happened between Abigail and myself, but she spoke before I did.

"You did well today, Parveen," she told me. At first I thought she was referring to the science lesson, but then I noticed she was still looking at the girls as they turned the corner. "You did very well."

12

FARIZAH ONCE TOLD me never to look directly at visiting spirits because if you saw their faces, they would haunt you forever. She said that they brought attractive gifts like coconut jam and cashew nut cookies to lure their victims, but the food was filled with poison. Her house had been visited by many spirits when she was young because the old man who had lived there before her family did was unwilling to leave. He apparently used to hold prayers and send spirits over to Farizah's house in the middle of the night.

A few weeks later, I saw the shadow outside our flat again and this was what got me thinking about the spirits that visited Farizah's house. It stayed still between the potted plants, as if it wanted to blend in. I rose from my bed and squinted, trying to figure out who or what it was. I wasn't sure if this was a visiting spirit because, according to Farizah, spirits floated and brought coldness into the air around them. This shadow stood firm in the corridor until I reached for the ruler on my desk and banged it against the window railings.

The shadow scampered but I still couldn't get a glimpse of who it was. I ran to the door but by the time I had unlatched it, the corridor was clear except for the plants that had been knocked over. Loose soil was scattered all over the ground. I waited outside for a while but then the fluorescent lights flickered a bit and I started getting nervous. When I walked back into the flat, Ma was coming out of her room.

"What happened?" Ma asked. She rubbed her eyes sleepily.

"Somebody was outside."

"You were dreaming, Pin," Ma said. "You used to sleepwalk when you were younger." She turned to go back into her room.

I went to sleep and I dreamt of the shadow figure stepping slowly towards my window. I still couldn't identify the face of the person walking down the corridor but I noticed how the feet gave loud, insistent knocks against the ground. They were so close to my ear that I could feel the floor vibrating slightly under me. The window grilles rattled. I strained my neck to see the person's face, then I heard Farizah's voice warning me not to make eye contact. "Don't look," she whispered, terrified. I was not scared. I was curious. "Hello?" I called out as if making friends with a stray cat. "Hello?"

·   ·   ·

Kristen tried to talk to me a few times over the next week, but only when she thought Abigail wasn't looking. On a pink scented piece of notebook paper, she wrote, "Are you mad at me? I still want to be your friend." She had dotted all of the *I*'s with hearts. I had heard from girls on the school bus that hardly anybody had shown up in the red cheongsams she had ordered everyone to wear. Only Abigail and Pui Fen had worn what Kristen wanted. She spent most of the time at the party whining that her birthday picture would look ugly and most of the girls ended up calling home to ask their parents to pick them up early.

Ma was cooking when I got home from school. The metallic

smell of fish stung the air. I made a face even though Ma didn't see it. We hadn't had fried fish in a long time. The taste and the prickling of tiny bones were bad enough, but fish had its own meaning in Ma's world. It was a punishment—not a punishment for me, but Ma's punishment for everything else. The stench of fish; the clumps of blood; the glassy eyes—they were all signs of Ma's frustration. Fish awakened our flat. It made us sit up straight and think about our actions.

"What happened?" I asked Ma.

Ma bit her lower lip for a long time before she spoke. "The more I think about your Fat Auntie and what she did, the angrier I become. At first I was sad. Now I'm just furious. I called her the other day, to try to reason with her. She had the nerve to call me a liar. She said I should be ashamed of myself, making up tales. And then she said that my mother's intentions had always been to give her the jewellery."

I could hear the words as they came out of Fat Auntie's mouth. I could see her spitting into the phone. The smell of fish blood filled my nostrils and when I tasted it, I suddenly knew how Ma could cook according to her emotions. The taste of fish was the taste of hatred, pure and simple. I could not connect it to anything else. This was how it must have started; this was the only way Ma knew how to speak to the world. When she said anything else, nobody listened. Her stories and her feelings and her intentions had to be conveyed through spices and recipes, sauces, oils and meats.

Ma turned on the stove and poured vegetable oil into a deep frying pan. She shook her head as if to shake the thought out of her mind. "I'm so damn angry, Pin," she said. "I don't know what to do."

I knew what to do. It occurred to me as I was standing in the kitchen and for a moment, I was too numb to move. I knew exactly what to do. I went to the storeroom and opened the door. Clouds of dust rose to greet me and entered my lungs. I stepped past an old toolbox and knelt between my four-wheel bicycle and a pile of sand buckets. There was God, sitting in the corner, still as tall and proud as He was the first day Ma had propped him up on our living room wall. I lifted Him up and brought Him out to the kitchen.

"I think you should put this back on our wall," I told Ma.

The look on Ma's face changed from anger to surprise to bewilderment. "And why on earth would I do that, Pin? After all the trouble He's put me through?"

I really didn't know why I wanted him back on the wall until I remembered His arrival with Nani-ji. Whether she believed Ma or not, Nani-ji would have wanted God sitting on our living room wall. And Fat Auntie could take Ma's jewellery and call Ma a liar, but we could honour and respect Nani-ji. I recalled something Mrs D'Cruz had said about forgiveness one day during morning devotions. She said it was important to forgive others for their mistakes because we, too, yearned for forgiveness. Nani-ji had had a hard life and she was gone now. It was time to show her we had no hard feelings. I also hoped that Fat Auntie would come to our flat one day so I could point to the wall and show her that we respected Nani-ji more than she did. But it didn't matter now if she never believed Ma. We were learning to give in even when we knew we weren't wrong. Fat Auntie never would.

As I explained to Ma, I found myself getting flustered. I thought she would laugh at me. But Ma stared at me intently as I spoke. I told her about Abigail Goh, Mrs Parasuram and Bus

Uncle, and even how I'd gone to the chapel twice to speak to a different God. I told her about Roadside, and how I had nearly drowned in the canal the day Nani-ji had died. I told her about how I had liked eating sugarbread at first, but then I gradually began to dread the evenings when it was all I had for dinner. I didn't plan on telling Ma everything but once I started, I couldn't stop talking.

Ma threw her arms around me and drew me close to her. I could smell the damp market vegetables on her clothes. "Oh, Pin," she cried. "I don't have to worry about you at all, do I?"

She cooked afterwards and served the fried fish with rice, cabbage and roasted nuts mixed with sambal. The sour, metal taste was gone, replaced by something sweeter. It filled my mouth and warmed my throat going down. It was a new taste and there was no way to describe it, but I knew what it meant: Ma and I had no more secrets between us. We knew everything we needed to know.

• • •

A few days passed before I saw the shadow again. The next time it appeared, I was prepared. I pushed aside the curtains and threw open the windows quickly. The shadow flinched, but stayed. It was Roadside.

I didn't have any words, and neither did he. We stared at each other, then finally, he said, "Pin." His face was bright with relief.

"Yes," I said tersely. Immediately, I thought of the canal's gushing waters, the pressure of the current pulling me further away from home. I thought of Roadside and the boys walking away.

"Pin, you're alive," Roadside said. "I thought maybe…"

"You thought I died?"

"After that day at the canal, I didn't see you again. Then when we came back from our holiday in Malaysia, the neighbour told us there had been visitors to your flat because of a funeral. So I thought…"

"It was my grandmother," I said. "She died the same day you left me in the canal."

Roadside swallowed. Under the fluorescent lighting in the hallway, his face was covered in ghoulish shadows. "I didn't want to leave you there," he said quietly. "But the other boys—"

"The other boys teased you. You didn't want to help me because they would say I was your girlfriend," I said. "You left me to *drown*."

Roadside stared at his feet. "I'm so sorry, Pin," he said. "I've been coming here again and again, to try and apologise, but I was too scared to knock on your door."

I pulled the curtains shut and sank back into my bed. At Nani-ji's funeral, I had stared at her still body and kept my eyes open until they burned with tears. I did the same now, focusing my gaze on the ceiling, but the hot tears came before I could summon them.

"Pin," Roadside said. He was closer to the window now. "I still want to be your friend. We don't have to play with those boys any more. We could become detectives again." He lingered at the window for a while, then I heard his feet shuffling down the corridor. I closed my eyes. Maybe one day I'd be able to forgive Roadside, but for the moment, the memories of the canal made my lungs ache as if I was underwater again.

IT WAS JULY again.

I searched for an empty table while Ma ordered cold drinks from a nearby stall. Men and women swarmed the hawker centre and disappeared into the lanes that led into the wet market. The heat was unbearable that morning; even Ma agreed. A thin sheen of sweat made her cheeks glow.

"One coconut and one grass jelly," she called. The stallholder paid no attention and kept his back turned. "Oi," she snapped. He whirled around. "I said one coconut and one grass jelly."

A young Malay couple with two toddlers rose from a nearby table and I rushed to chope it. I had a packet of tissue in my pocket just for reserving hawker centre seats. I took out two pieces, one for Ma and one for myself, and placed them on the table. Oil and water seeped into the tissues, making them stick to the table. Ma walked over with a wobbly tray and sat down with a sigh.

"You'd better finish that coconut this time. They keep raising the prices," she said, shaking her head. She cast a glance back at the stallholder, who was watching us through a neatly arranged tower of bottles and cans. Ma narrowed her eyes and the stallholder lowered his head. He suddenly became very engrossed in counting his coins.

"Why is he looking at us?" I asked Ma, taking the coconut

from her. The stallholder had chilled it in ice before slicing off the top and putting the straw in for me to sip the juice. She didn't have to worry about me not finishing the juice. It was sweet and cool, perfect for such a hot day.

Ma shrugged. "I told him I wasn't going to buy from him any more if his drinks got more expensive. I think he was watching to see if I was serious." The man should have known better. Ma was very serious.

Ma took a sip from her grass jelly. It was black, with long pieces of jelly drifting like snakes at the bottom of the glass. She offered me some, but I made a face. "What did I tell you about making faces, Pin?" she asked sternly. "It's rude to make faces at food."

"Even at drinks?" I asked, though I knew the answer.

"Even at drinks. Think of how lucky you are that you have something cool and refreshing to drink on such a hot day. Think of all the people who struggle even to get a glass of water." Her eyes suddenly filled with sympathy. She looked back at the stallholder again and her face softened.

This was my third time following Ma to the market since she had started making regular weekly visits again. For some reason, I expected it to have changed while we were gone. Singapore was like that—it seemed as if every time I blinked, new housing estates had been built, more shopping centres had been opened, and some streets had become so different that they were difficult to recognise. But the market stayed exactly the same, as if it had been frozen under a magic spell. The first time we went back, I was afraid I'd get lost, but I recognised the lanes and the stallholders even better than I had a year ago. Even Ma was impressed. "Pretty soon I'll be able to send you here to run errands on your own," she commented, watching me pick through vegetables like an expert. I beamed with pride, imagining myself among the ladies, haggling with the stallholders and haughtily strutting away when I was not pleased with their prices.

Strong sunlight glinted sharply off the glass windows of a bank building opposite the market, hurting my eyes. Two men hurried past us carrying large straw baskets and shouting at people to clear the path ahead of them. The crowds parted slowly. The men clucked their tongues and swore under their breath. Their baskets were filled to the brim with dragon fruit, a fruit that looked so bizarre I had never tried it. It was round and pink, with green flaps that curled out from the skin. But inside, it looked completely different. I had seen market stallholders selling cut dragon fruit slices. They were white or purple with little black seeds. I asked Ma if she had ever eaten it before.

"Once. I was pregnant with you and I was craving all sorts of funny things. I ate durian back then too. I don't even like durian."

"What's dragon fruit like?" I asked. I didn't need her to go on about durians. The foul smell was bad enough, like rotting fruit.

"It's…I don't know, honestly. I can't remember. Why don't you try it for yourself?" Ma asked.

I shook my head. "No thanks. I was just curious." I was afraid I would hate it, then I'd get a scolding for wasting food.

"Come on, Pin. I'm curious too. I haven't eaten it since before you were born. If you don't like it, you can give it to me," she said. I decided that this was fair, and I nodded in agreement. Ma sprang from the table and hurried into the market. I took another long sip of my coconut water, feeling my belly bloat. The sweetness was overwhelming. It blocked the smell of fish, raw meat, incense and wet cardboard that wafted out of the lanes. I didn't mind the mingling smells any more. I knew that if Ma was to trust me to run errands on my own, then I needed to get used to the market. When the smells entered my nostrils, I pretended they weren't so strong or I willed myself to taste something different in my mouth. The coconut water made it easier of course but if I didn't have a drink, I thought of rich chocolate or sweet sticky lapis sagu.

Ma returned with slices of dragon fruit on a plate. She picked up a satay stick and skewered a slice. "Try it," she said, handing the fruit to me. "And if you like it, then hurry up and finish. We have a lot to shop for tonight. Your Mama-ji is coming over for dinner."

Hearing Ma mention Mama-ji distracted me for a moment, and as my teeth sank into the crunchy slice, I couldn't taste anything. Then I remembered what had happened a few weeks ago and suddenly the sweet dragon fruit juices filled my mouth. I took another piece, then pushed the plate back to Ma.

"You finish it," I told her. She popped a slice into her mouth. Her eyes were glazed over. She was searching her mind for recipes. I knew she would have to invent something new this evening. She had never prepared a meal that stood for forgiveness, love and the erasing of bad memories all at once. For a moment, I dreaded entering the market, thinking of how frantic Ma would become when ideas began to flood her mind. But then I thought of Mama-ji laughing and chatting with Ma at our dinner table and a sense of peacefulness settled over me like a blanket.

•　•　•

Mama-ji had shown up at our flat the previous Saturday morning, ringing the doorbell. I was sitting down in front of the television, lazily flipping through channels. I thought it might be the karang guni man again but I sat up when I realised that I hadn't heard him call out or honk his horn. I scrambled to my feet and looked through the peephole. I was expecting so much to see a woman—either Rani or Fat Auntie—that I was shocked instead to see a man. He was looking down at his feet, so I could not recognise his face at first. Out of habit, I called for Ma but then I remembered that she was at her doctor's appointment at the skin clinic. Daddy was working a morning shift. I squinted and looked through the peephole again. "Who is it?" I called out. I tried to sound assured.

The man did not answer. He acted like he had not heard me, or maybe he really hadn't. The noises of traffic and construction from across the road made it difficult to hear anything through the doors lately. Daddy said it was just as well because he was starting to get tired of hearing the neighbours' arguments. "I shouldn't be listening to their family problems any more than they should be listening to ours, don't you think?" he asked me. For some reason, it had never occurred to me until then that the other families in our block had similar problems that seemed larger than life in their private worlds. I agreed wholeheartedly.

When I finally opened the door, I was so stunned to see who it was that I couldn't utter a greeting. The only words that threatened to spill out of my mouth were strings of questions and accusations. *What are you doing here? Are you going to scold me? Why didn't you believe my Ma? What do you want?* But Mama-ji did not look like he was there to stir up trouble. In fact, he looked slightly nervous. He rocked back and forth on his feet as if to keep his balance on unsteady ground. He kept his hands behind his back but brought them forward to begin a wave that he never completed.

"Hello, Pin," he said awkwardly. His arms hung by his sides like dead branches.

"My mother and father are not at home," I said. I tried to keep the iciness out of my tone but it was there anyway. I noted the slight raise of Mama-ji's eyebrow and I realised I had gone too far. "Please come in," I said, unlatching the padlock that held the gates tightly together.

Mama-ji stepped inside the flat and I remembered to ask him if he wanted a drink. "A glass of water, please," he said. "No ice." I went into the kitchen and poured water from the tap into a tall sea-green glass Ma reserved for guests. The rattan chair creaked as Mama-ji sat down, then I heard him chuckle. "Watching cartoons early in the morning, girl?" he asked me. I searched his eyes for sarcasm but he looked genuinely amused.

"I like them," I said defensively before turning off the television.

"How is school?" he asked. "You're in Primary Five now?"

"Yes," I said, pleased that he knew. Most people would have taken one look at me and guessed that I was still in Primary Three.

"You're still going to the girls' school?" he asked. "The Christian one?" I nodded. "It's a good school," he said. "Sometimes I wished I had enrolled your cousins at First Christian Boys' School. All they learn in their school is foul language from the other children." He shook his head. "Your mother was right to send you there."

"I like it," I replied. I looked at God, who was expressionless. He seemed to be looking at both my uncle and myself with the same blank stare. Silence followed. Mama-ji sipped loudly from his glass.

"My mother's not at home," I said again. *Why are you here?* I really wanted to say.

"Yes, I know," Mama-ji said. "I won't be staying long. I have somewhere to be, actually. I wasn't expecting to be invited in but I just realised that I haven't spoken to you since you were a little girl. And you've grown up so much since." The lines at the edges of his deep-set eyes crinkled as he grimaced. "I feel like I haven't spoken to your mother for an eternity."

I did not know what to say. "I'll tell her that you came looking for her," I said.

"Please do. I want to speak to her. Also, give her this," he said. He reached into his back pocket and with a slightly trembling hand, he presented the small velvet pouch. It bulged with an oddly familiar shape—Ma's jewellery. "Actually, this is a gift for you, isn't it? Mothers always pass the wedding jewellery down to their daughters when it's their time. Or these days they melt it down and shape it into something more trendy."

I opened the pouch and inspected the contents, feeling the weight of the jewellery in my hand. Mama-ji smiled at me. I was too surprised to smile back. "But Auntie…" I said.

Mama-ji's smile remained on his face but it was accompanied now by a loud sigh. "Oh, let me worry about your Auntie. Rani called us one day and asked to speak to her, but your Auntie was not home so I asked Rani why she was calling. She blurted out the whole story, then hung up before I had a chance to ask her anything. It was all I needed to know though. Why would somebody lie about something like that? Particularly Rani. She was always a sweet person. She wouldn't lie. In my heart, I never believed that she had run around with those Malay boys. I think Pra-ji wanted a reason to keep her from working for somebody else. Several wealthy families had gone to Pra-ji's house and seen what a hard worker she was, and had offered to pay her more to work for them. He knew that he couldn't match their offers so he made up stories about her. The poor thing. So many people talked about her after that, I think she herself started to believe their stories."

"If you believed Rani, then why didn't you believe Ma?" I asked angrily. I gripped the jewellery bag tightly in case this was a cruel trick.

"I believed your Ma, dear girl," Mama-ji said shamefully. "I always believed her. But I was too afraid to speak up. I'm sure your Ma has told you all about the Punjabis we grew up with. If Pra-ji insisted it was raining on a day when the sun was shining brightly and there were no clouds in sight, everyone would believe him and call you a fool. Or worse, a traitor. At the time, I thought it was important to have those people on my side. Our father was gone and people were already whispering behind our backs. One day, a group of teenage boys were saying terrible things about your Ma and I defended her. Instead of backing down, they shouted back that our whole family was a mess. They said, 'Your father left you, your mother's a maid and your sister's...'" At this point, Mama-ji seemed to remember he was talking to me and he cleared his throat. "They said I wasn't much of a man if I couldn't even keep my sister under control. They said nasty things about my wife, your Auntie, as well. I started keeping quiet because I didn't want to give them a chance to insult me any more. The more invisible I became, the less people bothered me."

Mama-ji patted my knee and rose from his seat. "You keep that jewellery safe and be sure to tell your mother I stopped by," he said. He paused and looked at God as if seeing Him for the first time. "I understand if she's still angry at me. The kind of betrayal I showed by not standing up for her in the first place... well, it takes more than a lifetime to forgive that. But I'm thankful that Rani spoke to me. She confirmed everything I already knew but needed to hear anyway." He shook his head and suddenly, his eyes became cloudy. He directed his gaze towards God again. "I only wish your Nani-ji had been around to find out the truth."

When he walked out of the gate, I was still speechless. I ran into my bedroom, stuffed the pouch of jewellery under my pillow and sat on my bed, my mind racing.

At first, Ma thought the returned jewellery was an elaborate joke. She called Mama-ji and the first words that came out of her mouth were, "Who do you think you are, coming to my house and telling your pitiful side of things to my daughter? Don't you think her mind has been poisoned enough? You would have been happy to see how terribly Ma portrayed me when she was living here. She made it sound like I gave Bilu that bleach to drink. You tell your wife—"

But then her voice fell away and she listened. I did not hear what Mama-ji was saying. Ma looked transfixed all of a sudden. I wanted to pick up the extension but then I remembered what Daddy had said about listening to other families' problems. This conversation was about Ma's family, the family she had long before Daddy and I became a part of her life.

Ma finally hung up an hour later. She entered my room, drying her eyes with her long sleeves. Tears streaked her face. I handed her the jewellery pouch and told her it was all there. She didn't bother checking to see if I was telling the truth.

"I'll keep it aside for you," she said, managing a smile. "We'll put it in a safe deposit box in a bank and when you're old enough, you can melt it down and get something really beautiful made out of it."

Rays of light from the setting sun poured in through the slats in my blinds, casting shadowy streaks across the flat. God sat

still, anticipating. It would be a long time before I could claim
the jewellery as my own but I already knew that I would keep it
exactly the way it was.

•   •   •

Ma twisted her lips now. "I can't eat any more dragon fruit," she
said. "More than a few slices and it just becomes too much."

"We shouldn't waste it," I pointed out. Ma began looking
around as if searching for somebody through the crowd. When
she finally fixed her eyes on something, I followed her gaze. She
was looking at the juice stall owner. "Wait here, Pinny," she said
softly. She brought the plate of fruit to him and kindly asked if he
wanted any. "Otherwise we'll throw it away," I heard her saying
in Malay. "And I hate to waste food." The man looked hesitant at
first but then he took the plate. "Thank you," he said. He gave me
a small wave and smiled. I waved back.

Ma gestured for me to get up. "All of the good vegetables and
meat are going to be gone by the time you're finished with your
drink," she lamented. "Bring the coconut with you." I picked it up
and followed her to the mouth of the lane, where people poured
out with their sagging shopping bags.

"Ready? I asked Ma. I grabbed her hand and we went in.

Ma and I shuffled from stall to stall without saying much.
She pointed at fruits and vegetables, and I picked them up to
inspect the skin for bruises and marks. I couldn't help but look at
Ma's arms when I did this. Her skin was improving now that she
was less stressed about the jewellery and her problems with Fat
Auntie. Scars and some redness still remained just beneath the
surface of her skin like ghostly shadows, always a reminder. She

was still diligent about applying her cream, and wore long sleeves out of habit. But I noticed that she did not worry as much about me as she used to. If I had a rash from scratching a mosquito bite or a swollen spot on my face, Ma did not panic. She just reminded me to take care and rubbed some mild lotion on the area before I slept at night.

"What exactly are you cooking tonight?" I asked Ma. It was an important night, the first time that Mama-ji and Ma would eat a meal together since they had lived together as brother and sister. Fat Auntie was invited too—I had heard Ma politely telling her at the temple a week ago that she would be happy to have her over—but she had haughtily told Ma that she had other plans.

"I don't know," she said. We were at the dry goods stall. Ma reached for a basket and began throwing in shallots, cloves of garlic and knotted ginger roots. She handed the basket to a woman who stood in shadow behind the wooden plank counter. "Give me the best price," she told the woman distractedly, tracing her finger along the sides of a crate full of plump rambutans at the next stall. The woman was expressionless as she weighed the contents of the basket and told Ma her price. It sounded too high to me but Ma quickly paid and we went on.

After the dry goods, we went to the chicken stall, then the fish stall, then bought more vegetables, leaves, spices and roots. I watched as stallholders raised their knives and chopped fruits. I turned away when I saw them sawing through the bones of dead animals, whose entrails were piled in a corner. We left the market with more bags than I had ever remembered carrying. I knew we'd have to stop to rest a few times on the way home. Ma strutted ahead of me, suddenly filled with a sense of purpose. I still didn't know what she planned on cooking and neither did she. But she was walking as if it didn't matter. She would figure it out.

"Hey!" Ma stopped and waved. I had to shade my eyes from the morning sun to see who she was calling out to. It was Daddy, walking out of the 4D shop. His head was down and he was concentrating hard on his tickets, willing them to become winning numbers. Ma kept on waving and she shouted his name, but he did not look up.

"Your father. Now he's bought his numbers, he'll be thinking of them all day," Ma said, shaking her head.

I laughed. "Yeah," I said. "That's Daddy."

"Pin," Ma said, her eyes still on Daddy as he slowly approached. "I want you to know something, in case you ever have any doubts."

A familiar sense of dread welled up in my stomach. Here we were, in the same place we had been the first time Ma told me she never wanted me to become like her. The canvas awnings shaded the shops below, and the windows from an opposite block reflected the glaring sunlight. "What?" I asked, wanting to close my eyes and ask her to stop.

Ma looked at Daddy, who had finally noticed us. He waved back with the hand that held his tickets so they flapped in the air like wings.

"I was never forced to marry your father. I know I said before that when people found out about me, my choices were limited… and they were. But I would have chosen your Daddy anyway. If I could go back to the past, I would change everything but that."

I breathed a sigh of relief. "I know," I said. The smile Ma returned lit up her entire face, making her look happier than I had ever seen her.

I looked at Daddy walking towards us now, tucking his tickets into his pocket, then pulling them out again to make sure the numbers hadn't changed while he wasn't looking. I blinked and I saw him again, this time a rail-thin boy with skin darkened by the sun, a mess of curls on his head, racing down a dusty path that wound through old houses. In my mind, he was chasing a football until it vanished, but he kept on going until he saw one house—Jini's house. He stopped outside, picked at the grass and even dared to touch the gate. Nobody came to chase him away.

Acknowledgements

Thank you to my family for their encouragement and support, especially when this novel made the Epigram Books Fiction Prize shortlist. Thank you to my husband, Paul, whose cooking skills rival those of Ma in this novel. I love you.

Inman Majors, Pinckney Benedict and Richard Bausch saw the earliest drafts of this novel when I was a student. Their faith in the story and their guidance made it possible to complete this book years after I left school.

Thank you to Edmund Wee, Sheri Goh, Melissa De Silva, editor Jason Erik Lundberg and the rest of the publishing team at Epigram Books for their vision, support and feedback. Thank you to the judges of the Epigram Books Fiction Prize for including this novel on such an esteemed shortlist.

About the author

Balli Kaur Jaswal is also the author of *Inheritance*, a universal story of family, identity and belonging, newly re-released by Epigram Books. Born in Singapore and raised in Japan, Russia and the Philippines, she studied creative writing in the United States. She has received writing fellowships from the University of East Anglia and Nanyang Technological University, and was named Best Young Australian Novelist of 2014 by the *Sydney Morning Herald*.

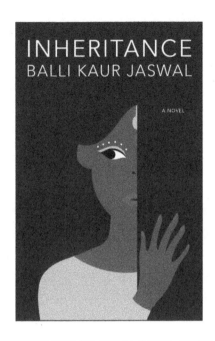

INHERITANCE BY BALLI KAUR JASWAL

- Winner of the 2014 Best Young Australian Novelist Award -

In 1971, a teenage girl briefly disappears from her house in the middle of the night, only to return a different person, causing fissures that threaten to fracture her Punjabi Sikh family. As Singapore's political and social landscapes evolve, the family must cope with shifting attitudes towards castes, youth culture, sex and gender roles, identity and belonging. *Inheritance* examines each family member's struggles to either preserve or buck tradition in the face of a changing nation.

ISBN: 978-191-2098-00-2
PUBLICATION DATE: May 2017

KAPPA QUARTET BY DARYL QILIN YAM

Kevin is a young man without a soul, holidaying in Tokyo; Mr Five, the enigmatic kappa, is the man he happens to meet. Little does Kevin know that kappas—the river demons of Japanese folklore—desire nothing more than the souls of other humans. Set between Singapore and Japan, Kappa Quartet is split into eight discrete sections, tracing the rippling effects of this chance encounter across a host of other characters, connected and bound to one another in ways both strange and serendipitous.

ISBN: 978-191-2098-72-9

PUBLICATION DATE: May 2017

NOW THAT IT'S OVER BY O THIAM CHIN

- Winner of the 2015 Epigram Books Fiction Prize -

During the Christmas holidays in 2004, an earthquake in the Indian Ocean triggers a tsunami that devastates fourteen countries. Two couples from Singapore are vacationing in Phuket when the tsunami strikes. Alternating between the aftermath of the catastrophe and past events that led these characters to that fateful moment, *Now That It's Over* weaves a tapestry of causality and regret, and chronicles the physical and emotional wreckage wrought by natural and man-made disasters.

ISBN: 978-191-2098-69-9
PUBLICATION DATE: July 2017

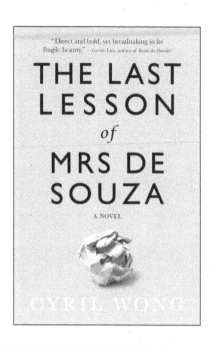

THE LAST LESSON OF MRS DE SOUZA BY CYRIL WONG

One last time and on her birthday, Rose de Souza is returning to school to give a final lesson to her classroom of secondary school boys before retiring from her long teaching career. What ensues is an unexpected confession in which she recounts the tragic and traumatic story of Amir, a student from her past who overturned the way she saw herself as a teacher, and changed her life forever.

ISBN: 978-191-2098-70-5

PUBLICATION DATE: July 2017

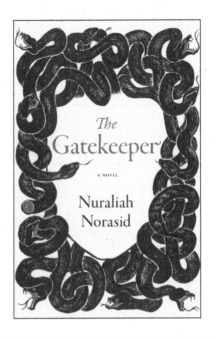

THE GATEKEEPER BY NURALIAH NORASID

- Winner of the 2016 Epigram Books Fiction Prize -

The Gatekeeper tells the story of a ten-year-old Gorgon girl named Ria, who petrifies an entire village of innocents with her gaze. Together with her sister, she flees the jungle of Manticura to the underground city of Nelroote, where society's marginalised members live. Years later, the subterranean habitat is threatened when Ria, now the gatekeeper, befriends a man from the outside.

ISBN: 978-191-2098-68-2
PUBLICATION DATE: September 2017

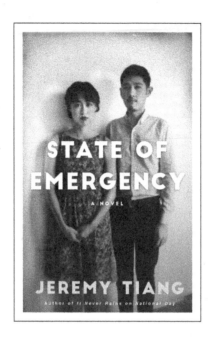

STATE OF EMERGENCY BY JEREMY TIANG

- Finalist for the 2016 Epigram Books Fiction Prize -

A woman finds herself questioned for a conspiracy she did not take part in. A son flees to London to escape from a father, wracked by betrayal. A journalist seeks to uncover the truth of the place she once called home. A young wife leaves her husband and children behind to fight for freedom in the jungles of Malaya. *State of Emergency* traces the leftist movements of Singapore and Malaysia from the 1940s to the present day, centring on a family trying to navigate the choppy political currents of the region.

ISBN: 978-191-2098-65-1
PUBLICATION DATE: November 2017

LET'S GIVE IT UP FOR GIMME LAO! BY SEBASTIAN SIM

- Finalist for the 2015 Epigram Books Fiction Prize -

Born on the night of the nation's independence, Gimme Lao is cheated of the honour of being Singapore's firstborn son by a vindictive nurse. This forms the first of three things Gimme never knows about himself, the second being the circumstances surrounding his parents' marriage, and the third being the profound (but often unintentional) impact he has on other people's lives. Tracing social, economic and political issues over the past 50 years, this humorous novel uses Gimme as a hapless centre to expose all of Singapore's ambitions, dirty linen and secret moments of tender humanity.

ISBN: 978-191-2098-67-5
PUBLICATION DATE: November 2017